GUILT IN THE COTSWOLDS

Thea Osborne's latest house-sitting assignment is a little different to the rest. Along with her spaniel, Hepzie, Thea finds herself in the village of Chedworth. She is tasked with creating an inventory of Rita Wilshire's possessions, requested by her son, Richard Wilshire, after moving her into a care home. All goes to plan, until Thea and her fiancé, Drew Slocombe, find Richard dead in a barn. When family members come knocking, Thea and Drew struggle to give them answers. Was Richard's death suicide? Or something more sinister? When the clues lead them in circles, Thea's relationship with Drew is put to the test.

GUILT IN THE COTSWOLDS

GUILT IN THE COTSWOLDS

by

Rebecca Tope

Magna Large Print Books
Long Preston, North Yorkshire,
BD23 4ND, England.

British Library Cataloguing in Publication Data.

A catalogue record of this book is
available from the British Library

ISBN   978-0-7505-4462-7

First published in Great Britain by Allison & Busby in 2016

Published in Large Print 2017 by arrangement with
Allison & Busby Limited

Magna Large Print is an imprint of Library Magna Books Ltd.

Printed and bound in Great Britain by
T.J. (International) Ltd., Cornwall, PL28 8RW

Dedicated to Pat and in fond memory of Beulah
Also with special thanks to Daphne Abbley
for help with Chedworth topography

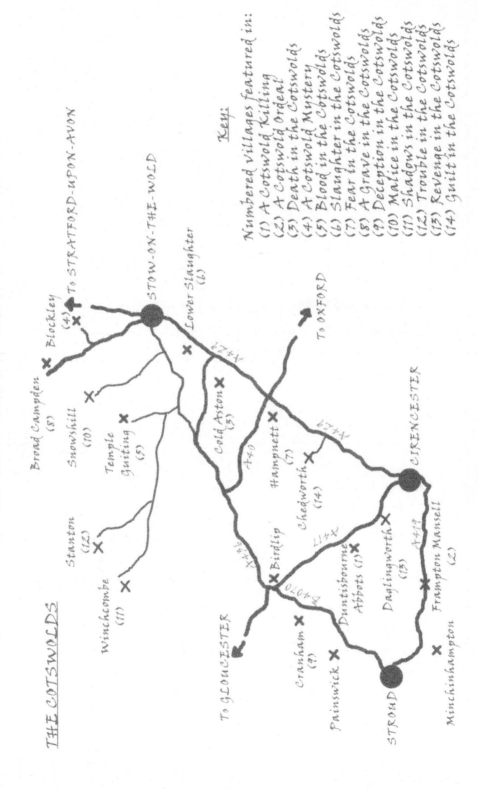

THE COTSWOLDS

Broad Campden (8)
Blockley
(4) TO STRATFORD-UPON-AVON
STOW-ON-THE-WOLD
Lower Slaughter (6)
Snowshill (10)
Stanton (12)
Temple Guiting (5)
Winchcombe (11)
Cold Aston (3)
A429
Hampnett (7)
A40
Chedworth (14)
TO OXFORD
A40
A429
CIRENCESTER
Birdlip
A417
Duntisbourne Abbots (1)
Daglingworth (13)
Cranham (9)
B4070
A417
B4436
Frampton Mansell (2)
A419
TO GLOUCESTER
Painswick
STROUD
Minchinhampton

Key:
Numbered villages featured in:
(1) A Cotswold Killing
(2) A Cotswold Ordeal
(3) Death in the Cotswolds
(4) A Cotswold Mystery
(5) Blood in the Cotswolds
(6) Slaughter in the Cotswolds
(7) Fear in the Cotswolds
(8) A Grave in the Cotswolds
(9) Deception in the Cotswolds
(10) Malice in the Cotswolds
(11) Shadows in the Cotswolds
(12) Trouble in the Cotswolds
(13) Revenge in the Cotswolds
(14) Guilt in the Cotswolds

Author's Note

As with other books in this series, the privately owned properties in the story are products of my imagination, with the exception of the large barn on the road to Yanworth. That does exist.

Prologue

Drew Slocombe was searching for a care home for the elderly on the outskirts of Stratford-upon-Avon, using a satnav for the first time. His daughter Stephanie, nine years old, had shamed him into it. His shame only increased as he realised how much easier it made the task than it would have been roaming the streets with the help of an inadequate map.

Mrs Rita Wilshire was waiting for him, along with her son Richard. Together they were to draw up a prepayment plan for Rita's funeral. When the time came she was to have a grave in Drew's burial ground near Broad Campden – assuming it was fully operational by then. Otherwise, she was content to rest in the Somerset field known as Peaceful Repose, where Drew had already buried close to seven hundred people in the years since Stephanie had been born.

It was early September and the sun was shining. At Richard's suggestion, they settled on canvas chairs under a handsome cedar and conducted the business in the open air. 'Rather as my funeral will be,' smiled the old lady. 'I do hope there'll be fine weather for it.'

Drew responded warmly, pleased to have such a stalwart customer, who accepted the certainty of her own death while expressing a hope that it would not be unduly soon. 'I would think I might last another five years,' she had said at the start. 'There isn't a great deal wrong with me, apart from my legs.'

'You'll see your centenary,' her son assured her, not quite so phlegmatic about the matter. Richard Wilshire struck Drew as a rather dull character, rendered uncomfortable by this deviation from the usual practice. Not so much the advance planning as the choice of an unorthodox manner of disposal. His mother insisted on a cardboard coffin and no religious input. As people so often did, she began to reminisce about previous funerals she had experienced. 'My sister died very young. There was a great deal of pomp and circumstance, no expense spared. But she was just as dead in the end. Poor Dawn. She'd be ninety-six now. I still remember her birthday every year.'

Drew ran through the costings of the services he could provide, but counselled against fixing too many details at this stage. 'Leave something for your son to do,' he said. 'Like deciding about music.'

'I've always liked the idea of a lone Scottish piper,' she said with a distant gleam in her eye. 'But I wouldn't insist on it.'

Richard Wilshire rolled his eyes, and gave her a gentle poke in protest. 'I make no promises,' he said. 'Since we don't possess a drop of Scottish blood between us.'

'Irish, then. Or even an English one. I don't see that our blood matters, anyhow. It's just a lovely haunting image.'

The business concluded, Drew stayed a little

while longer, because he was in no rush and he liked these people. Mrs Wilshire had only been in the home for a week or so, and was still intoxicated by the changes to her life. 'I seem to get the prize for the most compos mentis,' she laughed. 'But there are two other excellent bridge players. I've only won two rubbers so far. My partner isn't too hopeless, luckily. She was delighted when I arrived, and they could make up a table. We're both improving considerably.'

'It's a lovely spot,' said Drew, looking around. The town of Stratford was close by, but the home had generous grounds with several large trees and flower borders. 'Where did you live before?'

'In the Cotswolds. A village called Chedworth. I keep expecting to be overcome with homesickness, but so far everything's far too pleasant here for that to worry me. I admit I miss some of my things, and it's very strange knowing I no longer own the walls around me. I hadn't appreciated how much ownership matters. Probably a very incorrect attitude these days, but there it is. And besides, the house is still there, and Richard would never sell it while I live. Would you, dear?' There was a hint of challenge in her eye, thought Drew. Or perhaps something even darker, like a threat.

Richard sighed and shifted in his canvas chair. 'Not unless we run out of cash, and then there won't be any choice. This place isn't cheap, you know.'

'And the family isn't poor. You'll get the house eventually. I just couldn't bear to think of other people in it while I live.'

17

Richard sighed again. It was clear to Drew that he thought the old lady was being unreasonable.

The subject changed, and Mrs Wilshire pointed out her room, on the ground floor with a window overlooking the lawn. 'My pathetic legs qualified me for the ground floor,' she said. 'It's not long now before I'll be needing a wheelchair nearly all the time.' She had made it to the garden seat with the aid of two sticks, at a very slow pace, the two men following attentively behind.

Shortly afterwards, Drew made his departure, with Richard Wilshire accompanying him to his car. 'Back in a minute, Mum,' he said.

'No hurry, dear. I'm quite all right here. Thank you, Mr Slocombe. I don't expect I'll see you again, although that would be a pity. I very much enjoy your company.'

Drew nodded a rueful agreement. 'Perhaps I'll drop in on you one day,' he said. 'If I'm ever this way.'

'Oh yes – do. I'm sure we could always find plenty to talk about.'

Richard waited until they were out of earshot, standing beside his big Honda four-wheel drive. He bent down and felt underneath the chassis, below the driver's door. 'Sorry,' he said. 'It's a habit I've got into. I've lost so many car keys in my time. Now I just attach them like this.' He showed Drew a small metal box that had somehow stuck magnetically to the car. 'And I keep two spare sets at home for good measure.' He pulled a self-deprecating face.

'Seems like an excellent idea to me,' said Drew. 'So long as the magnet's nice and strong.'

18

Richard then began to speak rapidly. 'It was very good of you to come like this. I know you're based in Somerset. This must be taking up virtually the whole of your day.'

'No problem,' Drew assured him.

'The thing is, we're such a small family, and so many of Mum's friends have gone now, that it seemed to make sense to get all this settled. I just hope she hangs on until you've opened the new burial ground. She'd be so much happier close to her old home.'

'Chedworth – is that right?'

Richard nodded. 'You heard her. There's a great big house standing empty, except it's not actually empty at all. It's still full of all her stuff. She could only bring a tiny fraction of it here with her. I need to find somebody to deal with it, I suppose. Though Mum seems to think it's fine as it is. She's a bit irrational where that side of things is concerned. There's no way I can just get a clearance outfit to take it off our hands. I dread the day when we have to sell the house, but if she lives more than a year or so, we'll have to, to pay for the home.'

'So what would "dealing with it" actually entail?' Already Drew was having an idea.

'For a start, I need to know what's there. It goes back more than half a century. I was born there, and as long as I can remember there've been wardrobes and chests stuffed with all kinds of clothes and linens and I don't know what. Not to mention the attic, which has precious heirlooms, according to Mum. I can't just leave it all, can I? Much as I might like to,' he added in a low tone.

'I might know someone who could help,' said Drew. 'If you're interested.'

Chapter One

Thea was lost; lost and late. It was getting dark and the narrow lanes of Chedworth began to close in on her, the village seeming to come to an end only to start again a little further on. She should have paid better attention to the instructions, instead of blithely assuming she knew the area well enough by now to avoid any difficulty. It had become apparent in the past five minutes that there was both a Chedworth and a Lower Chedworth – which came as a big surprise. Small roads wandered off in all directions, including dramatic downward plunges. Richard Wilshire would be waiting impatiently for her in the stone house set on a small road that went nowhere, close to the church. He had ordained five o'clock as the required moment for her arrival. 'Then we can settle you in for the night,' he had said, with a laugh that had a trace of snigger in it. His instructions, taken down during a phone call, were scribbled on a scrap of paper beside her. 'Next left after Hare and Hounds pub. Right at the Farm Shop – straight through Chedworth until Seven Tuns pub.' No hint of distances or useful landmarks. She had met a T-junction soon after the right turn, of which there was no mention in the instructions. A defunct red telephone box beside the road had 'Defibrillator' blazoned across it, which made her smile. And then the road had carried on and on, around bends and up hills, passing the usual old stone houses with no lights on inside. Anyone, even the most unimaginative, could quite easily believe themselves to have slipped back a century in time. The existence of motorways, airports, bright lighting and high speed had all faded into a far-off realm. Here in this monochrome twilight world, it was easier to revert to a slower, simpler mode. As if to emphasise this, there were signs announcing 'Twenty is Plenty for Chedworth' in reference to the speed limit.

It was half past five in early October, which was still an hour short of the moment the sun sank over the edge of the world. But it was a cloudy day and there were trees and high banks and houses on all sides, closing out the lingering light. It felt later than it was. 'Not sure I like the atmosphere here,' she muttered to Hepzibah, her constant companion. The spaniel on the passenger seat gave her a liquid look of sympathy. But the houses were as lovely as those in most other Cotswold villages, some of them impressively old and weathered. As she hunted for the church, which surely ought to be on an elevation somewhere visible, she passed clusters of closely packed homes, with never a glimpse of a human being. Seconds later she found herself in virtually open country, with no buildings visible. This lasted only a short time before another typical house came into sight, followed by several more. The stop-start nature of the place was disorientating.

21

Chedworth, then, was nothing like Stanton or Daglingworth, Hampnett or Broad Campden – all of which she had come to know in the past year or so. All of which were also remarkably close by, many within walking distance. The way each settlement could acquire so distinct a character was a mystery.

Richard Wilshire was in his late fifties, a solid man of limited horizons. That much Thea had gleaned from information received from Drew Slocombe, her soon-to-be husband and acquaintance of Mr Wilshire. It was thanks to Drew that this commission existed in the first place.

'He's got an aged mother who's just moved into a residential home,' Drew had explained. 'She heard about the natural burials, and came to me to arrange her funeral when the time comes.' Drew had achieved the first stages of establishing a second burial ground in the heart of the Cotswolds, taking pre-planned customers, but so far only one grave lay there. In the process of funeral arranging, it had transpired that Old Mrs Wilshire was leaving behind a substantial house containing a lifetime's possessions. Her son found himself unequal to the task of sorting these items into any meaningful categories. Young Mrs Wilshire – Daphne – no longer regarded the fate of her mother-in-law as relevant. She and Richard had separated five years previously and she was living with a man called Nick. 'Are you keeping up?' Drew had checked with Thea at this point.

'Easily.'

'Good, because there's more.' He went on to report that there was a daughter named Millie who was twenty-five and – according to her father – so completely appalled by the treatment of poor old Granny that she couldn't bring herself to go near Chedworth ever again. 'All of which explains why a certain Thea Osborne is sorely needed,' he summarised. 'It might not be exactly house-sitting as we know it, but it's well within your capabilities.'

She had given him a look. 'You're telling me the job has expanded into that of house-sorter and house-clearer as well. Which might include heavy lifting. Do I get paid extra?'

'I left that to you to negotiate. I will, of course, come and help with anything heavy.'

Her reply was a familiar one. 'How will you find the time to do that?'

'I'll manage it somehow,' he said, as usual.

Drew and Thea had been together – emotionally if not logistically – for well over a year. The summer just ended had seen them spending more and more time as a family, with his two children rapidly accepting her as a fixture. Their wholehearted enthusiasm for her and her dog was almost unnerving. The first week of their school holidays that summer had been spent with Thea in a house-sit that had passed so idyllically she sometimes wondered if it had all been a dream. The four of them squatted in a large Cotswold house in Farmington in the most perfect weather with a pack of Siamese cats. On the last day, Drew had recklessly suggested marriage. In a surge of euphoria, Thea had accepted.

Three months later, she was still uncertain as to whether it would ever actually happen.

The Seven Tuns pub occupied a site near another T-junction. Peering at the final words of her directions, Thea read, 'Left, then follow road past church. House on left, easy parking.' Not seeing the church, she drove blindly to the left, up a steep little road that showed virtually no sign of having changed since before cars were invented. Suddenly, the church was right beside her, and all became clear.

She finally knocked on the door at five-fifty. Richard Wilshire brushed aside her apologies for lateness and led her into the living room. 'You come well recommended,' he assured her. 'Good in a crisis, they said about you. Ready for any-thing.'

She flinched at the *they*. Who else, other than Drew, had been talking? 'It isn't exactly what I'm usually asked to do,' she reminded him. 'There are professionals for this sort of thing. They take all the stuff in return for leaving a nice empty house.'

'I don't want that. This isn't about clearing the house. We're not disposing of anything other than absolute rubbish. First, I need an inventory.' He gave an embarrassed laugh. 'I lived here all my life, until I married, but I still have no idea what's in some of the cupboards and boxes. It never really occurred to me to wonder. But now – well, I can't leave it any longer.'

Thea attempted to look capable, sympathetic and responsible all at the same time.

24

'Be warned,' Mr Wilshire went on. 'My mother lived here for seventy years and there are places that probably haven't been touched for most of that time. How are you with spiders?'

'Not great,' she confessed. 'But better than I used to be.'

'The attic is the worst. Mum hasn't managed the stairs for a few years now. I should have gone up there myself, but I never got around to it. Take a killer spray with you, if you like.'

'No, no. I don't like to kill the poor things. I'll be all right if I'm forewarned. The dog sometimes catches them for me, if they're really huge.'

They went on to discuss the procedure she was required to follow. 'I don't think there'll be very much rubbish, but what there is can go straight into bin bags,' he said. Then he suggested she set aside items of obvious value; sort through papers (important and otherwise), make a list of items that were broken but potentially useful, and another list of whatever she found in the unexamined cupboards and boxes. She wrote much of it down and asked several questions.

'I understand Mr Slocombe's going to join you at some point,' he said.

She noted the formality with interest, having assumed the two men were on better terms than that. 'He'll try,' she said. 'It won't be easy for him to get away if things are busy.'

'I've prepared the main bedroom for you.' His tone implied that this had been a tremendous achievement, for which she owed him much gratitude. 'Turned the mattress over, so it ought to be okay.'

'Thanks.' Visions of an incontinent old woman sleeping on that mattress until a month or two ago made her uneasy. But it sounded as if all the other rooms were even less habitable.

'Listen,' he said with a tormented look, 'I know it'll be hard work, and I should be doing it myself. All this stuff – it doesn't matter to me. I'm not sentimental about most of it. But there's sure to be a few ... triggers, if you know what I mean. Things I've forgotten, from when I was a kid. There was a time when I tried to get her to throw stuff away, but I gave up long ago. Since then I've just closed my eyes to it, and stuck to the routine maintenance business. You know – making sure the electrics are okay and the plumbing works. The house is in a mess, basic-ally. It hasn't been decorated for decades. I made her take up all the rugs, in case she tripped and fell. They'll be up in the attic. But I know I could have done a lot more...' He tailed off miserably.

Thea looked around the living room, where they were sitting together on a shabby old sofa with the dog between them. Richard Wilshire evidently saw no reason to protest at a spaniel on the upholstery. The wallpaper was faded. There were piles of magazines and books on a window seat, and a clutter of old-fashioned furniture on all sides. The curtains were dusty and the skirting boards grimy. 'Didn't she have a home help or something?'

He shook his head. 'A girl came in once a week for a bit, but they fell out. My mother liked to think she could do it all herself. She never got the hang of the vacuum cleaner, though. Or the splendid new washing machine. She always loved the twin tub, but it died a couple of years ago. She's stuck at about nineteen seventy, in a lot of ways.'

'She washed clothes by hand?'

'Mostly, yes. I supervised a big wash in the machine whenever I came over – sheets and bigger things. She always used an antique carpet sweeper. It does work surprisingly well.' They both glanced down at the floor, which was quite acceptably clean.

There was something rather nice about it, Thea discovered. A little island of social history, ignoring such new-fangled developments as automatic washing machines. 'I don't suppose she has a computer?' she said.

'Oddly enough, she has. She had email almost from the start – must be twenty-five years or so now. She's kept everything on discs, all these years. Most of them are obsolete, of course. She's got a smart new laptop now. She's determined to keep up with relatives and old friends. Apparently half the residents in the home have got mobiles and tablets and the latest gadgets.'

'How old is she?'

'Well over ninety.' He sighed. 'The home's really nice, you know. But I still feel desperately guilty about it.' His eyes grew shiny. 'With the best will in the world, they can't let her take more than a tiny fraction of her stuff. She's going to be so lost without her things. She still has a very sharp mind.' He rubbed his face. 'Sometimes I think it's kinder when the wits go first, although I suppose it isn't. My mother's legs have let her down in the last year or so. And her sense of balance isn't what it was.'

'Does she know you've got me sorting out the house?'

He grimaced. 'I'm afraid I didn't have the courage to tell her. She would want to be consulted about every single thing. I mean well, believe me. I know some people think I should wait until she … you know. But she's never coming back here, so it seems silly to just mothball everything. Besides, we might need to sell up at short notice, although I hope not.'

'So what'll you do with it all?'

'No idea. I'll make a plan when I know exactly what there is. Nothing's going to happen soon.'

'You shouldn't feel guilty,' said Thea bracingly, aware that he was deeply unhappy. 'She'll have all her comforts there – all her meals provided. Warm. Safe. It must have lots of advantages.'

'All true,' he said. 'And she mostly likes the place. But it's such a huge change, and old people hate change.'

'No escaping it, though. There's nothing you can do about it.'

He gave her a look that startled her. It contained something close to dislike for a moment. Then he blinked and it was gone. 'It was her own decision. I never pushed her into it. But people will *think* I did. "Packed his old mum off into a home" – that's what they'll be saying. They'll assume I want to get my hands on the house. It's worth a small fortune, even in this condition. And I don't have to share it with anyone else.' The last words carried additional emphasis. Again, they both looked around the room. There were pictures on the wall, a Victorian clock on the mantelpiece, a piece of china that Thea thought could be Moorcroft, on a small table. 'But all that can wait,' he finished.

She opted for a change of subject, asking which services were still connected, and which not. 'No phone,' he said. 'But the power's on, and there's an immersion heater for hot water. I didn't think it was worth getting the Aga started, although I'm afraid the kitchen does get cold without it. You can have a log fire in here – there are still some logs in the shed at the back. It's very effective once it gets going. I hope it won't feel like an abandoned house that nobody loves.'

'It doesn't,' she assured him. 'Not with all the furniture still here. You could probably let it out to holiday visitors,' she mused. 'They'd keep it alive, so to speak.' She thought of Drew's neglected property in Broad Campden, which would feel much colder and more cobwebby than this one.

'Did you bring any food with you?' he asked.

'Not much. Milk, biscuits, tea bags and a couple of things to keep me and the dog going until I can buy something tomorrow. I thought there'd be a shop somewhere nearby.'

He frowned. 'There's the farm shop, that's all. It has pies and things. Bread. And there's the pub, of course. They'll feed you. Oh, and the Roman villa has a cafe, which I suppose is open for a few more weeks yet.'

'I'll manage,' she said airily. Food was seldom a high priority with her, although she was prone

29

to sudden attacks of insatiable hunger when nothing else mattered but to eat something.

'There are phone numbers on this list,' he said. 'You won't need them, I'm sure, but I always think it's good to have them. There's my mother, my daughter and the usual plumbers and so forth. Just in case.'

'Thanks,' said Thea flatly. The same thing had happened in almost all her house-sitting jobs. People thought a phone number could solve all kinds of difficulties. And sometimes they were right, she had to admit.

The man pumped his arms, as if winding himself up. 'Well, I have to go. I've got a visit to make. Then home, I suppose.' He didn't look particularly eager. 'I've left my dogs shut in, and they'll bark if nobody turns up. I think Millie said she'd be home tonight, but I'm not sure.' He tailed off, looking vague and distracted.

'Where do you live?'

'Stratford – half a mile from my mother's care home. It's only about forty minutes away from here, if you need me. But I'm going to be snowed under with work for most of the week, so try to manage, okay? If you do need me, I could drop by on Monday, at a push. Oddly enough, I'm back here again tomorrow, but I won't have a spare moment.'

'What do you do, by way of work?'

'Oh, I'm a vet.'

Thea thought of other vets she had dealt with in recent times, and tried to fit this one into the general stereotype. He had clean hands and tweedy clothes. But he didn't strike her as particularly outdoorsy. She cocked her head, inviting more detail.

'I work for DEFRA, mostly, testing cattle for TB. I'm officially part of a practice in Stratford, but these days I don't do very much with them. There's so much TB around now that it keeps me pretty busy.' He shook his head and sighed. 'Awful business. I have to go to farms and check their animals. I'm doing a follow-up visit in Yanworth tomorrow, before dashing over to Chipping Norton, and somewhere else I can't remember for the moment.'

Thea could not suppress a grimace. 'I bet you're popular,' she said with heavy irony. She gave him a considering look. His soft pink hands gave him a hint of vulnerability that could make him even harder to like or forgive if he landed some harassed farmer in trouble. 'Only doing my job,' he would plead, and they would fume helplessly rather than hitting him.

'They hate me,' he agreed. 'With reason, sometimes. The test is notoriously inexact, so we destroy far too many healthy animals. Nothing more heartbreaking, and there's nothing I can say to make it better. I seem to spend much of my time defending the indefensible.'

'Do you have to travel much? I mean – do you have an area to cover?'

He nodded. 'It's mostly the whole of the Cotswolds. I've got it easy compared to some. Farmers round here aren't half as curmudgeonly as in Yorkshire or Cumbria.'

'It certainly doesn't sound boring, anyway,' she said, having always believed that the very worst fate that could befall a person – except for getting themselves killed as her husband had done – was to have a boring job. 'And I'll try not to bother you. I'll have everything in nice piles and comprehensively listed for you by this time next week.'

'Thanks. I really do appreciate it.'

He left her then. She and Hepzie watched him disappear into the darkness, and then closed the door. 'Here we are again,' said Thea. 'Early start tomorrow, my girl.'

Chapter Two

Unusually, she had arrived on a Thursday. 'It doesn't matter to him what days you do,' Drew had said. 'And that means you can settle in and get started before I come over for the weekend. If I do,' he added, holding up crossed fingers, 'it'll be down to Pandora.'

The name always made Thea smile. It belonged to a temporary assistant who was standing in for Maggs Cooper, because Maggs had recently produced a baby daughter. Pandora was fifty-three and immensely efficient. She had no difficulty with dead bodies, coffins, grieving families or unreasonable requests regarding the positioning of a grave. She was equally good with Drew's children, and was infinitely available thanks to a recent divorce and her own two sons having left home. She had always lived in Dorset, the move to neighbouring Somerset a major midlife adventure.

The probability of having Drew to join her on the Saturday, albeit with his children, was a strong motivation for Thea to devote the whole of Friday to the house. She would not pause, she promised herself. Chedworth would go unexplored and Hepzibah unwalked. The dog could potter around the good-sized back garden and be thankful. Even with Drew, Stephanie and Timmy there, the work would have to continue, although they had agreed there must be a visit to Drew's property in Broad Campden at some point.

During the magical summer interlude at Farmington a great many elements had fallen into place. Dilemmas and complications had resolved themselves almost effortlessly. 'We'll live in the Cotswolds,' Thea had said. 'I'll sell my Witney house, and you can put Maggs in charge of Peaceful Repose. I'll work for you full time and we'll do good business.'

'But Maggs is having a baby,' he'd demurred.

'So we wait until she's ready to work again. It'll take a year or so, anyway, to get everything organised.'

Since then, some of the earlier difficulties had re-emerged; not least the appalled reaction from Maggs herself. Pregnancy had done nothing for her temper, which had always been short. Her association with Drew went back to a time just after Stephanie was born and the natural burial ground established. He freely acknowledged that he could not have done it without her. He owed her an impossible debt of gratitude for the support she had given him on every level, and she was not afraid to remind him of it regularly. Thea had stepped into the middle of a relationship that sometimes seemed more intimate than a marriage.

Maggs's reaction to Thea was itself an ongoing rollercoaster. At first ferociously protective, Maggs then opted to accept that Drew was at no risk after all. But she had come to see some of Thea's shortcomings in recent months, with the reappearance of earlier misgivings. 'You have to be *gentle* with him,' she said at one point, with a worried look. 'And instead you just expect him to be gentle with *you.*'

'Can't we be gentle with each other?'

'I don't know. Can you?'

Thea had gone away with a churning sensation in her stomach. When had she ever been gentle? she asked herself. She was so often impatient, intrusive, rude, reckless. Did she have to change her entire nature in order to be worthy of Drew Slocombe?

Drew himself didn't appear to think so, which was obviously the main thing. He showed every sign of finding her funny, independent, capable and trustworthy. It was all in the eye of the beholder, anyway, she assured herself. The Drew that Maggs knew and loved was a subtly different person from the one Thea was intending to marry. He knew what he was doing, she supposed. Everything would be fine.

As had become her habit, she phoned him at eight-thirty, after the children were in bed. She shared her observations of Richard Wilshire, the house and the shadowy glimpses she'd so far managed of Chedworth. 'First impressions?' he asked.

'I don't know. There's something elusive about it. I know I've said the same about other places, but this one really does have some strange levels. I mean – there *are* no levels. Everything pitches at an angle. And there are *two* Chedworths, which doesn't help. It took ages to find the house.'

'Which one's got the Roman villa?'

'Neither. That's off to the north, the other side of some woods.'

'I make that three, then,' he laughed.

'So it is. I have a feeling there's loads of good history attached to the place, but I won't have time to look any of it up. Tomorrow's going to be full on, sorting all the stuff that's here. I can't decide whether to start at the top and work down, or the other way round. Basically, I just have to open it all up and list what's here. But that'll mean moving lots of boxes and making heaps everywhere. Then I'll have to pack it all up again, with descriptions of the contents on the top of each box or whatever.' As she spoke, she felt a glow of anticipation at a task that would be full of interest. Who knew what she might find?

'I think you'll have to start in the attic, won't you? I can't see it working otherwise.'

'Why?'

'Well, if you have to put similar things together, you'll need to bring stuff down. Or have I got that wrong?'

'I wasn't planning to rearrange it. Just open everything up and see what's what. What's in the attic can stay in the attic. I was thinking I'd leave that for when you're here to help.'

'But all the most interesting stuff is likely to be up there.'

'I know. But there are spiders in the attic as well. I thought if I made a commotion downstairs, and Hepzie rampaged a bit, they might all decide to move out, before I have to face them.'

'I see. We should probably have thought of that sooner. A spider phobia rather disqualifies you for the job in hand, don't you think?'

'Certainly not. I'll just go carefully, and shake everything before I start. I can cope as long as they're not on me. It'll be fun, I'm sure, once I get started. I never dreamt of turning it down just for that. I need the money.'

'Yeah.' He sighed. 'We'll have to talk about money at the weekend, if we get the chance.'

'So you can come?'

'As far as I know, yes. Pandora's a treasure, you know. She even offered to come here and look after the kids all weekend, so I can come to you.'

Thea's heart jumped. 'Wow! And what did you say?'

'I was so surprised, I didn't say anything definite. In a way, it would be sensible. There's a lot of overdue paperwork in the office that she could get on with at the same time. And if there's a removal, she could easily get Den to help with that. She can call Harriet to babysit.'

'Harriet's the girl down the lane, right?'

'Right. But the trouble is, I'd have to pay Pandora properly for such a commitment. And Den's not keen on doing removals at the moment, with the baby so new. We're on a tight-

36

rope, in more ways than one.'

'When were you not? It's been the same since I've known you.'

'I know. But I really think I ought to bring the kids with me and keep Pandora on standby. I don't have to pay her at all then, unless she gets called out.'

They chatted for a few more minutes, until Drew instructed her to have an early night and face her fears with fortitude the next morning. Before obeying, she did a circuit of the house – all but the attic – trying to formulate a plan of operation. There were three bedrooms on the first floor, as well as a bathroom and a small area that might once have been called a 'dressing room'. It was piled high with cardboard boxes. When she peeped inside one, it seemed to be full of clothes.

Downstairs there was a large front living room, and two more rooms at the back. The kitchen ran along one side of the house, light and spacious, with a high ceiling and numerous built-in cupboards of a style long ago past. A back door led out to the garden, through a sort of porch. Another door led into an outside lavatory, which showed little sign of having been updated since the 1940s.

Involuntarily, she was acquiring a picture of the old lady who had spent such a large portion of her life in this house. The picture was coloured by personal experience, namely that her own widowed mother, in her seventies, was still occupying the family home. There had been six of them in it for a long time, but it was smaller than this handsome Cotswold property. The Wilshires had apparently only managed a single child, and he had duly grown up and left at a respectable age – probably not much later than twenty or thereabouts. There had been no reference to a Mr Wilshire Senior, and scarcely any evidence of him discovered so far. All of which led to a conclusion that the woman had remained here on her own as a widow for a considerable time, free to add clutter, pursue hobbies, with never any need to throw things away. It was in no way unusual. The land was full of similar scenarios. This was not the first instance that Thea had encountered, albeit with variations on the same theme.

This woman had a variety of interests, which were already apparent from the stacks of old magazines that toppled precariously in all the downstairs rooms. Historic houses and country living were not especially surprising. But pottery and medieval French history were more unexpected. There was also a small kiln at one end of the kitchen, with two shelves of dusty equipment close by: a cutting wire with wooden handles, a collection of spatulas and some plastic bottles containing coloured slip that proved to have dried up. No clay was to be seen, and no finished products, which made Thea think it had all been abandoned a long time ago.

Soon after ten, she took Hepzie outside for her routine toileting and then led the way upstairs. The bedroom was large and handsomely furnished with mahogany wardrobe, chest of drawers and dressing table. There was an oak chest, and the headboard on the big, high bed was a semicircle of painted wood that was like nothing she had seen before. However Richard had managed to turn the mattress without assistance, she did not know.

Hepzie jumped cheerfully up, despite the height, and Thea followed a few minutes later. She felt hesitant and oddly guilty. This was another woman's private room, the bed her own personal space for countless years. She, Thea, was a usurper, with no real right to be there. Mrs Wilshire wasn't dead. Instead she was in a kind of limbo, the twilight of her days, no longer the same autonomous person she had been, as she waited for the end. How would that feel, Thea wondered. Surely there must be resentment, sadness, resistance, and a craving for all the familiar things that this house contained. Could anyone truly possess the maturity to go willingly into that last phase, full of clean surfaces and excessively cheerful carers? If you still had your wits about you, didn't that make it worse? Would you have to pretend that it was all all right?

It was a very comfortable bed. Soft and deep, it offered a haven from the world. A person might live in such a bed, strewing books and biscuits across its considerable expanse. In the past, people had 'taken to their beds' and never got out again. It would have to be a bed such as this, to make any sense. There was something deliciously Victorian about it, and Thea felt she ought to wear a long cotton nightdress with tucks and ruches, and a flannel nightcap.

People really should be allowed to take their own mattress into the residential home, she thought. It was such a central factor in one's life. She remembered her father's affection for the big marital bed he and her mother had bought when they were first married. Maureen Johnstone regularly told the story of how carefully her new husband had selected the mattress and how important it had always been to him. Mrs Wilshire might well have felt the same. Perhaps her Richard had been born in this bed – almost certainly he'd been conceived in it.

She and Drew, she decided, would buy themselves a top-quality new bed, as soon as they finally came to live together.

Friday morning was there in a flash, after a fabulously good sleep. The spaniel hadn't moved a muscle all night, the sheets and blankets had moulded themselves to Thea's body perfectly, and her dreams had been full of contentment.

There were significant differences to this commission from the usual. Primarily, there were no animals to care for. No delicate elderly dogs or stand-offish cats. No lonely donkey or disconcerting parrot. Nothing downstairs needing food, exercise or love. Another difference was that the actual owner of the house would not be returning to assess her performance. Richard Wilshire might qualify as a replacement, but he would not have the emotional connection that his mother would. What was more, when he came back, everything would have changed. His reaction was uncertain, but Thea was determined to do a good job and earn the fee she'd been promised.

'To work!' she announced aloud, sliding regretfully out of the hospitable bed. Its height meant that she almost had to jump off the side, being a short person. It was a moment of nostalgia, taking her back to childhood days when she had barely managed to climb on and off her parents' handsome bed. She was liking it here, she realised. It was bringing philosophical thoughts that while not quite joyful, certainly weren't unduly melancholy or worrying. Mrs Wilshire had gone willingly, after all, if her son could be believed.

It was eight o'clock, and she allowed herself and the dog half an hour before the sorting began. 'Time for a little walk,' she said.

The house stood on a paved road, which only went a little way before morphing into a footpath – no less than the renowned Macmillan Way. The path crossed a large open field and then disappeared into a stretch of woodland. Thea let the dog run loose in the field, which undulated dramatically, showing evidence of ancient agriculture. There were no sheep or other dogs, and Hepzie ranged contentedly, nose to the ground. 'No time to explore the woods,' said Thea. 'That can wait for another day.'

As they turned back, she could see part of the village, with grey roofs and stone walls that were a weathered hue of a dark beige that was one of a wide spectrum of Cotswolds colours. In some villages they were much closer to yellow than they were here. Not only did age dictate the shade, but different quarries produced stone of different shades.

41

Chedworth was essentially an inward-looking place, she concluded. It was not on the way to anywhere, with no large roads within earshot. The A429 was a mile or so distant from the upper end of this long-drawn-out village. There was no enticement for tourists to come here either, with the Roman villa on a quite different road. Its railway had disappeared long ago, and the little River Churn was too small to attract any river-based activities. It offered nothing for visitors, other than a farm shop and the villa. The latter made no discernible impact on the village itself, as far as Thea could tell, although she did spot a faded iron sign at knee level, suggesting that by following the Macmillan footpath, it could readily be reached. She must not fail to go for a look at some point.

But work called, and she hustled the spaniel back and closed the front door behind them. Drew had assumed that the only rational way to proceed was to start with the attic and work downwards. Certainly, the attic contained the most mysterious items, not seen for ages. But they were also liable to be dirty, dusty, broken and spider-ridden. And wouldn't it make sense to clear some space downstairs first, before bringing stuff down to create more clutter? Richard had asked her to remove any objects that were un-arguably rubbish, giving little clue as to the quantity there might be. Even as he'd been speaking, she had resolved to err on the side of caution, consigning as little as possible to the 'to be thrown away' pile.

She had not anticipated the emotional consequences of the job, although the previous evening she had glimpsed something of the risk. The old lady's life was disintegrating before her eyes, as its component parts were sorted, boxed, and then stored for an indefinite time. None of them would ever be used or enjoyed by their owner again. There was a violence to it, a premature tidying away of a woman who still lived. No wonder her son felt guilty. Thea herself was aware of similar stirrings.

But she was being paid to do it, and if she gave it up, then someone else would be brought in. It would be no more ethical or sensitive to leave the house to moths and damp and rats. Now the owner was gone, the things were so much flotsam.

She went into the smaller of the two rooms at the back of the house, which had perhaps once been a sort of study or music room. It contained a substantial old bureau with a glass-fronted bookcase above it. There was also an upright piano against one wall, and two indistinct oil paintings hanging either side of it. She must get going on the first list, making an inventory of each room as she tackled it. The piano, for a start, was easy to log. She found a notepad left by Richard, and wrote 'Broadwood piano, mahogany. Fair condition.' Then she opened the flap of the bureau, feeling a great reluctance to examine the contents. There had been moments, during other house-sits, where she had done a spot of unauthorised snooping – opening drawers and lifting lids. But now, when it was expected of her, there was a foolish resistance.

There was nothing unduly personal to be seen. The cubbyholes were all full and in good order. A lot of chequebooks with just the stubs remaining; expired savings books and three old passports; bank statements and insurance policies. The sort of things that Mrs Wilshire's son or solicitor would perhaps need to sift through – and really not within Thea's remit at all. She closed it again, and turned to an inspection of the contents of the bookcase. There were two rows of hardbacks with their dust jackets still intact. They all had The Book Club printed at the base of their spines, and were novels by people such as Frank Yerby and Nevil Shute. She pulled a few out, for no good reason. Thanks to the glass doors, they were free of dust and perfectly dry.

'This isn't what you should be doing,' she muttered to herself. She wasn't being useful, inspecting items that were already in plain sight and of no great interest or value. She should be in the attic, or one of the smaller bedrooms. She should be upending boxes and emptying the wardrobes. The day would pass with nothing achieved, at this rate.

So she went upstairs and entered the second largest bedroom. Here was a big ottoman with a hinged lid, full of carefully folded cotton sheets with lavender bags tucked into the folds. Pillowcases edged with lace. Embroidered tablecloths. A silk counterpane. Lovely things that would never be used by the Wilshires again, but which might find homes if sold by specialists to those who collected such items. The ottoman itself was impressive, upholstered in red velvet and lined

44

with satin inside. Forgetting her instructions for a while, she simply indulged in the luxury of fingering the beautiful fabrics and imagining they were hers. They conjured a special kind of affluence, where quality was taken for granted, and no self-respecting lady would wear anything other than silk next to her skin. A time quite vanished now, of course. Personal items would be made of ivory and silver, largely handmade. Furnishings would be embroidered by wives and daughters with long evenings at their disposal. These days, if you were rich, you paid other people to make, choose and install all your possessions. You lived in vast empty monochrome rooms and thought only about how to accumulate more wealth.

With a sigh, she took up her notepad again and started a new page. The ottoman should be listed as a piece of furniture with a value, and then its contents carefully described. It took her over an hour. When done, she finally felt she had made some progress, moving to a wardrobe with a new sense of purpose.

Here were two fur coats, several outmoded suits and dresses, and a box holding a stiff canvas hat decorated with felt flowers. Again, it was safe to assume that Mrs Wilshire would not be wanting any of these garments again.

A yap from Hepzie, waiting on the landing outside the room, drew her attention. Next came a knock on the front door, which made Thea wonder if it was a repeat of a summons she had failed to hear the first time. There was a firmness to it that suggested impatience. She went down and pulled open the door.

Two people stood there, shoulder to shoulder, one of them disconcertingly recognisable.

Chapter Three

'Ah – you are in, then,' said the one she didn't recognise. 'We've been knocking.'

'Sorry. I was upstairs, half inside a wardrobe.'

A grimace of annoyance crossed the young face. 'Started already, have you? I suppose you're doing it for my father. I didn't expect him to waste much time, but this is obscene.' Thea waited for a foot to be stamped, but it didn't happen.

'Your father?' Thea was still magnetised by the familiar face of the other woman. Never a great fan of television, she nonetheless knew she had seen these features on a person from a prime-time drama series that had been running for years.

'I'm Millie Wilshire. This is my grandmother's house. I have to tell you that I find all this terribly upsetting. This is my friend Judith. Stop staring at her,' she finished crossly.

'Sorry,' said Thea again, dragging her eyes from the long Pre-Raphaelite face and the copper-coloured hair framing it. She looked at Millie, who had flyaway fair hair and a small pouting mouth. 'Your father said you weren't going to get involved. At least – that's what I understood.' She

46

realised that she had only heard this through Drew, and that it could have become exaggerated in the telling. 'Is there a problem with me being here?'

'Problem isn't the word. I absolutely hate the whole business. Gran should still be living here with all her things, instead of being carted off to a horrible home. And now it's being emptied and her valuables sold – and it's *wrong*. It's a disgrace.'

'As far as I know, nothing is going to be sold,' Thea corrected her. 'Your father just wants everything opened up and then listed, so he knows what there is. He's probably thinking about insurance and practical matters like that. Hasn't he discussed it with you?'

'We don't talk about it. He didn't ask my opinion, so now he's on his own.' She made a childishly spiteful face. Thea had an impression of an attitude adopted in haste and subsequently regretted.

'Have you been to visit her in the new place? It doesn't sound so bad to me.'

Millie paused and wiped away a tear. 'I can't *bear* to. She'll be so upset. It'll break my heart.'

Thea had quite a few things she'd have liked to say to that. *It's not your heart that matters,* was one. 'Don't you think she'd enjoy seeing you? If it's as bad as you think, she would surely appreciate a visitor.'

'You don't know anything about it. I have no idea who you are, but you obviously never met my Gran. She's a proud old lady – she'd hate me to see her so sad and *reduced*. My father is a *criminal* for doing what he's done.'

47

'It happened to my grandfather,' said Judith, speaking for the first time. Her voice was quite different from the one she used on TV. 'He only lasted two months. The place killed him.'

'See!' said Millie, as if this proved something

'Well...' Thea said, with no idea how she ought to respond. 'Do you want to come in?'

'Oh, no. I don't want to see it without Gran here. I only knocked because I saw your car and thought somebody must be here.'

This sounded odd to Thea, given that the little road led nowhere and couldn't possibly be passed accidentally. 'You obviously intended to come here,' she said impatiently. 'Have you got a key? Were you going to come in? Otherwise...' *Why are you here?* she wanted to ask.

'I thought I might catch my father, that's all. He's working around here this week, and I thought he might fit in an hour or two at the house, sorting things out or something.' She sounded hopelessly vague.

'But you knew he'd asked me to help? I mean – you didn't seem very surprised to see me.'

'He said he'd have to find someone to do it, if I wouldn't. I didn't think it would happen so quickly. And where *did* he find you, anyway? Are you some sort of girlfriend? Did he spend the night here? Because he never came home. I had to see to his dogs and he *knows* he can't rely on me to do that.'

Judith-the-famous-actor made a choked sound, as if the idea of Thea as Richard's girlfriend was too appalling for words.

'I am not any sort of girlfriend,' said Thea with

dignity. 'I met him through my fiancé, who knows him because he–' she stopped, afraid that a mention of Millie's grandmother's eventual funeral might be too much for her to cope with. 'He recently met your relatives,' she finished lamely.

'Is he paying you to dispose of the stuff, then? Are you in house clearance?'

'Not really – I told you, nothing's being cleared out. I'm usually a house-sitter. Your father just wants the stuff looked at. He says nobody's opened some of these boxes for decades. Long before you were born, anyway. It's a big job. I won't finish it for days and nothing's going to be thrown away unless it's utterly useless.' She took a deep breath in an effort to suppress her exasperation. Why did this girl need everything to be said three times? She went on more calmly, 'I think he'd be very pleased if you changed your mind about lending a hand. Have you got any brothers or sisters?'

Millie shook her head. 'There's only me. And Dad's an only, as well. I always think that's why we fight so much.'

Thea frowned at this remark, which made little sense to her. 'Huh?' she said.

'I mean, there wasn't anybody else to argue with. My mother never wanted to get involved. She said three was an awful number, and the only way to cope with it was for one person to stay detached. Very detached, is my mother.'

Judith laughed again. Thea was beginning to wonder whether she could actually function as a normal person, without a script to guide her. She had once before encountered a 'celebrity' during a house-sit; on the basis of that experience, she was prepared to believe that they were all inescapably peculiar.

'Well,' she said, wishing she was wearing rubber gloves, so she could brandish them to show how busy she was. 'There's a lot to do.'

'Just remember you're not to throw anything away,' said Millie passionately. 'It'll all come to me in the end. I want everything to stay in the family.'

This was at least a slightly different tack. From concern for her grandmother, Millie was now showing some good old-fashioned self-interest. But again, it struck a false note to Thea's ear. 'How do you know you want it, when you've no idea what there is?' she asked. 'Have you any use for antiquated curtains or lace bedspreads? Have you spoken to your grandmother about what she might want you to have? Is there a will?'

Millie flinched. 'Oh, I don't know,' she wailed. Then she seemed to gain more self-control. 'I did used to try sometimes, when I was younger. To find out what was in all those boxes and chests, I mean. She never wanted to talk about anything like that. She always managed to turn the conversation back to the other person. She's very clever, you know. Educated. But you could never get her to talk about the past. Family history and stuff like that seemed to annoy her. And my father's nearly as bad. He always says something like, "Best to leave all that alone. Remember Pandora's Box." He's always on about Pandora's Box,' she finished crossly.

Thea was reminded of Drew's new helper in his

50

funeral business, and wondered for a moment at the choice of name made by the woman's parents. Thea herself was something of a Pandora, she realised, with a rueful inward smile.

'Richard said she doesn't know I'm here,' she said, suddenly uncomfortable with that thought. 'I guess she wouldn't like it much if she knew.'

'Too right,' said Millie. 'She'd freak out if she thought anything was being thrown away or sold. But you've promised me that's not going to happen.'

'Well, of course it isn't up to me. And I imagine *some* things will go. Old newspapers and magazines, for a start. And there are vintage clothes that belong in a collection or museum or somewhere.'

Judith's eyes widened. 'Can we see them? Our wardrobe people are always looking for authentic old clothes.'

Thea hesitated. Millie was family, which obviously trumped a paid house sorter-outer – but Richard Wilshire's instructions hadn't covered such a situation. 'You should probably check with your father,' she said, again replying to Judith through Millie. 'I mean – he seems to think you've refused to get involved in anything here. If you want to look through the stuff, then maybe you should be doing the job instead of me.'

Millie gave an impatient huff, like a rich wife with a dim-witted employee. 'You don't know what you're talking about,' she snapped. 'This is *my* family's house. You can't keep me out of it.'

'I'm not trying to.'

51

'So why are we still standing here on the door-step?'

Thea closed her eyes against the powerful surge of frustrated helplessness. Again she'd have liked rubber gloves that could be torn off and flung on the ground. A gesture was certainly called for. She stood exaggeratedly aside and waved an arm. 'I asked you to come in, several minutes ago. Be my guest,' she said.

Neither young woman made a move. 'There's no time now. I want to find my dad,' said Millie. 'I've an idea where he might be. I'll phone him to check.'

Thea wondered just how close were this father and daughter, who argued and fought such a lot? The daughter said unkind things about the father, and yet apparently knew his daily movements in detail. 'Do you live with him?' she asked.

'Technically, yes. He's got a flat in Stratford and I'm there some of the time. Like last night. But he didn't come home and I don't know what to do with the dogs. That's why I'm here looking for him.'

'Where are you the rest of the time?' Thea asked, wondering as she did so why she was wasting time on fruitless curiosity. It was a constant need – to understand how people lived.

'I'm away a lot for work. On location.'

'You're an actor as well, then?'

Millie and Judith both laughed. 'No way! I'm in sound with the BBC. Outdoor stuff, mostly.'

'So that's how you two met?' Despite herself, Thea was curious about this unknown world.

'Actually, no. We went to the same college. High Wycombe. Judith's people were in Dubai much of the time, so she came to us in the holidays.'

'Vacations,' Judith corrected.

Millie rolled her eyes as if this was a recurrent argument. 'Anyway, we've been friends since then. It's like having a sister at last,' she added sentimentally.

'So...' Thea was losing patience – with herself as much as with these girls.

'All right. We'll go. Just don't throw anything away,' said Millie yet again, and the two of them turned to leave, Millie holding a mobile, presumably preparing to call her father.

Thea watched them for a few seconds and then looked around for her dog. Normally Hepzie liked to listen in to conversations with new people, and this time was no exception, although she was doing it from a short distance. She was stretched on a patch of grass under a small tree. 'Come on,' Thea ordered. 'Back to work.' An idle thought passed through her mind: *if Richard Wilshire hadn't gone home the previous night, then where was he?*

Before the dog could obey, a woman came across the small road towards her. 'Sorry to trouble you,' she said in careful tones, which in-stantly announced to Thea that this was someone who'd bettered herself and needed a voice to match her status. 'But was that Mrs Wilshire's granddaughter?' She indicated the car that was turning left to go back towards the village.

'Um...' said Thea cautiously.

'Oh, it's all right. I'm a friend. Norah Cookham's my name. I've known dear old Rita for over thirty years. Such a terrible shame, sending her off into a home. I saw you arrive last night. Do you mind my asking what it is you're doing here?'

I'll never get on at this rate, thought Thea desperately. She smiled faintly and said, 'Pleased to meet you.' Then she explained as briefly as she could what Richard had asked her to do. 'But I'm not removing anything from the house. Just making an inventory of the contents, that's all.'

Norah Cookham was about sixty-five, nicely dressed, with exaggeratedly large spectacles, well-cut hair and a confident manner. Thea strongly suspected that she had been observing the encounter on the doorstep for several minutes, from a front window of her house opposite. It was a magnificent house, with plenty of windows. There was a gravelled parking area containing a blue BMW. There were hundreds just like it across the Cotswolds.

The woman nodded, her eyes flickering in thought. Then she spoke in a jumble of comments that spilt out in a rush. 'The thing is, you see – I don't think Rita wanted to go. Not at all. I think she was coerced into it by that son of hers. Poor old girl never had a chance, with nobody to speak up for her. Where was that hopeless granddaughter when she needed her? Too late now, of course. *Much* too late to do anything about it.'

This little speech left Thea not knowing what to say. She could hardly argue the matter, quoting the various people who had given different opinions. All she felt was increasingly confused as to the nature and wishes of old Mrs Wilshire. Confused and rather worried. It made a difference, she found, to how she tackled the work set her. If the old lady was going to feel betrayed and violated by it, then that was horrible. But if she had willingly abandoned her house and its contents to her relatives to deal with as they saw fit, then that was perfectly comfortable. It seemed important to know where the truth lay, before she dived any further into the carefully packed and stored containers.

'In what way is it too late?' she asked. 'What do you mean?'

'Well, the deed is done, isn't it? The vultures are going to descend and nobody can stop them.'

This was too much for Thea. 'Mr Wilshire and Millie both seem extremely fond of her,' she objected. 'As far as I can see, they've both got her welfare at heart.'

'Not *them*,' said the woman. 'I'm talking about the *others*. That Martin and his children. I remember them coming here when they were tiny, especially that boy – Brendan, he's called. Rita spoilt him, having him to stay for weeks every summer with his little Arab friend. Thirty years ago, now, of course. But what does time matter when it comes to families? It all just sits there, doesn't it, waiting to jump out and bite you.'

Again Thea thought of Pandora, and what a fitting image that was, when she was herself opening lids on who-knew-what ancient troubles.

'I'm sure Mr Wilshire knows what he's doing,' she said firmly. 'I certainly can't see any reason to criticise him, and I have it from a quite independent source that his mother is perfectly happy in the care home. She has been very much involved in the decision to move. Nobody forced her into it.'

Norah Cookham narrowed her eyes. 'Is that what you think? Then let me tell you otherwise. I went to visit her yesterday, and I can promise you, she has *no idea* what's going on here. And if she did, it would make her very angry indeed.'

After a few more words of little consequence, Thea made her excuses and went back to her work. The bedroom was as she'd left it, and she sighed at her newly reluctant approach to the task she had agreed to undertake. If Norah Cookham was right, then she was party to something very unpleasant. But the emotions of the family were really not her concern. She might try to contact Richard Wilshire and explain that she needed firm assurances that she was not doing anything that would distress his mother, having heard what Mrs Cookham had to say. And there was also the fresh information conveyed by Millie to be factored in. Some of it was at odds with what Richard had told her.

She looked around the room, trying to decide what to do. There were four large drawers to be emptied after the wardrobe, with endless decisions as to how to arrange the contents. If Millie and her friend wanted them for a drama department, then wouldn't that be as good a fate as any other? Had Richard Wilshire categorically refused to allow her to have them? Was there some misunderstanding, whereby she had never actually asked him? Had he impetuously asked for Thea's help, only to realise that there really wasn't so much of a rush, and he should have listened more closely to his daughter? Would he turn up at lunchtime to tell her he was sorry, but she was not actually needed after all? And if he did that, would she still get paid?

The uncertainty had a slowing effect, but she decided to carry on as she had begun, although spending more time on each item she found. She piled the clothes from the wardrobe onto the single bed, in no special order. There was nothing that deserved to be thrown out. Every garment was in good condition, clean and un-damaged. When she moved to the chest of drawers, she found silk undergarments, thick knitted socks and big men's hankies and blouses neatly folded and separated from each other with tissue paper. Carefully, she wrote every-thing down on her list.

Inevitably, she drifted into reveries about Mrs Wilshire's life. Why would she keep all these things? They dated back to the 1940s, in many instances, when she would have been only a young woman – the age her granddaughter was now. Would she have worn the clothes then, and if so, how had they survived so well? Wasn't the normal thing for clothes to become worn out, torn and stained and finally used as rags? If they didn't suit you, or were the wrong size, you gave them to someone else or sent them to a jumble sale. These blouses in particular were perfect. Socks and hankies might never date, but almost everything else did. There was a suggestion of a sort of shrine in this room, Thea realised. Everything put away so carefully, protected from damage and never used. Perhaps they had never belonged to Rita Wilshire at all, but been rescued or bequeathed – kept because another woman had once owned them. Another woman who had gone away or died, leaving her lovely things high and dry.

Chapter Four

It was almost time for lunch, and Hepzie was getting restless. Another little walk might be a good idea. 'We can just do a quick circuit past the church,' Thea said.

This meant turning the other way from the earlier walk. The church was very close by, on a high point in a landscape of tremendous undulation. Just past the church gate, the ground fell away in a dramatic sweep down to the ancient pub on the main street. The way the hostelry squatted humbly directly below the grand serenity of the house of God was impossible to ignore. The church was in full light, nothing near it casting a shadow. But the pub gave the impression that it seldom saw any sunshine at all. The ground rose again behind it and large evergreen trees hemmed it in on either side. The facade was plain and dingy, although Thea surmised that this would not remain the case for long. The only place in Chedworth that offered any sustenance to visitors could not be permitted to present a

58

bad image.

She walked with her dog along a short stretch of the village street, passing a row of solid stone houses, many with attic windows projecting from their roofs, and no pavement for pedestrians. Since traffic was rare and slow, this caused very little worry on Thea's part. She had Hepzie on a lead, but as soon as they turned back up the little street that linked Mrs Wilshire's house to the main thoroughfare, she untied the dog and let her run free. They had performed a slow and crooked circle, more of a triangle in reality, and were back again within fifteen minutes. In that time, they had encountered not a single person. This was typical, and not at all surprising. There was, indeed, nowhere for people to go in the middle of a Friday. Somewhere towards Lower Chedworth, there was a primary school, sounds of playground games filtering across the valley. A dog barked in the distance and a plane flew overhead. Otherwise, the place was exceedingly quiet.

A quick snack comprising a sandwich made from the bread and ham she had brought from her Witney home, and then she went back upstairs for a look inside the third bedroom. This turned out to be the one Richard must have occupied before leaving home. Despite his assurances that there was nothing left in the house that he wanted for himself, there were possessions here that he had at least neglected to throw away. A guitar hung on the wall, for one thing. An odd home-made instrument, complete with strings, but with no hollow echo chamber, painted in swirly reds and purples. It must have been a short-lived interest – and besides, it would be unlikely to yield a good sound. There were two old transistor radios and a box containing obsolete wires and plugs. All rubbish, Thea assumed. She would have to start a pile for things likely to be destined for the tip.

The last and smallest upstairs room was the most cluttered. It contained old suitcases, a filing cabinet, a broken office chair and a lot of cardboard boxes stacked almost to the ceiling. Stuff that was too big or heavy to go up into the attic, Thea supposed, with a sinking heart. This was turning into a mammoth job, which would take more than a week to fulfil adequately. Professional house clearance people would presumably just bundle the boxes into a skip without checking their contents, along with the suitcases. From the little Richard Wilshire had said, Thea was expected to at least open them all, check for value or interest and then write down what there was. When she set about doing this, she found a few bundles of envelopes obviously containing letters, along with diaries and notebooks, sketchpads and postcards.

It no longer felt like a treasure hunt. When first explained to her, some weeks earlier, it had sounded like something that would be fun. With an interest in history, she had anticipated plenty of fascinating material to browse through. Now, the sheer weight of it all made her feel tired, along with the unease as to the consequences of all this disturbance. A nagging sense of guilt followed her every move. She should have phoned Richard for reassurance, but she kept hoping that his daughter would have found him and said enough to bring him back, without her needing to summon him. She was being more slow and careful than at first, conscious that she might have to put everything back as she'd found it.

At first she had assumed that a handful of old letters and photos would be delightful to examine. Now, with such a quantity of personal paperwork in front of her, she felt mostly sad. There was so much of it, inevitably containing a wealth of detail about the lives of Rita Wilshire and her family. Just one family out of millions, creating this great mass of recorded fact and feeling, which nobody was ever going to care about. Three suitcases and five full boxes was far and away too much for one person to leave behind. There were countless packets of old letters in their original envelopes that had been held together with rubber bands that had now perished, so that the bundles fell apart as soon as she tried to lift them out. They mainly seemed to date back to the 1950s and 60s, many of them typed. Nothing special – just the normal accumulation that anyone could produce, if they were not given to throwing anything away.

When she opened a drawer of the filing cabinet she found dozens of cardboard folders containing newspaper cuttings, recipes, knitting patterns, old theatre programmes, and huge numbers of leaflets and booklets garnered from visits to stately homes, museums, castles, exhibitions and other places of interest. It would appear that for one substantial period of her life, Mrs Wilshire had been an avid traveller, not just in Britain, but France, Italy and Germany too. Everywhere she went, she had gathered up colourful souvenir leaflets and kept them on file in perpetuity. A biographer would be in heaven, tracing her progress around Europe. But there was no biographer, and nobody else could possibly want to know all the places she had been.

Even more dispiriting was the discovery of a lifetime's worth of diaries. No fewer than twelve five-year diaries, all the same size, most of them secured with a tiny lock, piled in three layers inside the drawer. Sixty years, with a daily record of the weather, people met, films and TV programmes viewed, interspersed with momentous births, marriages and deaths. None of the locks was actually in operation, so it was simple to open them and read their contents. She spent half an hour flitting from 1957 to 1977, then on to 1994 and finally 2010. The writing was legible, and nearly every line in every book had been used. Four lines to a day. A page to a date, so the years came one below the last, and you could easily see what had happened on, say April 10th in 1957, 58, 59, 60 and 61. And very little of note had happened, it seemed. Again, only a dedicated biographer would ever take the trouble to go through it all.

But could you actually dump diaries in a skip? This was a woman's *life*, recorded meticulously. While she was still living, it would be essential to have her permission before discarding them. Similarly the hundreds of photos Thea found in one of the boxes, dating back to the monochrome 1950s and beyond. This was a more familiar dilemma to Thea. Just about everybody had a stack of old albums predating the digital age, and almost never looked at them. It was a relief, in most people's minds, that such albums would soon disappear entirely, leaving far less space-hungry methods of storage for one's pictures. It hardly seemed worth making a list of all this. She wrote 'Diaries, letters and photos' and left it at that.

Time swept by and she had little to show for it. Richard Wilshire would have to get more involved than he apparently wished to, because she, Thea, was not going to make irrevocable decisions for him. When the door knocker sounded at half past three, she and Hepzie exchanged looks of relief from the work that had at some point mutated from fascination into tedium.

Millie Wilshire stood there again, this time without a companion. She looked dazed and uncertain.

'Hello?' said Thea.

'He's not here, is he? My dad, I mean.'

'No. Why? Are you still looking for him? It sounds as if you really have lost him.' It was inappropriately facetious, she realised a second later.

'Yes, I have. He's not answering his phone, and nobody's seen him all day. In fact, I can't imagine where he's been since yesterday afternoon. What time did you get here? What time did he leave? Did he say where he was going?'

'Um...' said Thea, selecting the question she thought most relevant. 'It must have been nearly seven o'clock. He said he had a visit to make.

Something like that.'

'What does that mean? Where did he go? This *never* happens. He's completely predictable these days, and he *always* answers his phone, or calls right back. He *lives* for the phone. People call him all the time for work.' She fought down her anxiety enough to say more calmly, 'I thought perhaps you'd called him with a question and he'd popped in because he's in the area. He's supposed to be at Yanworth, then Stow, then Chipping Campden. In that order. He had appointments.'

'I haven't seen him or spoken on the phone to him. I did think of it after you'd gone this morning, but I decided not to.' It was impossible to know how concerned to be, but if the man's daughter was worried, it would seem that there was something wrong. 'Do you always stay in such close touch?' she asked.

'It's only because we live under the same roof. You do need to know where the other person is. Apart from anything else, there are the dogs. We don't bother each other much, in the usual run of things. But he has been a bit funny lately, and now he's vanished, it's like...' she tailed off. 'It scares me that I can't find him,' she finished.

'But you fight a lot? You didn't agree about your grandmother going into the home.' A faint hypothesis was developing in Thea's mind, in which the man was deliberately avoiding the accusing girl, his own guilty feelings already more than enough without her input. 'Could he have gone to visit her, perhaps?'

Millie blinked in confusion. 'No, of course

64

not. He has to *work*. He goes to the home at weekends – or early evening, sometimes.'

'You know all these farms he visits, do you?' It seemed highly unlikely that she would. 'And where did Judith go?'

'Can I come in if you're going to ask all these questions?'

'Sorry. I'm just trying to understand. And you asked me quite a lot, as well. Come on in.' They went into the front room together, where Millie stood looking intently around herself. Thea was unsure whether she was checking for missing objects or hoping to find her father hiding in a corner.

'I know which farms he has to visit. He's got a great big map up on the wall in the flat. I used to go with him sometimes when I was little. I like farms. I've got a thing about pigs. Not that you see so many these days. We don't really talk much any more. Our lives are quite separate. Just lately, we've hardly spoken to each other except about meals and that sort of thing.'

'Because of your gran?'

'Partly. That's been a real mess. Her friends have been vile about it. People who never lifted a finger to help now tell him he's a monster for doing what he's done.'

'But he says she *wanted* to leave. It was her own choice. And I thought you felt much the same as the friends.'

'It's not really true that it was her choice. She just couldn't see any way of avoiding it. Dad stopped fixing up the house like he used to. It was a *campaign* – that was the word he used himself.

A campaign to get her to see her situation the same way he saw it. It upset me every time he talked about it, thinking how miserable she must be about it. He said she'd fall downstairs, or set the place on fire, and then what would people say. She *has* been very wobbly on her legs. But she could have brought the bed downstairs and used the outside loo. I still think it's horrible.'

'Did she care what people said about her?'

Millie nodded. 'She did, rather. At least, she liked to keep up an independent image.'

'But you don't visit her?'

Millie flinched. 'I've been ever so busy. I took her out for lunch one weekend, not so long ago. While she was still living here, that was. And then it all seemed to happen really fast, and Dad got all quiet and withdrawn because of the guilt he was feeling.'

'But wouldn't her friends see that at her age a home is really the best place for her?'

'Some, maybe. Not others. There's a woman who lives opposite. Norah. She has this sniffy way of showing Gran what she thinks.'

'I met her today. Just after you were here. She said they'd been friends for thirty years, and she visited her in the home yesterday.'

'Yeah – I guessed she'd be watching. She always is. I'm surprised she visited, though – nothing better to do, probably. She and Gran email each other mostly. Even when they lived so close, they did it. Gran loves email. Norah and Dad fell out a while ago. She's been pretty unpleasant to him since then. I don't think Gran would count her as a friend, exactly. She keeps trying to set her against Dad, which is really stupid.'

'Has she got a husband?'

'Not any more.'

Thea was reminded of a house-sit she did in Blockley before she met Drew. There was an old lady with bothersome neighbours there, too. That was also where she'd met the celebrity rapper who had given the most bizarre comments on events going on around him. 'Where's Judith?' she asked again.

Millie frowned. 'She had to get back to London for something. She stayed the night with me at the flat last night and she and I had lunch today up at Kilkenny. Nice pub, that, by the way. Then the car came for her and she was off.'

'Car?'

'Right. Courtesy of the BBC. They all have their own drivers, like royalty. It's another world.'

'I suppose it is. She *is* awfully famous,' said Thea, thinking that if she recognised the actress, then almost everybody would.

'She's nice, though. It hasn't spoilt her. At least...'

'I suppose it must have an effect on a person.'

'It's mostly the being recognised all the time. People think they know her, and that's exhausting. There's never any peace.'

'Must be complicated for you as well.'

'I'm a haven from it all. Dad and me, that is. She loves coming to stay with us. She thinks my dad's perfect. We both think she's amazing, getting so successful before she's even twenty-five.'

An unworthy thought flitted across Thea's mind. Judith was young and pretty; Richard

Wilshire was divorced and appeared not to have a woman in his life. Did he harbour fantasies about his daughter's famous friend? Wouldn't it be odd if he didn't? And did Judith have a boyfriend of her own age?

'Well, I'm sure there's a simple explanation for him going missing. Did you say you'd been to the farms he was meant to visit?'

'One of them. He was due in Yanworth at eleven this morning, expecting to be there about two hours. I was thinking he might join us at the pub for lunch. I deliberately chose one that was more or less on his way. So Judith and I waited by the gate from about half twelve. When he didn't come, I went in to find him. The farmer was in the yard, all his cows assembled and waiting, but Dad had never shown up. The chap was furious. He kept me talking for ages. Said he could see for himself that he'd got at least four reactors. There's a lump that comes up on the animal's neck. He hardly needed Dad to tell him. He'd tried Dad's mobile as well, with no reply. I didn't know what to say to him. Something *must* have happened. I should call the police,' she burst out. 'I know he wouldn't let Andrew down like that if he was all right.'

'Andrew's the farmer?'

'Right. He was so angry,' the girl said miserably. 'The TB business is so cruel. I don't know how they bear it. Those poor cows, killed in their prime – and it's always the farmer's favourite that has to go.'

It would seem that this young lady was not good at bearing things, Thea thought. A sensitive

68

little flower, evidently. Even perhaps a moral coward. 'I imagine your dad has to take a fair bit of aggravation when he breaks the bad news,' she said.

'And the rest. They're always yelling at him about it, and how the tests are so inaccurate and there's no justice. He's had to get very thick-skinned about it.'

'Somebody has to do it,' Thea murmured, not really believing her own words. If nobody would do it, the system would have to change, and that might be a very good thing. 'Well ... I'm not sure what we ought to do now. As far as I'm concerned, I've got my instructions, and I'd better press on with the job. It's up to you whether you contact the police, but as I understand it, they're unlikely to worry too much about a grown man not answering his phone.'

'I know,' Millie said. 'Especially when he's done it before.'

'Pardon?'

'He went off with no warning five years ago. It was dreadful. He came back three months later and never said where he'd been. It ruined the marriage with my mum. Well – you can understand it, can't you? She was sure he'd been away with another woman, and he would never persuade her otherwise.'

Thea was lost for words. That ordinary, stiff-backed man had some kind of secret life, then. Other implications dawned on her, thanks to this astonishing piece of family history. No wonder Millie got agitated when he went off without saying where he was going. No wonder she was such a clingy daughter, well into her twenties. Because despite her protestations, she was clearly panicking at his unexpected absence.

'You said he was completely predictable now? And yet...?' she left the question hanging.

'I know – it sounds silly, doesn't it. But this time I know it's different,' Millie insisted. 'This time, I'm sure something awful's happened to him.'

Chapter Five

Millie left, saying she had no idea where she should try next in her search for her father. She still seemed dazed and unfocused. Thea could offer little convincing reassurance, still unable to grasp much useful information about the various characters in the Wilshire family. Her own position was uncertain if Richard didn't materialise. Who would pay her? The ethics of the business had become even more murky than before, and she wondered whether she ought to go and see old Mrs Wilshire herself. That might bring a very necessary enlightenment – but it might also be frustrating, painful and embarrassing.

The afternoon was waning, which meant she could decently abandon the work for the day. She could sit and watch TV, phone Drew and feed Hepzie. The absence of any other animals to care for felt more strange as time went by, rather than less. There should be a bewildered dog to console or a cat to befriend. Instead there was a void, which any amount of mysterious old possessions couldn't fill. Perhaps, she thought, she could bring a manageable pile of letters or diaries downstairs and sit with them on her lap, going through them slowly. Or was that too intrusive? There had been no vetoes at all. Nothing was said to be private or out of bounds. Besides, you couldn't just discard letters without reading them first. They might be from somebody famous, or have tremendous family significance. The problem, of course, was knowing significance when you saw it. The historian in her resisted the idea of binning any papers at all. But she had accepted the job, and at the very least she ought to produce a modest pile of totally superfluous and irrelevant business correspondence labelled 'To be thrown away'.

She ran much of this past Drew when she phoned him. He listened carefully and concluded, 'You haven't got time to read everything, by the sound of it. And if Millie's taking an interest after all, you should probably leave it to her to go through actual personal letters. Don't you think?'

'I'm not sure she is taking much interest, actually. I can't work her out. She disapproves of putting her granny in a home, but she doesn't go to visit her there. She doesn't seem to have much idea about other people's feelings. It's all about her. Admittedly she is worried about her dad, but that's because he's let her down in the past and she's not sure she can trust him. I expect he'll turn up again.'

71

'I hope he does eventually. I'll need him to sign things when the old lady dies.'

'Drew! That could be years and years away.'

He laughed. 'I was joking – sort of. In fact, I don't think I would need him, anyway. It's all prepaid, which is the main thing.'

She had a thought. 'Do you suppose he *intended* to go missing all along? I mean – he's got his ducks in a row, hasn't he? Nobody really needs him any more. He's free to go off to his secret life.'

'Sounds exciting. And Richard Wilshire did not strike me as an exciting sort of person.'

'Little do you know, he's got hidden depths,' said Thea, and told him about the man's disappearance five years previously.

'I had no idea,' Drew said. 'Where on earth can he have been? And has he gone there again?'

'Millie thinks not, for some reason. She's sure he's in trouble of some kind. The problem for me is – do I carry on as instructed, assuming he'll turn up next week and pay me?'

'Good question.'

'That's not helpful.'

'Wait till I get there. It looks as if I can be with you tomorrow afternoon and stay until sometime on Sunday.'

'With the kids?'

He paused teasingly. 'Not with the kids.'

'Pandora's having them?'

'Not Pandora. Not Maggs. Nobody you know. Timmy's got a friend, Jake, who has a birthday. They're going to a thing called Digger World, and there's a sleepover afterwards. Not to be outdone, Stephanie organised to go to *her* friend's house as well. I'm not sure she's altogether popular with the family concerned, but I've been on the phone to the mothers for ages, getting the logistics straight and promising to reciprocate sometime. How do people manage with five children, like your sister?'

'They don't need friends. They've got each other. They do music lessons, most of them, some sport, and that's about it. Anyway, you get special credit for being a single father. All those mums feel sorry for you.'

'So they should.'

'Well, I don't.'

'You're a hard woman.'

'Careful! I don't have to let you in, you know. But I will, because you're going to love the mattress on the bed here. It must be stuffed with angels' wings or something, it's so soft. You can drown in it.'

'Hmm. Doesn't sound very healthy.'

'Nonsense. Anything that ensures such a lovely deep sleep must be wonderfully good for you.'

She could sense his hesitancy when it came to talk about bed. Drew had a streak of prudishness that she found quite endearing. He never indulged in anything that could be remotely described as telephone sex during their nightly conversations, for which she was grateful. It could only lead to frustration and a feeling that something between them had been tainted. Besides, his children were in the house, and he could never be entirely sure they weren't hearing some of what he said.

73

She changed the subject. 'Any funerals booked for next week?'

'Two. One Tuesday, one Wednesday. Both small, with family carrying the coffin, so it'll be easy enough with me and Pandora. She's really doing ever so well, you know. I thought Maggs was unique and nobody could ever match her for enthusiasm and competence, but Pandora's getting very close.'

'Is Maggs jealous?'

'She would be if she noticed, but she's so wrapped up in little Meredith, she doesn't care what happens here.'

'I should go and see her.' Thea was in no great hurry to inspect the baby, although she was curious to see how it had turned out, with a short plump mixed-race mother, and a very tall fair-skinned Devonian father. Maggs had been adopted as a tiny baby, and her parents were, according to Drew, utterly besotted with the newcomer. 'Are the grandparents still around?'

'Oh – I forgot to tell you. They're planning to move house, to be closer. That's very good news for me and Peaceful Repose, if it means they'll mind the baby when Maggs comes back to work.'

'Aren't they terribly old?'

'Not really. He's seventy-five and she's about seventy. Maggs isn't thirty yet, you know. She's always seemed older than she really is.'

'Time for a whole litter of babies, then.'

'Could be. Den seems to think another one's on the cards, at least.'

'Already!'

'No, I mean theoretically. He's a different man

these days. It's as if something's got uncorked, and released all sorts of sentimental stuff he's been bottling up.'

'Sweet,' said Thea, injecting all the sincerity she could muster into her voice. She and Carl had only produced one child, in their early twenties, and never been especially demonstrative or sentimental about it. Jessica had turned out well, forging a career path through the Greater Manchester police force. Thea kept in touch, and saw her every couple of months or so, but they were nobody's idea of a devoted mother and daughter. Which made her think of Millie Wilshire again. 'Did you meet Richard's wife?' she asked. 'Millie's mother.'

She could hear his gulp of surprise at the abrupt switch. 'No. She's got a new man, or something, hasn't she?'

'I don't know any more than what you told me last month. Do you think she's got designs on this house at all? Is she actually divorced from Richard?'

'No idea. It's a very casual acquaintance, you know. I realise I should probably have vetted them in more detail on your behalf, but I assumed you'd work it all out for yourself, the way you do usually.'

'So you think I should leave the letters and things unread, then,' she concluded, ignoring his words. 'Just empty all the cupboards and boxes and try to sort everything out and make lists of it all?'

'Right. And don't forget the attic.'

'I'm leaving that until you get here. You can go

75

ahead and wrestle all the spiders into submission.'

'Very funny. I thought you could take a break, while I'm there.'

'You thought wrong. I'd never finish if I did that. You can help.'

'Providing we can go out in the evening somewhere – I've got a long list of things I ought to check. Won't you take Sunday morning off, either?'

'I might. Just get here as soon as you can, and we'll see.'

'I'll drive like the wind.'

'Good,' she said, not being superstitious enough to think that any injunction to be careful would make a difference. She had lost a husband to a road accident; she had little fear that the same fate would befall her fiancé.

Her second night on the blissful mattress went just as serenely as the first had done. She sank into it with a sigh of delight, compounded by the knowledge that Drew would be with her for the third night, and the old thing would be tested in quite a different way. The likely wallowing and floundering this could entail might add to the fun, she thought hopefully. A flash of memory of the unfortunate results of lovemaking with her previous boyfriend in a strange bed was quickly suppressed. Phil Hollis's back was something she definitely did not want to think about.

Saturday morning dawned dry and sunny, and it seemed a shame to be indoors. But there was no choice but to carry on with her unpacking, sorting and listing. She finally established a routine that speeded things up considerably. A pattern within the house itself came into focus, too. The main bedroom held clothes, shoes and magazines that were relatively current. Although quite tidy, it had obviously been a room in daily use, with much less care taken to preserve things in good condition. Drawers of jumbled headscarves, gloves, socks – it suggested normal life, as did the contents of the wardrobe. The second bedroom, however, was like a museum by comparison, everything packed away and then left to gather dust. Thirdly was Richard's one-time retreat, with boyhood possessions abandoned and forgotten. Lastly, the little dressing room was a personal archive, with the numerous diaries and packets of letters. It made perfectly good sense now, and Thea found herself making decisions more easily as she examined the things with a more cursory interest than before. There were still unanswered questions, it was true, but she had a feeling they would be explained relatively easily once she had a better look at the paperwork.

Overhead, the attic weighed on her like a threat. Attics were where the real clutter was generally to be found. Beloved objects that no longer worked; precious outgrown toys; overflow from bookshelves and cupboards; and anything that might one day come in useful. Although Rita Wilshire did not strike her as a woman who hoarded short lengths of string, used paper or plastic bags, empty envelopes or sheets of brown paper, she was still a woman who threw as little away as possible. There was sure to be a mass of stuff to be tackled on the top floor of the house.

Fortunately, Drew was going to be there to help. She was determined to employ him for much of the Sunday morning, despite his intention to visit his neglected house in Broad Campden.

But first there was Saturday morning, and that was rudely interrupted before eleven o'clock. The door knocker rapped insistently and Thea thumped crossly down the stairs, from where she had been trying to create some order, to answer it.

Millie Wilshire was there yet again, this time with two companions. Hepzie, following as always in her mistress's wake, was delighted to see that there were visiting canines: a pair of black and white sheepdogs, looking dauntingly intelligent and intrigued, squirmed around Millie's legs.

'Er... Hello,' said Thea. 'Is there any news of your father?'

'Not a word. Listen – these are his dogs. The poor things were on their own in the house all day yesterday. I decided – partly thanks to you, I should say – to go and see Gran. But I've got quite a few other jobs as well, and there's nobody to look after them. Up to now, Gran's always taken them, but she obviously can't now. I don't suppose you'd have them here, would you? They know the house and they're terribly well behaved. They just need to be kept amused. Dad takes them to work with him quite a lot, and they really are fantastically obedient.'

'Kept amused,' Thea repeated. 'How, exactly?'

'You can take them for a run. There's a big field just up there.' She pointed towards the footpath that Thea had found the previous day. 'Throw balls for them, that sort of thing.'

'How long do you want me to keep them?'

Millie heaved a dramatic sigh. 'Well, if my father doesn't come back, a day or so, I suppose. I'll leave him a note at the flat and send a text, to tell him where they are. If he shows up, he'll come and collect them from you.'

'But you don't think he will,' said Thea, noting the tone of the girl's words. 'And then what? What am I supposed to do? About the house, I mean.'

Millie merely gave her a blank look. 'I've stopped trying to guess what's happened to him. I don't see what I can do if the police won't listen to me. Either I just sit at home worrying, or I get on with my own life and assume he knows what he's doing. Judith thinks it's the stress of all this stuff with Gran that's sent him off the rails. That's what she says, anyway. She might just be trying to stop me thinking it's something more sinister than that.'

Thea heard the implications all too clearly. Like Judith, she was eager to avert any such line of thinking. 'I'm sure she's right. He's just gone off to sort himself out for a bit. Now it's the weekend, he can have a breathing space. And your grandmother might well know where he is, anyway. I don't expect anybody's asked her, have they?'

'That's where I'm going this afternoon. But he's never just abandoned the dogs like this. He

79

knows I've got to work. And he let Andrew and the others down yesterday. That's completely out of character.' She noticed Thea's sceptical expression, and went on defensively, 'It *is*. Last time wasn't the real Dad. Some madness came over him. He's not like that any more.'

Thea sighed and scrutinised the dogs. 'What are their names?'

'Betsy and Chummy. They're both girls, but they're not sisters.'

Thea continued her inspection. One was much longer-haired than the other, with a wider head and bushier tail. But the markings were similar. They were clean and looked very healthy. 'Did you bring food, and leads and bedding, and all that?' she asked.

'In the car. This is ever so kind of you. I know it wasn't what you agreed to, but we'll pay you extra, of course. How's the sorting out going?' she asked with a rueful expression, as if to convey that she had reconsidered some of her opinions on the subject.

'Better. I'm getting into the swing of it now. But I haven't been into the attic yet. I'm more and more worried that I shouldn't be doing it at all without knowing where your father is. If you're going to see your gran, maybe you could check it with her?'

'No, I can't. I told you – she doesn't know about you being here. I wouldn't dream of telling her.'

'Well, I might chicken out of doing the attic.'

Millie grimaced. 'I was always terrified of going up there. I remember when I was little

80

and came here one time, there were two boys visiting Gran and they shut me in and took the ladder away. I screamed the house down and the father of one of them thrashed them both.'

'Heavens!' said Thea. 'Who were they?'

'Cousins of some sort, I think,' she said with a frown. 'I was too little to understand how they were related.' Her face showed how hard she was trying to remember. 'I'd forgotten the whole thing until now. Now I think about it, one of them must have been Brendan. The other one was just a friend, I think.'

'Not Martin?' asked Thea, remembering something that Norah Cookham had said the previous day.

'Do you know Martin?' Millie's eyes widened. 'Has he been here?'

'No, no. I just heard the name.'

'He's Gran's nephew. Terribly rich and successful. Dad hates him.'

Thea did her usual mental gymnastics where family trees were involved. 'Cousins, then,' she concluded. 'Your father and Martin. His son is your second cousin.'

Millie shrugged. 'It doesn't matter. So you might leave the attic, then? Does that mean the job's almost finished?'

'That depends. It would take a while to put everything back as it was.'

'Well, don't go yet. I need you to mind the dogs. You'd probably enjoy the attic, and the ladder's much easier to use now. Gran had a few restructuring jobs done, including that staircase and the hatch at the top. It's got wiring and everything now. You could use it as a bedroom if you wanted to. There's a Velux window, as well.'

Thea had been resisting the prospect of groping in the dark roof space, accessed only by a wobbly ladder. Now she knew there'd be light and perhaps a proper floor, it took on a more inviting aspect. 'My fiancé's coming this afternoon,' she said. 'He'll help me for a bit.' She frowned as she thought over what Millie had just said. 'You wouldn't think the house needed any more bedrooms, even if your grandfather was still alive at the time. Why go to all that expense?'

'Grandpop wasn't alive. He died when I was three. I don't remember him. No – the idea was that we'd move in here and live with Gran, when I was about eleven. I don't know what went wrong, but it never happened. There was some falling-out, I suppose. I have a sort of memory of my mother shouting about it, and being in a foul mood for months. Probably she just refused to live with her mother-in-law. She was probably right that it would never have worked out. They never talked about it afterwards, but I think my dad was always disappointed. He really loved this house when he was little. I think he's changed his mind about it since then, though. The way he's neglected it is pretty bad.'

A momentary silence served to remind Thea that she should be working. 'Well...' she began.

'I have to go,' said Millie at the same time. 'Thanks ever so much for having the girls. They'll be no trouble, I promise.'

'You didn't give me much choice,' said Thea, with a weak smile to soften the words. 'And I must admit I was finding it a bit strange not to have any animals to look after. That's what people usually want me to do, you see.'

'Of course, if Dad turns up, he'll come and collect them right away. You might only have them for a few hours. Who knows?'

Who indeed, thought Thea. The disappearance of Richard Wilshire should probably be worrying her rather more than it was.

Millie made her escape, with a perfunctory farewell to the dogs – who watched her closely the whole time she carried the box of their things to the front door – got into her car and drove away out of sight. Then they sighed in unison and raised their muzzles expectantly in Thea's direction. They had ignored Hepzibah and her efforts to become their new best friend. Sheepdogs did that in Thea's experience. They were snooty and superior and impossibly clever. Always panting to be helpful and completely incapable of spending a quiet morning in peaceful contemplation. But they knew the house, and made their way shoulder to shoulder into the kitchen, where they sat on a handmade rag rug in front of the Aga, which was cold. Richard Wilshire had neglected to give instructions for firing it up, and Thea knew better than to tinker with it. At first glance, it showed signs of considerable age and was sure to be highly temperamental.

'You stay here for an hour or so, while I get back to work,' Thea told them.

Okay, they said resignedly. But make sure it's not more than an hour.

Did they know where their master was? Thea

wondered. They showed no signs of anxiety or distress at the change of routine. Perhaps he'd explained it all to them and they were perfectly content to wait for his return.

She went back upstairs, and managed to forget about the dogs and their absconding owner for a while. There was always a fascinating family history to be discovered in these sorts of circumstances, as Thea had learnt. Already absorbed by the biographical material kept in the little bedroom, she realised there was a story attached to the house itself, as well. Any house carried marks of the lives it had sheltered, but a beautiful old Cotswold house might have more than its share. She had noted two cupboards, as yet unexplored. One under the stairs, and a very big one in the main bedroom. Most families would have transformed the latter into a small bathroom, but the glance Thea had given it had revealed an almost empty space, rather to her surprise. Perhaps it had been the preserve of the deceased Grandpop, and nobody had ever taken it over after he died. It would come in useful as a repository for some of her sorted piles, she thought. Being able to spread things around made the operation a lot easier. She was inclined to return to the ottoman, and really examine all the lovely things again. Although she'd already listed them, she could spread them out and inspect them for holes or stains which ought to be noted on the inventory.

So she embarked on just that procedure, with a growing sense of achievement. The old satins and velvets were in excellent condition, for the most part. There was a fur cape in a rippling silvery colour that screamed *luxury* and was probably still quite valuable in the right market. Chinchilla, she thought. It sparked musings about the way humanity exploited other species for their own ends. Poor little animals, slaughtered for the warm pelts that nature had given them.

But she didn't dwell on this for long, distracted by the discovery of two flamboyant hats at the back of a high shelf in the wardrobe. Fit only for a dressing-up box, she judged. Perhaps her sister Jocelyn's children would like them – although they were probably rather old for dressing up by now. Noel, the youngest, was eleven. There had been some talk about a group of his friends getting together for some role play games. Presumably that involved donning outlandish garb to represent various warriors and goblins. The last time Thea had visited, Noel had talked relentlessly about the latest fantasy series he was reading, with detailed descriptions of dozens of characters.

And all the time, she was mentally counting the hours and minutes until Drew would arrive. He had deliberately avoided naming an exact time, knowing how unpredictable his schedule would be. All she knew was 'afternoon', which meant he wouldn't want lunch – but an evening meal was definitely going to be required, especially if she made him go and ferret about in the attic as soon as he arrived.

Those dogs would want exercise, too. Could they wait until Drew arrived, so they could all go out together? She wanted to get a better idea of how Chedworth was arranged. All she had managed to glean so far was a long straggling main street with numerous loops and cul-de-sacs leading off it, and a myriad of public footpaths going in all directions. To the north was woodland and a Roman villa. At least she had found the two significant landmarks for any village – the church and the pub. From there, everything else ought by rights to fall into place.

It occurred to her that she had not given Drew any instructions on how to find the house. Then she recalled that he had recently started to use a satnav, with all the zeal of the convert. 'The road signs will all fall into ruin before long,' she'd said irritably. 'They don't think anybody needs them any more.'

'That might be true, but honestly, it is fun. The thing knows *exactly* where you're going. It's like magic.'

'You're being deskilled,' she said. 'You'll be sorry one of these days.'

She must find distraction, she told herself. It was barely midday. He would most likely not even have left home yet.

So she thought about Richard Wilshire instead. Where, for heaven's sake, had the man disappeared to? His daughter struck Thea as an unreliable witness on a number of levels. She had initially refused to ever come to Chedworth again, according to Drew's original report on the commission. Then she had casually appeared on the doorstep with her famous friend, but declined to enter the house. She was vague and volatile by turns, swinging from anger to anxiety, then back to a relatively businesslike answer to the problem of the abandoned dogs. She had poured out a mass of information that would take a lot of sorting out, if Thea ever decided she wanted to understand even the basic structure of the Wilshire family.

The absence of Millie's father was clearly of deepening concern to the girl – and if she was honest, Thea herself was growing increasingly worried about him. And yet there was a sense of a family that did not share information very readily. Rita didn't know her house was being ransacked. Millie wasn't sure about anything in the past – even the identity of her own cousins. Judith was an additional complication, and the dogs were stark reminders that something irresponsible and perhaps alarming was going on.

But Drew would shed some light, she was sure. He knew the Stratford addresses of Richard and his mother, for a start. He would take a clear view of the ethics of the situation, as regards how much more delving into Mrs Wilshire's possessions they should do. Without him, Thea might have been tempted to feel a degree of resentment. She might conclude that she was being taken for granted, for example. And that might tempt her to think it would serve the Wilshires right if she bundled up some of these gorgeous old clothes and took them home with her. If nobody paid her, that could be rationalised as nothing more than her due. But Drew would never permit such an act. Knowing this made her smile ruefully, as she covetously fingered a velvet jacket.

She would have to go down and see to the

dogs. They'd be bored soon and that might lead to bad behaviour. She could at least take them to the nearby field and give them a bit of fresh air. Not that she dared let them run free – that way led to all kinds of terrible trouble, as she had learnt in Lower Slaughter.

'Come on, then,' she invited them, having found their leads in the box still sitting in the hall. 'Heps, you can go loose, if you're good.' Keeping three dogs from tangling themselves around her legs was not an inviting prospect. She opened the front door and ushered them all out. Before she reached the gate, there was a loud voice signalling urgent annoyance, coming towards her.

'What does she want this time?' Thea muttered, as she waited for Norah Cookham to get close enough to speak normally.

Chapter Six

'What are those dogs doing here?' she demanded, without preamble.

Thea ran quickly through a selection of responses: flippant, defensive, outraged or placatory. None of them felt quite wise. 'Why?' was all she ended up with.

'The last time they were here, they killed my cat. They're demons, the damned things. Rita never had any control over them. It wasn't her fault, I know. Her selfish beast of a son foisted them onto her whenever it suited him. I thought at least I'd never have to see them again, once Rita went into the home. And now here they are, large as life. It's a disgrace!' Her voice rose into a squeal of protest.

Thea could only blink and hold her ground. 'They killed your cat?' she managed. 'That's incredible.'

'I assure you it's true. She let them out, and they just shot after poor Sammy like wolves. Tore him to bits. It was appalling.'

Thea looked to the dogs for an explanation, but none was forthcoming. The story was hard, but not impossible, to believe. Whilst there were other breeds – which were most likely to be of the hound variety – with tendencies towards the murdering of passing cats, rabbits or lambs, even the highly humanised and disciplined shepherding ones could forget themselves on occasion. Two bitches together were notoriously unpredictable. 'Oh dear,' she said feebly. 'I'd better not let them off their leads, then.'

'You can't let them out of the house,' the woman insisted. 'They're banned. It went to court. There's an injunction.'

'Blimey!' Again Thea looked at the dogs. 'That's going a bit far, isn't it?'

'They were lucky not to be put down. Now take them in again. I can't bear the sight of them.'

There did not appear to be much choice in the matter. Betsy and Chummy would have to make do with the garden behind the house, until somebody came to retrieve them. It seemed a harsh fate for two such pleasant animals. Perhaps when Drew arrived, they could be smuggled out of Chedworth in a car and allowed a bit of freedom in the woods. Chasing squirrels was surely allowed and with a second person to help, it might be safe to give them a run.

With a mixture of resentment and doubt, she made herself a sandwich and let all the dogs out into the back. The aborted walk had confused them and they milled about indecisively, waiting for the next surprise. Norah Cookham had supervised, with arms folded, the retreat into the house and Thea did not doubt that she would be keeping a close watch to ensure there were no infringements of the extraordinary injunction. Had Millie not known about it? Presumably not, or she would have said something – or never even brought the dogs in the first place. Again, Thea wondered how closely the Wilshire family communicated, and what events there might have been in the recent past to lead to the current situation.

She went back to the upstairs sorting with a heavy tread. The enjoyment had gone out of it, thanks to the woman living opposite and the multiple visits from Millie. There were undercurrents and mysteries that bothered her. Richard Wilshire was beginning to look like a man disliked by many people – neighbours, the farmers he worked with, and possibly even his mother. Drew had seen them together, and reported no animosity, but perhaps they had deliberately presented a bland public face especially for him. There had even been a flicker of emotion on the features of Famous Judith, when his name was mentioned. Was he a bully? A coward? A heartless bureaucrat? Had he ridden roughshod over the wishes of his mother and his daughter? And had he selfishly taken himself off without warning, leaving other people to pick up the reins in his absence?

And perhaps, if he really had disappeared, it was foolish of her to continue with the work he'd given her. Perhaps everything was now different. It was highly likely that the old lady who owned the house would instruct her to put everything back exactly as she'd found it, once she learnt what was going on.

The old lady might even have some useful explanations for the way the little family was behaving, Thea realised. In the absence of Richard, his mother was inevitably the next in line for consultation, and Thea would feel much more comfortable morally if the owner of the house knew she was burrowing through its contents. She really ought to be told. Thea liked to think that if she had known the old lady was in ignorance, she would have refused the commission in the first place. Impatiently, she waited for her fiancé's arrival, when she would suggest they go and see Mrs Wilshire in Stratford. They could do it the next morning. There'd be time to go to Broad Campden as well, if they made an early start, and abandoned any attempt at exploring the attic.

At half past two, she felt sorely tempted to phone Drew and ask him where he was. It took about an hour and a half to drive from his Somerset village to the Cotswolds, up the M5 and then following one of two routes they had devised, depending on whether Thea was occupying a house in the north or south of the area. Chedworth was towards the south, not far from Northleach. On Thursday, approaching from the east, she had turned from the A40 onto the A429 and found herself in Lower Chedworth quite easily. But for Drew, it would prove more complicated.

Chedworth on the ground in three dimensions was bizarrely unlike the comparatively straightforward depiction on the map. It was mainly to do with the switchback levels, the ground plunging bumpily down to the valley carved by the little River Churn, and boasting more than the usual quotient of small streets running at odd angles. The place was a lot bigger than first expected, too. Even a satnav might find it tricky. Maybe she could phone him and offer advice. But if she did that, he'd feel patronised – or annoyed because he could not legally answer it.

While these ditherings were filling her mind, she heard a car pull up outside. Hepzie yapped in recognition, and in half a minute she was hugging her man on the doorstep.

Conversation was postponed while they indulged in a joyous reunion for a while. Then Drew pulled away and looked around. They had somehow got into the kitchen, where three dogs were paying close attention. 'Lovely old Aga,' said Drew. 'Why isn't it on? It's chilly in here.'

'I don't know how to work it. The living room's got a log fire, so we can make it nice and warm. But we have to take the dogs out first. I hope you had some lunch? There's loads to do. What shall we have for supper? There's absolutely no food here, except for bread and a bit of milk. And stuff for the dogs.'

'Why are there so many dogs?' He frowned down at the unfamiliar animals. 'Who do these belong to?'

'Richard Wilshire. I told you he's gone missing. His daughter dumped these two on me this morning. They're not supposed to be here – there's an injunction. I have to take them somewhere in the car for a walk.'

'What?'

'They killed a cat, according to the woman over the way. She's not very nice. I haven't met anybody else.' This was unusual, she realised. Even in the empty little streets of a typical Cotswold settlement, Thea Osborne generally managed to make the acquaintance of at least three or four locals within her first day.

'Let me get straight. I need the loo. And I should bring my bag in. Will the woman over the way object to my being here as well?'

'Probably. If she thinks you're a friend of Richard Wilshire's, that'll put her against you. She dislikes him, apparently.'

'Poor chap. He seemed quite harmless to me.'

'And me. But he's got form, according to Millie. He went missing for three months, five years ago.'

'Yes, you told me.'

'Did I? Sorry. It's intriguing, though. How can somebody get away with such mysterious behaviour these days? No wonder his wife couldn't cope with it. It wrecked the marriage.'

'Maybe that was the intention. A cowardly way to do it, of course.'

'And cruel. If she had any feelings for him, she must have been desperately worried. And his mother. Even worse for her, in a way.' Thea tried to imagine how she would feel if her daughter disappeared without trace, succeeding so well that she began to shake. 'It would be so ghastly, not knowing what had happened.'

Drew folded his arms around her. 'Maybe he kept her secretly informed and swore her to secrecy.'

'I was wondering if we could go and visit her? You know where her care home is, don't you?'

'The satnav does,' he said proudly. 'It worked perfectly coming here, you know. I can't believe the difference it makes.'

'Shut up,' she said fondly. 'You're just trying to pick a fight.' She made herself think about the Wilshires. 'Why didn't his mother move in with him? He must have quite a big place – Millie lives there, and her friend's been staying as well. And if it's too small, why don't they sell this house and get somewhere big enough for all of them in Stratford?'

'They did explain it all to me. I think he'd have preferred something like that, but the old lady insisted on doing it the way they have. She really likes the home, you know. I had a little note from her this morning, in with a paper I asked her to sign. She made a point of telling me how happy she is there.'

'Hmm – Stratford's a bit far to go, I suppose.

But it sounds as if she'd really like to see you.'

He looked doubtful. 'I don't think she has any special liking for me. It might seem a bit odd, dropping in on her without warning.'

'We'll think of an explanation. I really do want to meet her. How long have you got tomorrow?'

'If I leave here at five, it should work. I can collect the kids and get them to bed in reasonable time for school. I feel a bit guilty about it, but they seem happy enough.'

'I feel guilty taking you away from them,' she admitted. 'But we don't do it very often, do we?' she added defiantly.

'Not often enough. I haven't had you to myself for ages.'

'Just wait till you see the bed,' she teased. 'It's like magic.'

'What if I can't wait? Why don't we...?'

'What? Now? We can't, Drew. There's too much going on. At least–' She had heard herself sounding prudish and less than enthusiastic, and wondered what she was thinking. An hour of afternoon passion with the man she loved would break no laws, and the dogs had no urgent need for an outing, after all. 'All right, then,' she said, with a laugh.

'Women!' he complained. 'Never know their own minds.'

'Careful! One wrong word, and I'll change it again.'

She led him upstairs, where he paid a quick call to the bathroom, and then put his head into each bedroom in turn. 'Just checking there's nobody here,' he said. 'It feels as if there's a presence somewhere.'

She looked at him, unsure whether or not he was joking. 'Must be a ghost, then,' she said. 'I expect a few people have died here over the years.'

'That room—' he indicated the second bedroom '—looks as if a bomb's hit it.'

'That was me. Come on, Drew. You're meant to be consumed by passion, not exploring the house.'

The lovemaking was good, but nowhere near their best. Thea felt uneasy using the big old bed in such a way and Drew picked up on her mood. 'It's rather awful of us,' he said. 'Don't you think?'

'A bit,' she agreed.

'I'm her undertaker, for goodness' sake. It's macabre, when you think about it.'

'More like a very black joke. You could make a funny film out of it – an undertaker who always has sex in his clients' beds.'

He groaned. 'Stop it. Even *Six Feet Under* didn't do that. Not as far as I can remember, anyway,' he added.

'Well, we've done it now, and it was very nice, and I am extremely happy that you're here. Let me show you the house properly. It's not really haunted at all. It's got a lovely welcoming atmosphere, actually.'

They dressed, still slightly self-conscious about it. Thea pushed aside a niggling thought that the real truth was that she and Drew functioned best together when they were talking, making plans, and exploring new places. He was approaching forty and she was some years senior to that. Young enough for a vigorous sex life, but too old for it to be the mainstay of the relationship. She could easily envisage a somewhat tepid middle age, in which they settled into a routine where the sex was more of a habit than necessity. And yet she definitely loved him. Looking at him now, she swelled with it. His boyish looks concealed a maturity that she was still discovering. He was stoical about the death of his wife, honest about his uneven feelings towards his children. Stephanie was inescapably more special to him than Timmy was – a small tragedy that he did not try to hide from himself. Timmy had been an accident, born uncomfortably soon after his sister, and cheated of proper parenting by his mother's long-drawn-out illness and death. Drew hoped that the role played by Maggs Cooper had compensated in some way. Maggs had immediately observed the situation, and taken it upon herself to focus on the child and his needs. But now Maggs had her own baby, and Timmy was nearly eight and increasingly inscrutable.

The second bedroom was indeed a mess. The contents of all the various drawers, chests and boxes were laid out on every surface, including the floor, despite many of them having been moved to the little closet off the main bedroom. 'There's *masses* of it,' Drew said. He fingered a silk camisole. 'I don't think I've ever seen a garment like this before. And look at this hanky. It's got some sort of crest embroidered on it.' He smiled. 'I always think it's weird to decorate something you use to blow your nose on. This stuff must be fifty years old.'

'More like eighty. It's pre-war, some of it, I think. I don't understand what it's doing here. People don't keep their old clothes as long as this. They hardly seem to have been worn. I started packing it all away again, but then I thought you might like to see it.'

'They're not hers,' said Drew suddenly. 'They must be the sister's.'

'What? What sister?'

'She died young. Mrs Wilshire told me about her. People do that,' he explained. 'They go back through all the funerals they've known. It's a sort of instinct. And it helps them decide how their own should go. Makes sense.'

'Okay,' said Thea thoughtfully. 'So, assuming she was born in the 1920s and died as a young adult – old enough to wear these clothes, anyway – that would be the forties or thereabouts when she died.'

'She was older than Rita. She'd be in her late nineties now. She had a grand funeral. That's all I can remember. She said her name ... something nice. It's gone.' He shook his head as if the name might be dislodged.

'But why would anybody give house room to a dead sister's clothes?'

'For lack of any other idea, probably. I mean – what else should she do? She probably intended to dispose of it, and never got around to it.'

'For seventy years? That's insane.'

Drew shrugged. 'Time rushes by, you forget about it, and then it doesn't seem to matter any more. I can imagine how it might be. Rita had her own life to think about. Husband. Son. Interests.'

Thea had a thought. 'Have you still got Karen's things somewhere, then?'

He lifted his head, aware of a moment that mattered. 'Her mother took it all away. There wasn't much. In the last year or two, she hadn't bought anything new. She wasn't interested, and we hardly had any money.'

There was a sadness gathering in the air, which was far from what Thea wanted or expected. 'Enough!' she announced. 'We're having tea and cake, and then we'll go for a little drive with the dogs. It'll be dark otherwise and we won't have done anything.'

Brooking no further distractions, she bustled him through this plan, so that shortly before four o'clock they were piling three dogs onto the back seat of her car. Drew had refused to use his, on the very reasonable grounds that the child booster seats would get in the way.

Almost at random, Thea drove down to the lower street and turned left. 'Where are we going?' asked Drew.

'No idea. But take note, because we might never find our way back again. The place is pretty confusing and I have no electronic assistance.'

'This road goes to Yanworth,' he said with confidence.

'It's not the main village street, is it?' she said, a moment later. 'I thought it was.'

'No. For that you need to turn right past the

pub and then left. I think. It's the other side of the river. I did take notice, despite having the gadget telling me what to do. That's where people go wrong,' he added piously.

They were climbing a steep hill, which ended in a tight bend to the right. 'Blimey!' said Thea. 'This must be grim in winter.'

'Indeed. We need to find a footpath, don't we? Those woods look appealing.' He gazed out of his window with interest. 'And look at this amazing old barn! Slow down, Thea. Let me have a proper look. I want to take some photos of it.' He produced his phone and began to fiddle with it.

On the left was a jumble of buildings, oddly conjoined and centred around a large stone barn with a very high red-tiled roof. Thea stopped the car, and immediately the dogs in the back went wild, scrabbling at the car windows to be released.

'Let's walk from here, then,' she said. 'Don't open your door until I've got them on leads.'

Awkwardly, she leant over and grabbed each dog in turn, attaching leads to their collars. 'Okay,' she panted. 'I've got them. Hepzie can go loose, so long as there's no car coming.'

They scrambled out in a tangle, the sheepdogs showing extraordinary excitement. 'What's got into them?' asked Drew. 'They've gone mad. I'm going over there to take my pictures.' He started walking to a point where he could see the whole building.

The behaviour of the dogs was certainly excessive, Thea agreed, as the animals hauled her along the grass verge towards the buildings. 'I

100

think they must know this place,' she called back to Drew, who had his phone in his hand, apparently ready to take photos. 'Oi! Dogs! Slow down.'

But there was no stopping them. Through a field gate adjacent to the barn and across a small ditch they dragged her, then onto the yard in front of the barn. Drew trotted some distance behind her, protesting weakly that they were trespassing. 'What's the matter with those dogs?' he demanded again.

Thea was rather enjoying herself, not trying very hard to slow the animals. They were so sure of what they wanted, so determined in their trajectory, that she was caught up in the quest for whatever it was they were heading for. They towed her up to the vast stone-built barn, which had a wide-open hole where a door might be expected. Hepzie followed, though not showing anything like the enthusiasm of Betsy and Chummy. 'We're going in!' called Thea to the distracted photographer. 'It's like a cathedral in here.'

She had time to stand in awe on the threshold, looking up into the immense height of the roof, and wondering why it had been built on such a vast soaring scale. There were big bales of straw stacked against the back wall, and a modern-looking tractor parked near them. The dogs were straining and yelping even more desperately than before. Almost without realising it, she dropped the leads. Her arms were hurting, and she saw little risk that they would suddenly turn round and dash away over the fields.

She was right. They flew to a shadowy corner and started nuzzling and whining at something on the floor.

'They've found something,' she shouted to Drew, who was still aiming his phone at the barn from outside. He had gone some way back towards the road, to get a good angle. 'Come and see.'

He came unhurriedly to her side. 'A rats' nest, probably.' He was standing as Thea had done, his head tilted back as he stared upwards. 'You know what's so amazing about this place – it's still being used as it was first intended. It must be the only working barn in Gloucestershire. Why hasn't somebody converted it into a house?'

'You wouldn't want a roof like that in a house. And I doubt if you'd be allowed to change it. It's gorgeous.'

'But they've ruined it outside, adding all that modern concrete blockery.'

Thea didn't reply. She had moved closer to the dogs, thinking she ought to recapture them before they ran off. There was a small niggling worry dawning as they whined in unison. Hepzie had joined them, and kept looking back at Thea as if asking for advice.

'What is it, girls?' she asked. 'Why are you so upset?'

Then she saw it, as if a spotlight had suddenly been switched on. A round shape with close-cropped grey hair, and a chin. Shoulders. Hands.

'God, Drew. It's a body!' she gasped.

Chapter Seven

Drew was supposed to be good with bodies, having seen so many of them. But he let himself down quite badly on this occasion. 'It can't be,' he said, flatly.

'It is,' she insisted. 'Look!'

He approached at a pace that felt glacial to her. 'It's a man,' she said.

'Must be a tramp, then.' He finally got there, leaning down, careful not to touch. 'Amazing the way the dogs knew.'

'Drew, look. I think it's … it is, you know. That hair. It's Richard Wilshire. The dogs have found their owner.'

The body was lying awkwardly, not quite flat on its back. One arm was under the torso and the head was twisted sideways. One leg was bent, the other straight. Blood was congealed on the forehead and cranium. The nose looked flatter than it should.

'No!' He took a few steps back. 'How can it be? That's insane.'

She could see that he was shaking with shock. 'His poor mother!' Drew gulped. 'This is going to kill her.'

Thea was more immediately concerned for the dogs, and how to deal with them. They had already scrabbled at the body, moving it fractionally. They undoubtedly understood that this was their master and had probably known he was lying here in the dark since the car stopped in the road. The strangeness of it was set aside in the more pressing need to remove them from the scene before all hope of an effective forensic examination would have to be abandoned. 'We'll have to put them back in the car,' she said.

Drew was still paralysed by the implications of Richard Wilshire being dead. He cared nothing for subsequent police investigations, and little for explanations of what had happened. 'It's impossible,' he spluttered. 'How can it be him? It's all *wrong.*'

'You can say that again,' Thea agreed. 'About as wrong as it gets. He's been murdered, Drew. Look at his head.'

Drew looked reluctantly. 'He might have fallen from up there,' he said, looking at the open-edged platform far above them. 'And landed on his face, somehow.' He grimaced painfully. 'You'd probably twist and turn in the air, in the panic. Don't you think? It looks to me as if his neck's broken.'

'So he dived head first from up there.' She was still staring upwards. The roof space was partly occupied by sturdy flooring, originally designed to hold corn, most likely in hessian sacks. 'I suppose he must have,' she said slowly. 'But what was he doing up there, if so? And there's no ladder. How would he have *got* there?'

Drew shook his head. 'Not our problem. We have to call the police.'

Thea had managed to get the resisting dogs a few feet away, relieved to see her own spaniel nosing about in a distant section of the barn and ignoring the fact of a dead man. 'Help me with these two,' she ordered Drew. 'Then make the phone call. This is such a...' She wanted to say *nuisance* or *pain,* but they would both sound outrageously insensitive. Nonetheless, they were the words that best fitted her feelings.

'Quick, then,' said Drew. It was obvious that in his opinion the animals were quite definitely a nuisance. Impatiently he took both leads and heartlessly dragged the orphaned dogs outside. 'We can tie them up here, look.' There were horizontal and vertical metal poles creating barriers alongside an odd construction that Thea had noticed on her rapid rush into the barn. 'What is this?' Drew asked.

'Could be where they dipped the sheep,' she ventured. It was a long narrow alleyway made of concrete blocks, about the width of a sheep, with a parallel section running alongside. It was weedy and rusty and clearly long disused. But it offered a useful place to tie dogs, for the time being.

The 999 call took the usual protracted time while details were laboriously repeated and fatuous questions asked. For a man who conducted sensitive business on the telephone every week of his life, he made something of a mess of it, offering irrelevant information and finally shouting, for the third time, that he had no idea what the road number was. As far as he was aware, it was far too small to have a number at all. Thea itched to take over from him, despite knowing nothing more than he did about the geography of the place.

Finally, he ended the call, and said irritably to Thea, 'You know these people. Detective Inspector whatshisname and that nice woman I met in Stanton.'

'Gladwin. She's a superintendent. The other one is Higgins. They'll probably only get involved if it really is murder.' She spoke distractedly, struggling to get to grips with the appalling turn of events. It had been so far from what she had expected, her mind was taking its time in catching up.

'You think it might not be, then?' he sounded hopeful, as if a reprieve had been offered.

'I don't know, Drew. He's got dreadful injuries. A broken neck and his skull – what can have done that to his skull?' She flinched at the vivid image of the crusted crack in the front of the man's head. His very short hair had done nothing to cover the stark sight. 'Let's not go back in there, okay.'

'We have to watch out for the police car, anyway. That's if they ever manage to locate this road.'

'It's not a very efficient system, is it?' she said. 'It's not the first time I've almost given up explaining to some girl in Bristol or Birmingham how a little village works. They never listen properly, that's the trouble.'

'They think it can all be done by satellite.'

'It probably could, if they used the right technology. I mean – doesn't your phone send a signal that gives the location? The police are always talking about finding criminals through their phones.'

'I think that's more on TV than in the real world. They only use it for very high-powered terrorist stuff.'

'Ironic, really,' she said, mainly for the sake of talking about something other than a dead man with a cracked head. 'I hate all this surveillance and CCTV and stuff, but when you *want* to be found, everything falls apart.'

Drew was more than willing to keep up this line of conversation, finding it helpful in soothing his own distress. 'We don't know it's fallen apart, yet. They could turn up at any moment and prove us wrong.'

'The trouble is that Chedworth really is hopelessly complicated. I'm not even sure I could get back to the house from here. I certainly wouldn't like to do it in the dark.' She looked around. 'Come here, Hepzie. Don't go back in there.' The spaniel was idly sniffing the ground, retracing their steps back towards the barn. The whole incident appeared to have left her unmoved and incurious. Upstaged by the sheepdogs, Thea supposed, with their superior skills on every level. Hepzie had seen dead people a time or two before, and might have developed associations of stress and confusion with such discoveries. She was also liable to be left shut in a car or a house for long periods when something like this happened, which did not suit her at all. 'Poor old girl,' said Thea. 'Things never go smoothly for you, do they?'

'You said he wasn't liked,' Drew said suddenly.

'What?'

107

'Richard Wilshire. Nobody liked him, you said.'

'Oh. Farmers, mostly. His job made him unpopular. Bringer of bad news. Telling people their cows had to be destroyed because of TB.'

'So a farmer did this?'

'Probably.' Just at that moment, it didn't seem very important. Waiting on a darkening October afternoon for people to come and examine a broken body, then bundle it away to a horrible sterile mortuary to be dissected by a pathologist: it was all sickening and stupid and she wished herself a thousand miles away. 'There's one called Andrew, round here somewhere. Except...' She gave it some reluctant thought. 'He says Richard never showed up. That's what Millie told me. All the cows were gathered and waiting, but Richard didn't come.'

'Perhaps he did, after all, and this Andrew person killed him, and then pretended he'd never seen him.'

She shivered. 'Seems unlikely. What about his car? And there must be other people on the farm as well.'

'What's happened to us?' he asked, wonderingly. 'We used to find all this sort of thing fascinating. We were ace detectives, only a few months ago.'

'We grew out of it,' she said. 'Or something.'

'That must be it. It's all so *sad*, isn't it.'

She stroked one of the sheepdogs. 'What'll happen to these two, I wonder? Millie isn't going to take them on, I bet. And there's nobody else.' Again, she thought back over the dreadful fates that had befallen dogs she had known. In Winchcombe, Hampnett, Lower Slaughter, Cranham, dogs had become incidental casualties of human wickedness. Throughout history, there were similar stories she could not bear to hear. She knew it was a failing, but there had been times when she cared more about the dogs than the people. Human beings, after all, had a choice. They were meant to have enough brains to foresee the consequences of their actions, whilst animals were merely victims. She sighed miserably, and felt oddly guilty at the way she was thinking.

'That might be them,' said Drew suddenly. Until then, they had not noticed a single passing vehicle. He trotted down to the road, only to find a large metal gate firmly locked, between him and the approaching car. He and Thea had entered from the side, jumping over a ditch and onto the concrete forecourt of the barn. But Thea's car was parked in full sight on the verge. That would be enough, surely, to announce their presence.

It was, and before another minute had passed, Thea had gone to wave at the two uniformed police officers who emerged from a squad car. 'Over here,' she called.

With squared shoulders and determined chins, the men followed her directions and disappeared into the barn. They quickly came out again and set in train the usual processes necessary for dealing with a sudden violent death. Questions, explanations, all conducted with a stiff formality that barely concealed the excitement and nervousness that came with the drama of such a rare event. The officers were young and un-familiar to Thea. Charged with a first response, they knew they would very soon be elbowed aside by the detectives from CID, and given no more importance. They would carefully write their report, and be lucky if they had any further involvement. Possibly some house-to-house questioning, or computer searches, would come their way. But for the moment, this was their pigeon, and a dead man in a barn did not come along every day. They were intent on doing a thorough job.

Questions were muttered as they carried out their unfamiliar duties. 'Where's his car? How long's he been lying there? Have the dogs messed him up much? Who's the CID on duty this evening?' They threw the queries at each other with little expectation of answers. Thea heard them but refrained from participating in the conversation, such as it was. She had sup-plied the man's name and a brief summary of how the body had come to be found. More than that could wait.

But the policemen could no longer delay the handing over of the business to more senior officers. As evening approached, more cars arrived, blue tape was strung in all directions, and Thea and Drew made their escape with the dogs. They had hovered on the sidelines for longer than was strictly necessary as it was, un-sure as to what was required of them. Because of the dogs, they were not given warm haven in a spacious police car, but left in the open as the temperature fell. When Drew announced that

110

they were leaving, nobody took much notice. 'Okay, then,' said a newly arrived detective. 'We've got your details. We'll be in touch – in the morning, most likely.'

'Can't wait,' muttered Thea. 'Come on then, dogs.' Only then did she remember that she had Millie Wilshire's phone number at the house – but of course it would be entirely unthinkable to call her and ask what should be done with Betsy and Chummy. She would have to explain her reasons, and that really wasn't her job.

'They thought it was odd, the way we found him,' Drew worried in the car. 'They think it's too big a coincidence.'

'Well, it sort of is, when you look at it objectively. Of all the people in the area, why should it be us who found him?'

'Exactly. I mean – nothing was further from our minds.'

'Although we did know he was missing. Maybe we were subliminally looking for him.'

Drew snorted. 'You mean sub*consciously*, I believe. Surely you don't think that?'

She was negotiating the disgracefully sharp bend on the way back into the village, finding it even more alarming now they were going steeply downhill. 'It makes a sort of sense. We knew he was missing, and we had his dogs. We also knew he was supposed to be in Yanworth yesterday. I did, anyway,' she amended. 'It's possible that's why we headed in that direction to start with.'

'Nope,' he said, firmly. 'You're rationalising. It was just a very nasty coincidence, that's going to cause us a whole lot of aggravation. I'm not

111

looking forward to tomorrow one little bit.'

She sighed. 'I don't even want to think about it,' she said.

Chapter Eight

They were hungry and shocked, worried about the dogs and all the other implications of what had happened. 'I feel stupidly responsible,' said Thea. 'I didn't take Millie seriously enough. I didn't do a thing to help her.'

'There was nothing you could do. And actually, when you think about it, you did a huge thing by finding her father.'

'By mistake, and too late.'

Drew was cutting a thick slice from a somewhat dry loaf of brown bread. 'I'm starving,' he said. 'Is there any butter? Jam? Cheese?'

'Butter and cheese in the fridge. I brought it from home. There's not much left.'

'Want some?'

She shrugged. 'We'll have to go out for a proper meal. There are pubs.'

He frowned. 'I'm not sure I want to go to a pub. Can we get a takeaway from somewhere?'

'Cirencester. It's not too far away.'

Drew was obviously thinking as he chewed. 'I had an idea,' he said. 'Just now. Don't you get a sense of being *directed*? By Millie, I mean. She dumps these dogs on you, and burbles about Yanworth and her dad disappearing. Couldn't it all be a very subtle way of ensuring that it was you who found the body?'

She puffed out her cheeks, in an expression of sceptical disbelief. 'That's pushing things,' she objected. 'She'd have to be a mind reader or a hypnotist for that to work. I wasn't thinking about her father at all when we set out towards Yanworth.'

'You know – people are very predictable. If she's clever enough, she could quite easily feed you suggestions that led to something very like what actually happened.'

'No, Drew. How could she *possibly* predict that we would stop at that very barn? Besides, I don't think she is particularly clever.'

'I expect you're right. It might be absolutely mad to even suspect it. There's just a niggle about it all. Something too neat.'

'But why would she? If she killed him, she wouldn't want the body discovered. It's not logical.'

'No.' He looked dubious. 'But if she knows who did it, and is scared to say anything directly to the police, she'd have to find a devious way to get to the same point.'

'You know what you're doing, don't you?' she challenged him. 'You're reverting to your old self. Drew Slocombe, detective. I thought we'd decided he was gone.'

'Does that annoy you?'

She thought about it for a moment. 'A bit. It makes me feel tired and peculiar. Unclean, almost. This whole thing – the Wilshire family, the house, the weird celebrity girl–'

'What? Who?'

'I forgot to tell you. Millie's friend is an actor on *Random Road*. She's one of the four sisters. Millie calls her Judith, but she's Jayjay Mason to the rest of the world. It did take me a while to remember that,' she admitted. 'The point is, she's about as famous as you can get if even I recognised her.'

'Why is she weird?'

'I don't know. She didn't say much. She gets driven about by a chauffeur. It's a whole other world.'

'Lots of famous people around here,' he said, as if it was too obvious to be worthy of comment. Other thoughts were taking priority and the next one turned him pale. 'You don't think they'll suspect *me*, do you?'

'What?' Thea was more concerned with food, and dogs and the mess the house was in. Her remark about feeling unclean had to do, in part, with the ransacked chests and cupboards and the decisions about the contents that might not now be made. She had intruded and interfered; and even though asked to do so, it was still un-savoury. The knowledge that a bereft old woman was probably even now being informed of her son's death only added to the feeling. Drew's sudden panic struck her as rather beside the point.

'It happened before, remember? They thought I was a murderer then. Why not now?'

'What possible reason could they have?'

'I've got a contract with the Wilshires for a funeral. I introduced you to them. And I found the body. They always suspect the person who finds the body.'

'No, they don't. That's rubbish. Anyway, you must have a good alibi. Lots of people must have seen you yesterday.'

'He didn't die yesterday,' he said, to her surprise.

'How do you know?'

'Rigor mortis. He wasn't entirely stiff, which means he was probably dead for only ten or twelve hours. It was probably quite cold overnight, which slows it down, but his legs were hardly stiff at all.'

'You didn't touch him, did you?' Alarm began to flicker through her.

'I *nudged* him a bit. With my foot.'

'Yuk!' It struck her as a very odd thing for an undertaker to do, trained as they were in total respect for the dead. 'You *kicked* him?'

'Not at all. What a dreadful idea. It was done very gently. It's a sort of instinct. When we go to collect a body, we always check for rigor. It affects how we carry them. And I was trying to fend off the dogs, as well. Anyway, I would guess he died sometime early today. Not that it matters what I think. The pathologist will figure it out better than I can.'

'So where was he all day yesterday?' Her insides began to flutter. 'Oh, Lord, Drew. I wonder if anybody has seen him since Thursday evening, when he left me here. What if I was the last person to see him alive?'

'You mean he was hiding away somewhere the whole of yesterday, all by himself?'

115

'That's what it looks like. But why go to the barn like that? And where was his car?'

'These, dear Watson, are the big questions. But you're right – we don't have to find the answers. Once the cops have interviewed young Millie and the farmer chap, it might all fall into place. Our work is done. We found the body for them. They can take it from here.'

'Brave words. But we've still got the dogs and the house and no idea what we should do next.'

'What we do is find a Chinese place in Cirencester, phone an order and feast ourselves on lemon chicken and beef satay. My favourites, as I hope you remember,' he twinkled.

There were quite a few subtexts to this suggestion: Thea's poor showing as a cook; the hint of celebration and indulgence; the reluctance to show themselves to the public gaze, and more. 'We can find somewhere with Google,' she said. 'They might have the menu, as well.'

It was readily accomplished, thanks to the Digital Age. So easy and smooth was it that neither thought back to a time in their youth when the process would involve digging about for a printed menu in a messy drawer, and ransacking pockets and purses for cash to pay for it. Only when Drew had set off to collect the order did Thea pause to acknowledge how convenient life had become in so many areas.

And he wouldn't even get lost on the way back, with his trusty satnav to keep him straight.

'I could do it with the map,' she insisted, as if it was an argument she might yet win. 'You turn left off the 429 after the Hare and Hounds pub,

116

then right at the farm shop, and aim for the church.'

'Can you see the church in the dark?' he wondered, with feigned innocence. 'I rather fancy not.'

'Just go,' she said.

He had been gone ten minutes when the door knocker ominously shook the silence of the village. Someone was very eager to gain entrance, by the sound of it. Wishing there was a way of seeing who it was, Thea cautiously opened the door.

'What's been going on?' demanded Norah Cookham.

Thea acted dumb. 'How do you mean?'

'My brother-in-law just called me and said there's been some dreadful find at the barn on the Yanworth road. You and those dogs were there, he says. And a man,' she added with a narrow-eyed accusation.

'How does your brother-in-law know me? Where does he live?'

'That's irrelevant. But if you must know, he saw your car when you arrived here on Thursday evening. He never forgets a car.'

'For heaven's sake!' said Thea angrily. 'It has nothing to do with you. Or if it has, then you should speak to the police and do what you can to assist them. It sounds as if your brother-in-law could be extremely useful, with his encyclopedic knowledge of where every car in Gloucestershire was at any given time.' She was quite proud of this quick piece of repartee, but Norah Cookham was unimpressed.

'How *dare* you?' The narrow eyes glittered with a rage that far outdid Thea's. It conjured visions of catfights in East End pubs, with scratching and hair-pulling. Norah Cookham's inauspicious roots were still very near the surface. 'Who do you think you are?' she finished.

Thea almost laughed in the woman's face. Throwing caution to the wind, she continued in the same defiant vein. 'I think I'm a person who's been landed in a very difficult situation, with nothing to feel guilty about. I have no obligations whatsoever towards you. You obviously have some sort of problem that has nothing to do with me.' Never inclined to prevaricate or skirt around an issue, she relished the provocation that had sparked this speech.

It was highly effective. Norah Cookham's mouth opened and shut and her face turned red. 'You have no idea,' she gasped. 'No idea at all.'

'That's absolutely true. And I'm hoping to keep it that way. Now please leave me alone.' She began to close the door, forcing the woman backwards. Her own anger was flaring almost out of control at the realisation that the Cookham woman had waited until Drew left before accosting the undefended house-sitter – or whatever she was. It was an act of aggression, against which Thea felt fully justified in defending herself.

When it was finished, and the dogs were belatedly showing solicitude, she thought it over. One stark impression was that Norah Cookham was obviously someone to treat with care. For a few moments, it was tempting to cast her in the

118

role of killer – pushing Richard Wilshire to his death in a fit of rage. But the same doubts arose as had done where Millie was concerned. Would anybody be such a fool as to show themselves in such an aggressive and untrustworthy light if they really had just committed murder?

It had to be an infuriated farmer who'd done it. There was no other credible explanation. The police would quickly grasp the facts and pinpoint the perpetrator. It was even tempting to hope that she and Drew would not be required to make any further testimony. They had given every detail to the detective sergeant who'd questioned them at the scene. Drew's worries about being under suspicion were clearly silly.

He was a long time coming back with the food. It was almost nine when he finally appeared. Thea had warmed plates and wished there was some wine to go with the meal. She fed the dogs from the supplies left by Millie, and worried a little about what was going to happen to them. They were subdued and anxious, glancing towards the door every few minutes. Their fate might be a tragic one, if there was really nobody in the family to take them on. They were not really suited to domestic life, anyway. Their instincts were to work outdoors with sheep; lying around all day in a house would drive them to bad temper and destructive behaviour. For the hundredth time, Thea wished people had more sense than to take such animals into their urban homes, when there were far more appropriate breeds available.

Richard Wilshire had not been entirely urban,

of course. He had visited farms, where the dogs were probably allowed to explore and meet others of their own kind.

All was bustle as they opened the foil containers and dived into the delayed meal. To Thea's great approval, Drew had acquired a bottle of white wine on his foray into Cirencester. 'You clever thing!' she said.

She then reported the visitation from Norah Cookham, proudly repeating her own response. 'She was so cross,' she said with a smile.

He shuddered. 'You've made an enemy,' he said. 'Doesn't that worry you?'

'Not really. I don't expect I'll ever see her again. I'm leaving here tomorrow. I've decided.'

'Have you?' He nodded to himself, as he considered the implications. 'I suppose you should, by rights. I'm sorry, love. This is all my fault for suggesting you come here in the first place. I do feel bad about it.'

'You meant well.'

'That makes it sound even worse. Meaning well is seldom a good thing. The path to hell, and all that.'

'I didn't have to agree to it. Anyway, it sounded perfectly all right. Neither of us could have anticipated the way it turned out.'

'Except you didn't really like it, even before this afternoon – did you? It isn't a very pleasant job.'

'And now I've got these dogs to worry about. I'll have to find somebody to take them, before I can leave.' This gave her cause to worry about her decision. 'I hope we can get hold of Millie tomorrow.'

Drew had a worry of his own. 'I really have to go to Broad Campden. I can't come up here and not even look at the house.' He blew out a long breath. 'Every time I think about it, I feel burdened with obligation. I wish, really, she'd never left it to me. It's an awful thing to do to a person, when you think about it.'

'She meant well,' said Thea, and they both laughed.

'I know it's all going to work out right in the end. It's mainly a matter of timing, with Maggs out of action. Moving house is so *violent,* don't you think? Uprooting the children, packing up all your possessions, and dealing with estate agents. Except I won't have to do that, of course. That's one blessing. I don't think I could ever face trying to sell a house these days. It sounds a totally insane business.'

'I've got to sell mine,' she reminded him.

'So you have. I forgot. Are you sure...?' He gave her an anxious look.

'Stop it. It's all going to be all right.'

Somehow the reassurance had the opposite of the desired effect. Just at that moment, the future felt treacherously unreliable.

Thea's phone pinged, and she found a text message. 'We're to go for interview in Cirencester at nine-thirty tomorrow,' she announced. 'Summoned by text. What's the world coming to?'

'Do you have to reply?'

'Doesn't look like it. They'll assume we'll obey.'

'At least it's nice and early. We can be away by

coffee time, with any luck – straight to Broad Campden.' He looked relieved. 'That should work quite well.'

'Except for the damned dogs,' she said glumly.

'Hand them over to the police,' he advised. 'There'll be a procedure.'

'Yes – they'll be locked up in kennels somewhere and then destroyed. I can't let that happen. You know what I'm like.'

'It's a mental illness,' he told her. 'Dogophilia. You need therapy.'

'Probably.' She glanced down at her spaniel, contentedly curled on the blanket that they'd brought with them for her comfort. The dog always spent the night on whatever bed Thea was in – except when Drew usurped her place. Tonight would be one of those rare instances. There was likely to be trouble as a result. 'Where are they going to sleep?' she wondered. The house was not equipped for dogs in any way. 'Millie didn't bring them any bedding.'

'In your car?'

'No way. If they're banned from Chedworth, somebody might see them and take unilateral action.' *Somebody* meaning Norah Cookham, she realised. 'I suppose there are plenty of blankets and things upstairs. I can make them a bed in the living room.'

'What if they widdle in there?'

'Let them. But I doubt if there's much risk. They're terribly well behaved, poor things.'

'And Hepzibah?' he asked warily.

'I thought she could come up with us. She's a lovely bedfellow.' It was at least worth a try, she

122

calculated. After all, when Drew married her, he'd have to take on her dog as well, just as Thea would have to incorporate his children.

'I don't approve of dogs on beds,' he said mildly, and not for the first time.

'She'll whine if we shut her out. I can probably persuade her to stay on the floor.'

Drew sighed. 'Love me, love my dog,' he muttered.

'Yes. What's wrong with that? She's been a life-saver these past years. I'm not going to cast her off now – not for you or anybody.'

'I'm not asking you to. I get it. You're a package, like me and my kids. But I don't intend to have Timmy or Stephanie in bed with us all night, either. There are limits.'

She felt wrong-footed. As always, the inescapable fact of Drew's decency and niceness made her feel guilty. She was not really a nice person – certainly not compared to him. She did not deserve him. She might not be good for him. And yet, they did seem to get along so very well. She sighed, too. 'You're right,' she said. 'As usual.'

After a short interval, he changed the subject. 'I really think I must go and see Mrs Wilshire,' he said. 'I feel so sorry for her.'

Thea frowned. 'Won't that seem a bit ... ghoulish? She'll associate you with funerals, remember. She'll think you want to do Richard's, and are chasing the business.'

He went pale, his jaw slack. 'Good God, so she will. It never even crossed my mind. Not once.'

'Sorry.' Again she felt guilty. 'My mind works in nasty ways.'

123

'No, it doesn't. It's the obvious sensible con- clusion to draw. I was just too thick to realise. But I really do want to see her. Maybe if you came with me, that would put a different light on it?'

'And maybe she really would like you to do the funeral. Somebody has to, after all.'

He nodded slowly. 'And I understand better than most how terrible it'll be for her. She won't have to explain that she'd assumed that Richard would be eulogising her, at some point not too far off. Now all that's turned to ashes. All her plans about money and property are thrown into chaos. Another undertaker would struggle to grasp all that side of it.'

'How will we have time, though?' She quailed at the lengthening list of obligations for the coming day.

'Tricky, but not impossible. Cirencester first, then Broad Campden, for a couple of hours, then straight up to Stratford in the afternoon. We don't have to stay long. Then I can bring you back here, grab a cup of tea and be off on schedule.'

She remembered that undertakers – especially the big ones – routinely constructed complex timetables, with ten funerals a day. Drew had worked for one like that before setting up on his own. He was accustomed to calculating dis- tances and timings and fitting everything in. Where most people flapped and dithered over one engagement, he calmly managed his time and motion with impressive efficiency, even when it did not involve conducting a funeral.

'I'll be guided by you,' she said, biting back yet another reminder about the dogs.

They washed up, Drew complaining how cold the kitchen was. Thea remembered a house-sit in the well-named Cold Aston in a property that had stood empty for a while and had very little heating. She had been with Detective Superintendent Phil Hollis at the time; the parallels that came to mind with the current situation were uncomfortable. It made her feel almost promiscuous. Having been faithfully married for nearly twenty years, it was still strange to find herself with somebody other than Carl. Drew very probably felt the same, she supposed.

They sank into the big soft bed, rolling together for a friendly cuddle. Hepzie obediently compromised by settling onto a warm rug on the floor close to Thea's side. 'Poor Mrs Wilshire,' sighed Drew. 'I can't stop thinking about her.'

Downstairs Betsy and Chummy were whining restlessly, bewildered and anxious about the whereabouts of their familiar people. 'We'll never get to sleep,' said Thea. But ten minutes later they were both dead to the world.

Chapter Nine

The police interview was entirely different from what they'd expected. There was no atmosphere of tension or urgency that Thea had come to associate with a murder investigation. 'Oh, yes,' said the man on the desk when they introduced themselves. 'Thank you for coming. Just a few loose ends the DI wanted to tie up. Take a seat, and I'll tell him you're here.'

Drew and Thea exchanged a surprised look. She opened her mouth to say, 'You caught the killer, then?' but closed it again. Something had changed dramatically since the previous afternoon and it was probably sensible to stay quiet until enlightenment dawned.

'Loose ends?' Drew muttered, when they were left alone.

She widened her eyes and said nothing.

It was five minutes before the familiar figure of DI Jeremy Higgins emerged from a door behind the desk. 'Mrs Osborne,' he smiled. 'And Mr...' He shook his head apologetically.

'Slocombe,' said Drew.

'Right. Well, come through for a minute. I won't keep you long. Sorry we called you in at all, really. Not necessary, as it turned out.'

They trooped through to a small room, where they sat round a table and Higgins smiled again. 'The good news – if we can call it that – is that there was no foul play associated with the death of Mr Wilshire. We're satisfied that he took his own life.'

The shock was considerable. Thea rocked back, her mind whirling. Had she and Drew been such complete fools as to jump so wrongly to the idea that it had been murder? Why had they done that? Were they so hardened by repeated involvement in deliberate killing that they could see nothing else, whenever someone died? She frowned – no way could that be true of Drew, the undertaker. 'Oh,' she said.

'That surprises you?'

'It hadn't occurred to me,' she admitted. 'And now I feel really stupid. You think he jumped off the ledge in the barn?'

'It's consistent with his injuries. And there's no sign of a struggle or anyone else being present.'

'How did he get up there?' Drew asked. 'We didn't see a ladder.'

'There was one at the back of the barn, up against an opening onto that higher floor.'

'Have you found a suicide note?' asked Thea.

Higgins gave her a look of reproach from under his brows. His big square head tipped forward. She had seen the same look more than once. 'Sorry,' she said. 'You're not at liberty to tell us that sort of thing.'

'The man on the desk said there were some loose ends,' Drew prompted.

'Not exactly. But we are somewhat puzzled as to how you came to find him. That is – how it came to be you two.'

'It was really his dogs. We stopped the car to

have a better look at the barn, and they went mad.'

'Why would you want a better look?'

'It's such an unusual sight these days – a barn still in its original state, and not converted to a big house. And there was just something intriguing about it. We like that sort of thing.'

'And why did you have his dogs?'

Thea answered with deliberate patience. 'Because he went missing on Friday, and his daughter couldn't have them.' She paused, trying to assemble her thoughts. 'You know – it really can't be suicide. Where's his car? Where was he all day Friday? Those aren't just loose ends, are they? They're great big questions that ought to be answered.'

'They will be answered,' said Higgins, through a tight jaw. 'Now please tell me why you're in Chedworth.'

'I was employed by Richard Wilshire to make an inventory of the contents of his mother's house. His daughter Millie came to see me a number of times on Friday and yesterday, more worried each time about her father. His dogs needed somebody to look after them, so I guess it made sense to her to dump them on me. I need to know, actually, what I ought to do with them now.'

'Hand them back to Miss Wilshire,' he said, as if this were obvious. 'They're her responsibility.'

Again, Thea wondered at her own dim-wittedness. Much that Higgins evidently thought perfectly clear had never even occurred to her. Although, she had in fact thought about and then

128

dismissed Millie as a viable custodian of two sheepdogs. She worked away; she was young and inconsiderate. She really didn't qualify as a long-term owner.

Drew was very quiet, his hands folded in his lap, and his gaze thoughtfully directed onto them. 'Drew?' said Thea.

'Consistent with his injuries,' he said slowly. 'Broken neck, cracked skull. Perhaps other fractures. How high was that platform? Twenty feet or so?'

'Over thirty, sir, as it happens.'

'But a soft floor. Bare earth, with no stones or concrete slabs or anything to land on. He couldn't be sure it would kill him.'

'By that reasoning, a murderer couldn't be sure, either. That's if you're suggesting he was taken up there by force and then pushed off the edge.'

'You're certain he died there, are you? He wasn't dumped there post-mortem and arranged to look as if he'd fallen?'

Higgins sucked his lower lip and sighed. 'He was not, sir. There are *no* suspicious indicators of any sort.'

Thea interrupted. 'I think there are a lot, actually. How do you explain his movements since Thursday evening?'

Higgins turned his head in a sideways tilt. 'Pardon?'

She swallowed. 'From what Millie said, I think I might have been the last person to see him alive. Unless you've found someone else, of course,' she added hopefully.

Higgins spoke with unusual formality. 'We are

129

acting on the assumption that the man took his own life. Although it helps the family to have a picture of the final hours, it is not incumbent upon the police force to investigate them. As I see it, the man found a quiet spot in which to consider his situation. Perhaps it took him all day Friday to summon the courage to do what he did. His car is most likely somewhere close by and will be reported at any moment.'

'I suppose that could make sense,' said Drew, with no sign of apology for his earlier argument-ativeness. As one professional to another, he habitually treated the police with a distinct lack of deference. An unfortunate experience the year before, in which he found himself suspected of killing a man, had done nothing to increase his respect. They had a job to do, and they mostly did it with fair efficiency – but he saw no reason to abase himself before them. Thea's own approach was very much the same. She had a daughter and brother-in-law in the police force; she knew they were all too human.

'But he wouldn't do that to his mother,' Drew went on. 'There is no way he would inflict such suffering on her.'

The look on Higgins's face implied that he recognised this sentiment, but was not swayed by it. He said nothing.

Drew persisted. 'I've met her twice, both times with her son. They were very close. It is simply unthinkable that he would put his own unhap-piness before a wish to protect her.'

'On the other hand,' Thea interrupted, 'he did feel very guilty about putting her into a home.

130

It's possible he found that unbearable.' She was tempted to add that she had detected something less than pure affection in the man towards his mother, but held it back. She had only spoken to him for a few minutes, after all.

Both men gave her words due consideration. 'Betrayal of her trust, letting himself down in his own eyes,' said Higgins. 'That sort of thing.'

Higgins wanted it to be suicide, Thea realised. While nothing to celebrate, it did make the police work easier, by a long way. Suicide was unpleasant, but murder was very much worse. She saw no reason to argue about it, other than a strong sense that something wasn't right.

'He wouldn't do that to his mother,' Drew repeated, with even more certainty. 'If he felt as guilty as that, he could have done something about it. And everybody keeps ignoring the fact that Mrs Wilshire *likes* the home. It was her own choice to go there. He had no *reason* to feel guilty about it.'

'And yet he told me he did,' said Thea impatiently.

'That was more to do with her possessions and the house. All the ramifications, and his decision to have you do it, instead of tackling it himself – he felt bad about that part of it.'

Higgins leant forward. 'It *was* suicide,' he said. 'There is no scrap of evidence to suggest anything else. Once we've got the PM report to confirm it, the case will be closed.'

Drew absorbed this without speaking. Thea was reminded of her younger sister, Jocelyn, when being reprimanded by their father. She would clamp her lips together and look at a point on a distant wall, making it clear that while she heard the words, she found the message unacceptable. Drew was doing much the same thing.

'Well, then. Is that all you need from us?' she asked, thinking it could have easily been managed over the phone, instead of wasting over an hour of their time. Then she remembered it was a Sunday, and Higgins might well be conscious of his own family life running along without him. He had mentioned a daughter, some time ago, and she suspected there were other offspring. He had the look of a family man.

'I think so,' he said, with a little frown. 'Just tying up the loose ends.'

'Yes, you said that before,' Drew snapped. 'Loose ends that seem to me to point every bit as logically to unlawful killing as they do to suicide.'

'All right, Mr Slocombe,' said Higgins heavily. 'I think that's enough. We're grateful to you for your assistance. It was helpful to have the man's name provided so quickly.' He turned to Thea. 'Please don't worry. The whole picture will become perfectly clear in time.' He gave a humourless smile. 'I would think you'd be glad not to be involved in yet another murder.'

The reproach was impossible to miss, and impossible to refute. Guilt flooded through her at the implied criticism. 'I'm sorry,' she said meekly. 'I'm sure you're right. But it isn't easy to just brush it all away. For a start, Richard's dogs are still with us. His daughter has made no attempt to contact us about them. And it's complicated because the woman across the road thinks they're the spawn of the devil.'

Higgins blinked. 'Pardon?' he said.

'Oh, it's nothing important. Mrs Wilshire's neighbour, lives opposite. Norah Cookham, she's called. She hates the dogs. Says there's an injunction out against them being in Chedworth. Is that even possible?'

Higgins pulled a laptop towards him and activated it. 'Cookham – is that what you said?'

Thea nodded.

'Let's see. Um ... Chedworth. Attack on a cat. Made a strong complaint. But nothing as extreme as an injunction. Just a warning. She's exaggerating. People do that a lot. In fact she was close to getting into trouble herself, given all the disturbance she caused. It was only a cat, after all.' He gave Thea a meaningful look.

'Does that mean I can take the dogs for a run in the woods?'

'If you can be sure they're under control. In reality, of course, we all know that once a dog is off its lead, it is very much *not* under control. Even the best behaved ones will run off given enough incentive.'

Thea suspected that he knew the story of an incident she had brought about in Lower Slaughter. She was forced to agree that he was right, when she thought back over that awful time. 'So what's to become of them? I want to leave here later today.'

'I told you. Return them to Miss Wilshire,' Higgins repeated. 'What's the problem?'

Drew patted her arm none too gently. 'We decided that already,' he said. 'Stop obsessing

133

about damn dogs, will you?'

He was angry. Drew Slocombe, the mildest of men, was so angry he used the word *damn* to her, his beloved. It hadn't ever happened before. She took a deep breath, before saying, 'She told me she wouldn't be there, though. That's why I've got them in the first place.'

'I would imagine her plans have changed somewhat since then,' Higgins suggested. 'In fact, I know they have. She might even be expecting you to return the dogs. She could be glad to see them.'

'Oh. Am I obsessing about them?' she wondered aloud. 'I suppose I am, a bit.'

'It's what you do,' said Higgins, adding hastily, 'I mean, the house-sitting. You're accustomed to being in charge of people's animals. You're just following the usual pattern.'

Drew had slumped unhappily in the chair, saying nothing.

Thea stood up. 'Come on, then.'

He obeyed with an effort. 'What's the matter?' she asked him.

Most men would have snapped, *Nothing*. But he was not most men. 'I don't believe it was suicide,' he said. 'You haven't listened to me, either of you. I hate to think that he'll go down in history as a man who killed himself, when I'm sure he did no such thing.'

Higgins got up and walked around the plain table until he could put a hand on Drew's shoulder. 'No evidence, though. Not a whisker of evidence. It's often like this. Nobody can believe it. Even when there's a note trying to explain, there's always a daughter or brother or someone who refuses to accept it.'

Drew raised a hand to prevent further assurances. 'I know all that. And you'll say I wasn't close enough to Richard Wilshire to understand what was going on inside. That's true. But the whole picture is wrong. It doesn't *solve* anything, do you see? He didn't need to escape from anything now. He'd done the hard stuff, already.'

'Guilt,' said Thea. 'He must have been escaping from his own feelings of guilt.'

Higgins shook his head as if he had said all there was to be said.

'We should go,' Thea urged. 'Lots to do, remember.'

'Yes, I'm coming.' Drew was still just as angry, but not with her, she realised. The whole situation had got under his skin for reasons that were most probably connected with his line of work or a past experience she knew nothing about. Or simply because he was acutely aware of the grief and despair that must be gripping Richard Wilshire's mother since hearing her son was dead.

They left Cirencester with no more delay, Thea driving unthinkingly northwards. They were going to collect the dogs and take them to Stratford, where they would be returned to Millie Wilshire. Then she and Drew would go to the residential home and see Millie's grandmother. Thea's own dog would be taken along, because it would be unkind to leave her alone in the Chedworth house.

'Where's the turning?' she asked, as they sped along the arrow-straight A429. The road was still not entirely familiar to her, and she was decidedly hazy as to how Chedworth related to other places she knew, such as Northleach. It all looked so deceptively simple on maps, making her feel stupid when she failed to interpret the geography on the ground. The ongoing controversy concerning satnavs made it important that she save face by finding the way unassisted. 'Oh yes – I knew, really.'

'Not this one, but the next,' Drew said, ignoring her bravado. 'Left, and then a right fork into the middle of the village. Except – why are we going back into Chedworth at all? We should be heading straight for Stratford.' They had rejigged Drew's masterly itinerary for the day, putting Mrs Wilshire ahead of the Broad Campden visit. 'Then we can spend all afternoon there, without any pressure,' he'd said.

'Dogs.' She refused to apologise or explain, even if he was annoyed with her so-called obsessing. 'We'll dump them on Millie, whether she wants them or not.'

'Assuming she's there.'

'We could phone her. Richard gave me the number.'

'Did he? Isn't that a bit odd?'

'Not really. He gave me his mother's, as well. People always do that when they leave me alone in a strange house. It's automatic. They think I'll flounder, or be scared, without them.'

'Did he give you his own as well?'

'Of course.'

'Hmmm. Well, I've got the full set, too. It's in my car. I brought the whole Wilshire file with me.'

'Well done.' She remembered that she had told Drew about Richard Wilshire being missing when she phoned him on Friday. 'You expected we'd be doing some detective work, then?'

'It did seem likely. Not that I'm happy about it.' He smacked the side of the seat, beside his thigh. 'He would *never* kill himself at this particular moment. Nobody would. Leaving you in the house with all that stuff to deal with. He wasn't that irresponsible.'

'I know. Even leaving that farmer with his cows waiting to be examined was entirely out of character, according to Millie.'

'Your Higgins chap *wants* it to be suicide,' Drew accused. 'Just to save the police some bother and expense.'

'I don't think it's as deliberate as that. He's thoroughly decent. And anyway, it won't be his decision. He's only an inspector. There are plenty of people higher than him who'll have to authorise an investigation – or not.'

'Well, let me brainstorm for a minute, okay? It works better if I do it out loud.'

They were entering the south-eastern corner of Chedworth. Thea recognised the farm shop, and remembered to take the next right, which would pass the primary school after a longish meandering stretch of road. 'I'm getting the hang of this,' she said, with a sense of relief. 'All right, then. You've got a few minutes.'

'Okay. So let's say somebody spent all day

137

Friday with Richard on some pretext. Maybe it was all quite amicable at first, or perhaps there was something important that he felt he had to see to ... but what could be so important he couldn't phone Millie and the farmer and make his excuses? That in itself suggests he was under the control of somebody who wanted him to keep quiet. Anyway, this person then lured Richard to that barn probably very early yesterday, and up into the top storey through that back opening. They could easily say there was a litter of kittens or a rare bat or something up there. Richard was a vet, after all. Or maybe they forced him at gunpoint, or with a knife. Then, at that open front edge, it would be simple to push him off. A quick check to make sure he was dead, and away, leaving absolutely no evidence. He landed face down, which implies he was pushed from behind.'

'Not the same way you'd land if you jumped. Wouldn't you go feet first?'

'I don't know. You might just sort of *dive*, with your arms out. And he had broad shoulders, and a big head. Top-heavy,' he summarised with a twist of his mouth.

'It's all about the physics,' she said. 'I used to be quite good at physics.'

He ignored her. 'But for a determined suicide, it's not high enough. You wouldn't expect to die falling thirty feet. Two broken legs, yes, but nothing fatal.'

Thea sighed. This was going over old ground. 'Yes, and the same goes for a murder. Maybe somebody just lost their temper with him and never meant to kill him.'

'Maybe. The police seemed in no doubt that he died on that spot where we found him, but if the body was moved very soon after he died, or even just before, that would be difficult to detect. Especially when they're not really trying.'

'These lanes are designed to confuse people,' she complained, as they approached a sharp junction just below the church. 'You have to go back on yourself here. I can't imagine how I ever found it on Thursday evening.'

'You should have gone up there.' He pointed to a small single-track road ahead. 'That's called Church something. You're heading for Gallows Lane. Lovely name. Anyway, it all comes to the same thing, but you're making it more complicated for yourself.'

'What?' She frowned up at the barely visible church tower.

'Never mind. We're there now.'

They weren't, quite, but a right turn at the top of Gallows Lane took them onto familiar territory. Fields and woods stretched ahead and above, with the village falling away southwards. 'I can't remember a more confusing place,' she grumbled. 'I generally have a pretty good sense of direction, but all these hills and valleys have me foxed.'

'We're not stopping – okay?' Drew warned. 'Gather up the dogs and off again.'

'No problem. But you have to get that file from your car, don't forget. We should try to phone Millie now. What if she's not there?'

'We find the nearest dog rescue and give them

two fine sheepdogs to look after.'

'We most definitely do not do that,' she said, with no notion of what they might do instead. 'Maybe Mrs Wilshire's home would have them for a bit? They are sort of hers, after all. Some homes are okay with dogs these days.'

Drew made no reply, heading for his car. Thea was left to collect the animals, who all greeted her joyfully. 'Poor things,' she crooned over them. 'What an awful mess this is. What's to become of you?'

Hepzie nudged forward for her share of blandishments, the sheepdogs politely giving way to her. They were such benign, innocent creatures, Thea thought. Always doing their best to please, striving to understand what was required of them. Did they remember that their master was dead? Did they have concerns about their own future? They were probably well known in the farming community, and might be lucky enough to find a new home amongst sheep and other livestock, where they would be fully utilised as their natures intended. But would they be kept together? And were they really such goody-goodies? Not if Norah Cookham could be believed. Higgins had confirmed that they really had attacked her cat.

Drew came back, his hands full. Not just the folder, but his trusty TomTom and a jacket he'd left in the car all night. 'Might turn cold,' he said.

'Come on,' she urged. 'Let's see what happens next.'

Chapter Ten

'We could have stopped for coffee,' Thea grumbled, halfway to Stratford. It was eleven o'clock and she was thirsty. Millie Wilshire had not answered the phone, so the three dogs were still on the back seat.

'We'll get some somewhere,' he promised vaguely. He was still fiddling with his gadget, trying to make it stick to the dashboard where they could both see it.

'Carl would be horrified,' said Thea. 'I think it might be his fault that I'm so slow to accept technology. He always insisted on having everything as natural as possible.'

'I'm with him, as a general approach to life,' said Drew. 'But in this instance, I've joined the rest of humanity quite cheerfully.' References to Thea's dead husband caused him no discernible discomfort, just as Thea remained quite relaxed when Karen was mentioned. 'I'm definitely going to teach my kids how to read a map, just so they can have the fun of getting lost once in a while.'

'I should hope so too.'

They found the care home with almost magical ease. A handsome red-brick building, three storeys high with discreet annexes set on either side, much lower. A freshly painted noticeboard gave its name, with a reassuringly straightforward account of itself. 'Residential Home for the Elderly' it said, with no hint of shame. In recent times there had been so much shocking publicity for such places that Thea had half expected them to be shy about announcing themselves. 'It looks gorgeous,' she said. 'I'm going to sign up for a place now.'

'Very funny. You might mention it to your mother, though.'

'Too far from everything she knows. And about ten years too soon for her, as well, the way she's going.'

'It'll be lunchtime soon,' he observed with a grimace. 'They won't want visitors then.'

'Would they give us some coffee, do you think? And we'll have to give the dogs a bit of a run. We haven't really made any progress at all today, have we?' All their plans marched past her inner eye – the visit to Drew's house in Broad Campden was receding fast, and yet he remained determined to fit it in.

'If only dratted Millie Wilshire would show herself, it would be a lot easier.'

And then, by a further piece of magic, the girl herself came into view, emerging from a door at one side of the building. Walking slowly, head bent forward, she was a picture of misery. 'That's her,' said Thea in amazement.

'Stay there,' Drew ordered, apparently addressing Thea and the dogs together.

He got out of the car and trotted up to Millie. 'We've been looking for you,' he called. Thea opened her window electronically, on the second attempt since the ignition was turned

142

off, hoping to catch everything that was said. One of the sheepdogs pressed urgently over her shoulder, snout against her ear, with the same intention.

Millie looked at him in bewilderment. 'Who are you?' she asked.

'Drew Slocombe. I know your grandmother. I knew your father. I am so sorry about what's happened. How's Mrs Wilshire coping?'

She frowned. 'Slocombe? You found my dad, then? Is that right? You and her.' She indicated Thea with her chin, showing no sign of pleasure. 'God knows what you thought you were doing there at the barn.'

'That's right, but–'

'And the *dogs*. You've got his bloody dogs.' She slumped bonelessly, looking liable to land in a heap on the ground.

Drew moved to support her. 'Hey! Steady on,' he encouraged her. 'Let's go to that seat for a minute.' There was a wooden bench under a large cedar tree, the other side of a lawn. It was where he had been sitting a month before, with Mrs Wilshire and her son, arranging her funeral.

Thea got out of the car. 'Are you okay?' she asked.

Millie took a few shallow breaths. 'I'm not coping too well, I admit,' she said, with a weak smile. 'And the last thing I need is those beasts. What am I supposed to do with them?'

'They'll have to go to a rescue place if you don't want them,' said Drew. 'We can't have them any longer.'

'As if they *mattered*,' said Millie savagely.

143

'They're only dogs.'

'Would your father think that?' Thea demanded. 'He was a vet – he spent his whole life giving animals as healthy and happy a life as he could.'

'Rubbish! He sent most of them for slaughter. The best you can say is they died without too much suffering. And even that wasn't always true.'

'The dogs loved him,' Thea persisted. 'They found his dead body, for heaven's sake.'

'Thea!' Drew warned. 'Don't be so–'

'I'm sorry,' she said, without quite meaning it. 'But they did. Now they're your responsibility. I'm going home this evening, so there's no way I can keep them any longer.' Again, she felt a lurch of sadness and resistance at the bleak prospect for Betsy and Chummy.

'Judith can have them,' said Millie. 'She's got a dirty great mansion standing empty near Chipping Norton. She can pay somebody to feed them. At least that'll do for a while.'

It sounded marginally better than a rescue centre, at least. 'Good,' said Thea. 'Now we have to go and see your grandmother.'

Millie looked from Drew to Thea and back again. 'Why? You can't. What *for?*'

'I wanted to tell her how sorry I am,' said Drew.

'Why – you didn't kill him, did you?' The words were shot out angrily, very far from the joke they might have been coming from another person.

Drew smiled stiffly and said nothing. Thea was

less restrained. 'That's a horrible thing to say,' she accused.

'Everything's horrible anyway.' Millie's voice broke and tears began to flow. 'My poor dad! I still can't believe it. It's changed everything. I feel as if I'm drowning, sinking through the earth, with nothing solid to stand on. How could he do such an awful thing? I never had any *idea* he was thinking of killing himself. How could I miss such a thing?'

Drew patted her arm. 'People always say that. It can often be a terrible shock.' He threw a look at the building in front of them, plainly wishing he could leave Millie and make his planned visit as soon as possible. 'Is your friend staying with you?'

'Who? Oh – you mean Judith. No, she's working for the next two days. Nothing can get in the way of that.' She glared at Thea. 'And don't start about the dogs again. I'll take them back with me for tonight and sort something out tomorrow. Wretched things. I *told* him not to get them. They always have to be taken into account, every time we go anywhere.'

'They seemed to know he was in that barn,' said Thea. 'It was uncanny, really.'

'They'd been there with him plenty of times,' dismissed Millie. 'He taught them some tricks there. They probably just wanted to go and play.'

'Tricks?'

'Agility sort of stuff. Those sheep races are useful – where they used to dip them, ages ago.'

'They're quite overgrown,' Drew commented.

'So?'

'It didn't look as if anybody had used them for anything for a long time.'

'Well he did,' she said flatly. 'You can't possibly think I would tell lies about it.'

'It doesn't matter,' said Thea loudly. 'I'm going to get Betsy and Chummy now. They're all yours from here on. Be nice to them. They're confused, poor things.'

Millie, whose demeanour had brightened slightly during her conversation with Drew, slumped again. She was very young, Thea reminded herself, and she'd had a dreadful shock. She'd been kind enough to visit her grief-stricken grandmother, too. Perhaps they had managed to comfort each other. She collected the dogs and handed the leads to Millie. 'There's a bit of food left. Everything's in the bag.'

'Come on then, girls,' said Millie. The dogs looked at her trustingly, and Thea was reassured that all would turn out better than she had feared, where the animals were concerned.

'Will they let us see your gran if it's lunchtime?' Drew asked. 'We do have quite a busy schedule for the afternoon.'

'Oh, you can't see her,' said Millie. 'I told you. They wouldn't let me, so they definitely won't let you.'

He stared at her blankly. 'Why not?'

'You just can't. I've got to go now. I expect I'll see you again. You'll be doing Dad's funeral, won't you?'

Drew and Thea were both taken aback by this. 'Will I?' said Drew stupidly.

'We'll phone you about it tomorrow. Bye.' She

146

ushered the dogs onto the back seat of her car and was quickly driving out of the big double gates of the home.

'Well, part one of the mission is accomplished,' said Thea. 'Now let's see what she meant by saying we can't see the old lady. If you're doing her son's funeral, then you *need* to see her, anyway. They'll have to let us in.'

They became aware of a woman standing in the main doorway, looking as if she had been watching them for a while. Together they walked up to her. 'Morning,' said Drew. 'We'd like to see Mrs Rita Wilshire, if that's all right.'

The woman, who wore a blue nylon garment over ordinary clothes, shook her head. 'Not now, you can't. It's bridge.'

Drew glanced at his watch. 'In the middle of a Sunday? Isn't that an odd time for it.'

'Eleven to one. It's their brightest time. Then a sherry and roast lunch.' She smiled. 'Life of Reilly, here. They live like lords. Literally.' There was a definite trace of resentment in her tone.

'You work here, do you?' Thea asked.

The woman nodded. 'Just meals. Some of them need extra help then. The pay's not much, but I get my dinners as well. Suits me well enough.'

She was in her late sixties, Thea guessed. Probably surviving on a pension in a small house on the outskirts of Stratford. The prospect of a residential home for herself might not be terribly far away. She might even be calculating on a discount at this one, if she made herself useful.

'And you can't interrupt a game of bridge,' said Drew with a sigh.

'That's right. They don't even talk to each other, except to cast blame at the end if somebody thinks their partner let them down. It can get nasty then. One or two of them are rubbish players, which the others find annoying. And that's silly, given that the poor things were bullied into joining in, at the start. Rita's been very forceful about it. But it's not just her. There's one old chap who can reduce people to tears the way he speaks to them.'

'We've come quite a long way to see her,' Drew tried again. 'And after the dreadful news yesterday, I'm surprised she's still playing cards. She must be desperately upset.'

'News?'

'Her son. He died.'

The woman went white. 'No! Who told you that? I haven't heard anything.'

'I assure you it's true.'

'They can't have told her. She was just the same as usual when I saw her ten minutes ago. I always pop in to say hello when I get here. I was a bit early today. I've got to get cracking now. Thirty full dinners. Roast chicken with all the trimmings.' Her mouth worked as if she was salivating at the prospect. 'They won't have told her,' she repeated. 'That happens sometimes.'

'But the police will want to interview her. They can't just not tell her.' Thea spoke angrily, suspecting a patronising attitude of overprotectiveness. 'She's not demented or anything, is she?'

'She's ninety years old. She's here because she needs looking after. The boss will want to be sure it's done properly.'

Drew made a sound of comprehension. 'Typical,' he said. 'These places are terrified of death. I've seen it dozens of times. They try to hide it from the inmates. Pretending it's never going to happen to any of them.'

The woman pushed her face towards him. 'And what's the alternative?' she demanded. 'Let them think they're here just waiting to die? On a sort of conveyor belt, waiting their turn to tip off the end? Never knowing which one will go next. That's no way to carry on. The last thing a very old person needs is to have dead bodies pushed under their noses.'

Drew was wrong-footed. 'You could be right,' he said. 'I'm an undertaker, you see. I probably have a distorted view of things.'

'I *guessed* as much. You've got that look.'

Drew grimaced, obviously wounded by this remark. 'I suppose I can't help it,' he tried to joke.

'It's not a bad thing, exactly,' she tried to reassure him. 'Something about the eyes. As if you know more than ordinary people.' She shrugged. 'Well, I should go. I came out for a smoke, and then stayed to keep an eye on you. Thought it was a bit funny, standing around with those dogs, the way you were.'

'They didn't let Millie speak to her grandmother, in case she broke the news,' Thea realised. 'And she would have done, obviously. She couldn't possibly keep it a secret, could she? That would be ghastly.' She thought of the imagined consolation the old lady and girl could provide for each other and how some official had thwarted them.

'She didn't see her,' the woman confirmed. 'The boss lady caught her and took her into her sanctum. That's what we call it – the sanctum.' She repeated the word with relish, giving it a wealth of significance. Thea had a glimpse of a woman who refused to adopt the usual jargon with which the care industry was imbued. Even 'care industry' was horrible, when you thought about it.

'She did look very downhearted when she came out,' Drew said. 'It seems very ... high-handed, though. People have a right–'

'Don't start that again. Go and see for yourself, if you must. You've got half an hour, nearly, before they're wheeled in for lunch. End of the corridor and the second door on the left. She'll be in there, most likely.'

'Who? Mrs Wilshire?'

'No, silly. Mrs Goodison. The Chief.'

'Right. Thank you.' All three mounted the shallow steps into the building. Inside was a carpeted area like a small hotel lobby, with two doors and an open archway leading off it. The assistant pointed them through the archway and left them to fend for themselves.

They found the office easily enough, its door standing open. Inside a woman sat at an antique desk, reading a magazine. Two armchairs and a low coffee table were arranged at one end of the room. 'Hello,' she greeted them, as if they'd been expected.

It was clever, Thea realised. The very friend-

150

liness was guaranteed to disarm any complaint or uncomfortable questions. 'We've come to talk to you about Mrs Wilshire,' she said, not waiting for Drew to speak first. 'We've just seen her granddaughter outside.'

'And you are?' smiled the woman, perfectly unflustered. She was about the same age as Thea, with a halo of very curly hair. Frizzy, you might even say, thought Thea.

'I'm Thea Osborne and this is Drew Slocombe. We found the body of Mrs Wilshire's son yesterday. We came to offer her some sympathy on her loss – but it would appear that she hasn't been told about it. Isn't that very strange?'

'Perhaps it seems strange to some people,' Mrs Goodison nodded. 'To me, it seems exactly the right thing.'

Drew took over, with a small glance of irritation at Thea. 'When do you intend to tell her? She's going to notice he's not visiting her. Presumably he'd have come today, in fact?'

'And that would have been our cue. You perhaps don't appreciate the extreme delicacy of the situation.'

'I'm an undertaker,' said Drew with an obvious expectation that this would change the tenor of the conversation. 'I've been here before, but you and I didn't meet on that occasion.' His formality was almost funny, and Thea had to clamp her mouth shut for fear of grinning.

'So I understand,' the woman said, cutting the ground from beneath his feet. 'I know who you are, Mr Slocombe. I had the police here for some time yesterday evening. I am well acquainted

151

with undertakers, as you might expect. It is not my experience that they ever get to be the ones to break bad news to bereaved relatives. I, on the other hand, do it roughly once a month.'

Drew floundered. The polite and friendly manner of the woman made it impossible to take an aggressive stand. As Thea watched, it was obvious that they had no grounds at all for criticism. Mrs Goodison knew her business. She was open, frank and not even slightly defensive.

'I see,' said Drew. 'Of course.'

'I'm sure you do.' The smile remained sweet. 'But you perhaps are not aware that Mrs Wilshire's nephew is on his way, to be with her when we tell her the news. He's joining us for lunch, after which we will speak to her together. It will be extremely painful.' A hint of reproach struck Thea forcefully. What, actually, did she and Drew think they were doing, she asked herself.

'Nephew?' Drew frowned. 'I wasn't aware of any other relatives than Millie. They never mentioned a nephew.'

'He's her sister's son. He has lived most of his life in the Middle East, but has retired back to the UK now, and been in touch since then. He's a lovely man,' she finished girlishly. 'She'll be very glad of him now.'

'You've met him?'

'Once. He brought two of his three children to see Rita, a week after she came here. Well, they're not *children*, of course. All in their thirties, I would think. Lovely people. All doing extremely well for themselves.'

Typical Cotswolds folk, then, thought Thea,

before bringing to mind the scraps of information she and Drew had already gleaned concerning the family. The dead sister; an aristocratic husband and now a gaggle of great-nieces and nephews. 'He'll be Dawn's son,' she said thoughtfully. 'Is he called Martin?'

The others both looked at her gravely, as if a child had spoken out of turn.

'That's right,' said Mrs Goodison.

'How did you know?' asked Drew.

'The woman across the road said something about him. His son's called Brendan. I don't know about the others.'

'I should probably meet him,' said Drew firmly.

'He'll be the one to deal with when Mrs Wilshire dies, now Richard is dead.'

Mrs Goodison's assurance appeared to waver. Her eyes bulged slightly, and her cheeks paled. 'You ... aren't you running ahead somewhat? Rita is in excellent health. This blow will certainly come as a great shock, admittedly, but I wasn't anticipating that it would be fatal. We don't say "dead" or "die" here, Mr Slocombe,' she finished in a low hissing voice. 'We prefer to keep the atmosphere positive.'

'That's what your kitchen woman told us, just now,' said Thea. 'I suppose you know best, but it does seem somewhat ... artificial, to us. Drew has instructions to handle the funeral when Mrs Wilshire ... goes. And we thought she might want him to do Richard's as well.'

'There's a term for people like you,' said Mrs Goodison sharply. 'I think it's "ambulance chasers".'

153

'That's a vile thing to say,' Drew protested.

She closed her eyes for two seconds, her head lowered. 'All right,' she said. 'Perhaps it was a bit strong. But I have seen some very undignified behaviour in my time here. I found it shocking, I have to say.'

'I haven't met any undertakers in this area, so I can't comment. But I have never seen any poor behaviour from anyone in my line of work. Over-charging, maybe, but always totally sensitive and discreet with the families.' He shook his head. 'Anything else would be unthinkable.'

'All right,' said Mrs Goodison again. 'I take it back. But I can't let you see Rita. Not until her nephew's been. Come back tomorrow, if you must.'

Drew and Thea both started to say that was impossible, when a figure appeared in the doorway. A large and rather elderly man with an oval head stood smiling in at them. 'Am I early?' he asked. 'Or late?'

'Mr Teasdale.' The greeting was imbued with relief, as Mrs Goodison got up and almost trotted towards him. 'Your timing's perfect. Lunch is in about ten minutes. Rita will be so pleased to see you.'

'Poor old Auntie. How is she?'

'She's disconcertingly well. I hope we can keep the shock to a minimum – although it's difficult to see how. She and her son were so very close.' She sighed. 'It's a cruel thing to do to her.'

He came in and reached for her hand, ignoring Thea and Drew completely. 'I know. It defies our understanding. But at least I can offer to do

154

my poor best to fill the void for her. I'm here now, with acres of time on my hands. I can be a regular visitor – take her out for a drive now and then. And Brendan will do all he can. He's very family-minded for a chap his age. And he only lives in Cheltenham. No distance away.'

'You're Richard Wilshire's cousin?' Thea interrupted. 'My name is Thea Osborne, and this is Drew Slocombe. We found his body yesterday. At least, his dogs did, initially.'

The Teasdale man swallowed back his bonhomie and turned rather pale. 'Indeed?' he said faintly. 'Why are you here?'

'We assumed your aunt had been told of her son's death and we came to offer condolences. And perhaps to answer any questions she might have.'

'And to try to get her business,' Mrs Goodison added. 'He's an undertaker.'

'Ah, yes,' said the cousin. 'Of course.' His lack of reaction was unsettling. 'But your condolences are premature,' he smiled.

'They were just leaving.' The administrator, or matron or whatever she called herself, spoke firmly.

There did not seem to be any alternative, so Thea and Drew removed themselves from the room and headed along the corridor. Nobody was going to escort them, evidently, and Thea had a wild idea of doubling back and finding Mrs Wilshire. Her head was full of muddled anger, mostly on Drew's behalf.

Drew, however, was intent on making the best of things. 'Next stop, Broad Campden,' he said.

'No, please. I must have some lunch first. Can we stop at the next pub we see?'

'Certainly not. I don't like Sunday lunches in pubs. They make you buy a full roast dinner with all the trimmings. I'm not spending that sort of money.'

She might normally have agreed with him, but just at that moment it felt highly unreasonable. 'So what do you propose?' she demanded.

'We can stop at a garage shop or something and get sausage rolls and some juice. I'll have to do a proper meal at home for the kids tonight, anyway.'

Drew's wife had been a devoted follower of good-quality country food, at one time. She grew wholesome vegetables and bought local meat. Fast food, takeaways, microwaved pub lunches and supermarket ready meals would all have been anathema to her. Thea's incompetent negligence where catering was concerned would have annoyed her. And Thea herself wished she could summon more interest in the subject. All she knew was that she was rumbling with hunger and dry with thirst. 'All right, then,' she sighed. 'But make it soon.'

'You're driving,' he pointed out. 'You can choose where and when we stop.'

'On condition it isn't a pub, of course.'

'Apart from anything else, we haven't got *time*. The day's half over and we haven't done anything useful yet.'

'How is going to Broad Campden useful?' she wondered. 'What can you actually *do* in an hour or so?'

156

'Make sure the roof is still on, for a start. Prune a few roses, and dig up any obvious weeds at the front. It mustn't look completely neglected, or there'll be squatters moving in.'

His tone was firm and decisive. Any idea she might have had of talking him out of the detour to his house was quickly abandoned. She wasn't even sure why she should want to dissuade him, except for a restless feeling that they ought to be concentrating on Chedworth and the Wilshire family. The attitude of the woman at the residential home had created a brick wall through which she and Drew were unable to pass, or even see. She had joined forces with the nephew whose sudden appearance was both convenient and suspicious.

'He'll inherit the house, I suppose,' she said. 'The Teasdale man.'

'Surely not? Much more likely to be Millie, I would think. But while the old lady is alive, it's still hers, anyway. She can leave it to whoever she likes.'

'Not you, I hope,' said Thea with a laugh. 'You can have too much of a good thing.'

'Definitely not me,' he said, still sounding uncharacteristically sharp.

'So we don't think the nephew killed the son to get his hands on the family home?'

'Good God, Thea – you can be so thick-skinned sometimes. Aren't you sorry for her – that poor old lady, kept in the dark, completely unaware of what's happened? I can't stop thinking about it. They'll be eating their big roast lunch, trying to hide the truth, and then they'll drop it on her afterwards. How's she going to feel, knowing what a pretence they've been keeping up?'

'I have no idea. I never met the woman. Of course I'm sorry for her. It's awful for her. But I'm just as sorry for her son – however he died, it was wrong. I'm annoyed that we weren't allowed to talk to her, as well. And if I am thick-skinned, it's because I've been forced to be like that, over these past years since Carl died. And let me remind you that you don't think Richard killed himself. If a killer goes free, that's an injustice that neither of us will be happy with. Stop being such a prig,' she finished, in a low voice.

To her surprised relief, he laughed. 'There we have it, in a nutshell,' he said. 'Our worst faults exposed within a couple of minutes. I *am* a prig, sometimes, I know.'

'And I'm a tactless selfish cow.'

'You are. I guess nobody's perfect.'

She swallowed the lump in the throat that these words gave rise to. The fragility of her self-confidence seemed to be increasing, along with a tendency to tears. Hormones, she diagnosed fiercely to herself. There was a sense of exposed flesh – in fact, the very opposite of being thick-skinned. When Drew was nice to her, as he almost always was, it could make her feel un-worthy. She so seldom gave him any assurances to match those he gave her.

'Hey – where are you going?' he demanded suddenly. 'We want the A429, remember.'

'So what's this one?' She had been driving on autopilot, simply following the road they had come into Stratford on. Drew had turned the TomTom off, with a remark to the effect that they at least knew how to find Broad Campden.

'This one goes to Chipping Norton and Oxford. Too far east. We need the turning to Chipping Campden.'

'Too many Chippings,' she said. Then she tried to visualise the route. 'This is off my usual patch. I can't think how it links up.'

'It's easy. You're only confused because we usually approach it from the other direction. We can forget Chipping Sodbury, for a start. That's miles away.'

'I'm still hungry,' she said humbly.

'Okay. Stop at the next garage. There's sure to be one along here somewhere.'

There was. Less than a minute later they were on the forecourt of a fully equipped petrol station, offering a shop, toilets and every sort of fuel. 'I need the loo as well,' said Thea.

'And you're low on petrol,' he pointed out. 'Let's do it all in one go.'

They spent some minutes seeing to their various needs, including letting Hepzie out for a quick pee on a handy patch of grass. The spaniel plainly considered that she had been cruelly neglected so far that day. Her sheepdog companions had disappeared and the people hadn't given her a single word or glance for hours. Sometimes she was less than thrilled at the very existence of Drew Slocombe.

It took very little time to reach Broad Campden. The house was on a small side road that ended as a footpath, just as the Chedworth one

159

did. In fact, it was a regular feature of several Cotswold settlements that the roads simply stopped, with a hedge or gate or stile offering no further progress except on foot. It happened in Blockley as well and contributed to the sense of an earlier time, before motor-driven vehicles claimed dominance. Even bicycles were regularly thwarted.

Drew stood back and gave the building a thorough scrutiny. 'Doesn't look too bad,' he said. 'Will you be okay, living here with me, do you think?'

She hesitated. The plan had been so slow to take shape, and was still so fraught with complication that she hardly believed it would really happen. But now it hit her with some force. *Did* she really want to spend the next phase of her life – perhaps all of it – here in the complacent Cotswolds? This village was as silent and deserted as most of the others she had experienced in her time as a house-sitter. Drew would have to erect a special building for storage of coffins and dead people. There would be awkwardness with neighbours: rich and famous individuals who kept their country mansion in mothballs except for a few weeks each year, when they chose to retreat to a secluded idyll where nothing nasty could happen. There would be a hearse standing in full view. There would be night-time call-outs to remove a body. There was a whole lot more to the funeral business that she still didn't know about.

It was almost a crisis, in those moments. The day, which had been cool and cloudy thus far, suddenly brightened, and the sun burst forth, turning the stonework of the house to a rich honey colour. The previous owner, who had died naturally, if somewhat younger than expected, had created a future for Drew that he had little choice but to follow. She had exerted control from beyond the grave, which Thea had felt, even at the time, to be unsettling. However generously meant, it had been an almost aggressive thing to do.

'I'm not entirely sure,' she said, with more honesty than tact. 'I can't quite imagine it yet.'

'Neither can I. It's so different from Somerset. But look at it.' He swept a wide arm to embrace the fields and woods on every side. There were bumps and dips in the landscape, concealing the waterways and many of the buildings. The very emptiness could be seen as a rare asset on a crowded island. There was nothing ugly or threatening about it. The little rivers behaved themselves perfectly, finding no reason to burst through living rooms or gardens when there was so little new building to frustrate them.

'It's lovely,' Thea agreed. 'I suppose I wonder whether we can hope to live up to it. I mean – everything's so *tidy*.'

'Superficially, perhaps. But there's just as much cruelty and pain and anxiety here as anywhere else. You've discovered that for yourself, surely.'

'True. I've met plenty of real people, along with the millionaires and celebrities. There are farms with cattle and sheep, as well as horses. There are even some children,' she smiled. 'We have to remember the children.'

'We do,' he said, with only a faint hint of the earlier sharpness at any suggestion that he might forget Stephanie and Tim.

'But ... to really settle and make our lives here. Could we make it work?'

'Absolutely we could, if that's what we put our minds to. People would come and visit. We can join some of those clubs and things in Blockley.' He shook himself. 'Come on. Let's go in.'

He found a key to the front door in his jacket pocket, which impressed Thea. 'You remembered to bring the key!' she said admiringly.

'Why wouldn't I? This is top of my list of things to do this weekend.'

She punched him lightly on the shoulder. 'Before taking me to bed?'

'Not *before*, exactly, but of greater importance in my business life. Obviously.' He gave her a direct look, which said *Let's not play games*.

The house smelt dusty and stale. It was chilly and their footsteps echoed in the hallway. Although there were still a few pieces of furniture, they were not enough to give a soft absorbing effect. The main room was missing its carpet, because Drew had agreed to let a member of the family have it. He felt bad at inheriting the house over the nephews and nieces who had assumed it would come to them. Thea went upstairs, hoping to remind herself of just what it provided. There were four bedrooms, though one was very small, and a single bathroom. 'The kids can have a room each,' she called down. 'And we can just about squeeze a visitor in, if they don't want to stay too long.'

'It's not really typical of the area, is it?' he said. 'Only one bathroom, and the kitchen hasn't been updated for about forty years.'

'There are plenty of places like this,' she told him. 'The Chedworth house, for a start. I've looked after some extremely unfashionable homes in my time. It's not all glass and chrome and white walls, even in the Cotswolds.'

'Thank goodness for that.'

'Mm.' She came downstairs again, and prowled through the living room and kitchen. Hepzie followed her, sniffing in corners. 'She can smell mice,' Thea said. 'I can hardly remember being here, you know. I mean – I remember the funeral in the field, and *you*. I suppose that's the thing. All I could think of was you, and what fun you were to talk to.'

'It is a nice house,' he said, with a hint of melancholy. 'A bit dark at the back, maybe.'

'We could make it lovely. We could make *anywhere* lovely, between us. We'll have enough money, once I sell my place. The funerals might take off tremendously.'

He pulled a face, baring his teeth in a kind of anxious wince. 'That's the trouble. I'm really not sure they will. There aren't enough old people living here any more. They've sold up and gone to be closer to their children. They've moved out of the villages and into new developments in Cirencester and Cheltenham. They're not committed to the land, like they are in Somerset and Dorset – and even that's changing. I depend on people who want to spend eternity in the open air, under trees they've always loved.'

163

'Oh dear.' She gave it some hard thinking. 'I've met quite a few old people, actually. Isn't that what we were just saying? Tucked away in unreconstructed cottages, surrounded by empty properties with security lights and alarm systems. I bet there are thousands of them.'

A loud male voice interrupted them, causing Hepzie to bark and rush to the front door. 'Who's there?' came the voice. 'What's going on here?'

The door was open and a man stood on the threshold. The light behind him made it difficult to see detail, but he appeared to be of average size and to be carrying a stick.

'Hello, there,' said Drew with exaggerated affability. 'Do come in.'

The man made no move, apart from flinching away from the spaniel, which was greeting him with little jumps. Where she would normally stand up and paw at a person's knees, she was plainly too intimidated by this person to risk it.

'Are you a neighbour?' Thea asked him, as sweetly as she could. She and Drew were going to extract all possible fun from this encounter.

'Umph. Across the way. Shipley's the name.' He peered down the hallway. 'Bought this, have you?'

Drew laughed. 'Surely you're aware of the story? Mrs Simmonds left the house to me when she died. I'm Drew Slocombe, and this is Thea Osborne. We intend to come and live here with two children.'

'And a dog,' said Thea, patting Hepzie with lavish affection.

164

'Good, good,' said Mr Shipley. 'Well, I'm sorry to intrude. We're a close community here, you see. Keeping an eye on things for each other.'

Rubbish, thought Thea. Any claim to a genuine community in many of these silent little villages was sheer self-delusion. A few exceptions came to mind – Blockley and Temple Guiting, especially – but in others, there was almost no social interaction that she had discerned.

'Very considerate of you,' said Drew. 'And now you'll know us another time, won't you?'

'You're an undertaker, is that right?' the man went on, with a narrow look. He was perhaps sixty, dressed in the usual Cotswold uniform of expensive jacket and sturdy boots.

'I am. You'll probably know that I have permission to establish a natural burial ground in a field just outside the village. On the road to Blockley.'

'You buried Greta there,' Mr Shipley nodded. 'You'll be keeping a hearse hereabouts, I suppose?'

'Indeed. But the details are yet to be decided. I have no wish to cause any upset or annoyance.'

'Umph,' said the man again. 'It's not going to go down well, I warn you.'

'You think it'll lower the property values,' said Drew with a laugh.

Thea was less forgiving. 'You realise that Broad Campden has a proud history for arts and crafts, of course,' she said. 'It seems to me that simple natural funerals are exactly the sort of thing that would fit with the village. It'll add character and meaning to the place. You should be *grateful*.'

'That was all a long time ago. It has a very different atmosphere these days.'

'Then it's time we rescued it,' said Thea with asperity. 'Gave it back some of its former glory.'

Drew made a sound, part caution, part admiration. She was quite impressed with herself. Mr Shipley had clearly had enough. He retreated through the door, with a little wave of his stick, and was gone.

'Is that really what you think?' Drew asked.

'I suppose it must be. I came over all missionary and evangelist, for a minute.'

'I noticed. I remember when I was like that.' Again, the faint whiff of melancholy accompanied his words. 'But it'll be such a struggle,' he sighed.

'We *like* a struggle. It'll be our thing, together. We can build on what you've learnt at Staverton, and add a lot of new bits and pieces. We'll hit the headlines and convert everybody in Gloucestershire.'

'I loved the way you told him he ought to be grateful.'

'There you are, then. Have faith, Drew. We can't go back on it now.'

He pulled her to him and wrapped her in a warm hug that lasted so long that Hepzie yapped in protest at being left out.

On the face of it, they agreed, there was no reason to stay any longer in Chedworth. They could simply drive away, leaving the house key under a flowerpot and a note to say Thea would waive her fee, under the circumstances. Drew would write to Millie, with a formal confirmation that he was expecting to hear from her if she chose to use him for her father's funeral, and certainly he would meet her again at some future date, when her grandmother died. The Teasdale nephew was an irrelevance; the death of Richard Wilshire a nasty little mystery that they would be forced to forget.

The A429 was beginning to feel like an old friend. 'We could turn left where it says Yanworth,' Drew suggested, 'and approach the village from the north.'

'Let's not,' Thea demurred. 'That would take us past the barn again, wouldn't it? We don't want to do that.'

'No,' he said. 'I suppose we don't.'

'You don't sound very sure.'

'Something might come to mind. I mean – some detail we've forgotten.'

'A detail that would prove it was murder, not suicide?' she challenged. 'Is that what we want?'

He sighed. 'Sorry. You're right.'

So they carried on, following the same road a few more miles, with a substantial stone wall running alongside for much of the way. 'Must have been a grand estate at one time,' he remarked.

'Probably still is. It's in excellent repair.'

They swooped downhill, past the big pub at the bottom and then up again to their turning. 'We're getting good at this,' said Thea. 'Even from a different direction.'

But the way through Chedworth was still surprisingly long and meandering. There were so many small turn-offs where an unwary driver might venture. The village stopped and started again, the sense of being hemmed in and over-looked quite strong in places. At the top, it was still a muddle of sharp angles and cockeyed levels. 'This is nothing like any other place I've been,' Thea marvelled. 'How is it possible?'

'We can spend our lives walking every foot-path, perusing every plaque in every church, sampling every pub,' he said dreamily.

She laughed at the prospect. At that moment it felt perfectly feasible. 'I can't wait,' she said.

Then they were back at the Wilshire house, where Drew's car was waiting. But it had a com-panion. Beside it sat a large new Nissan four-wheel drive, with tinted windows. As Thea awk-wardly parked her own car behind it, a woman got out.

'Recognise her?' Thea whispered.

'No,' said Drew blankly. 'Who is she?'

'The most famous face in British soap opera. I wonder what the hell she wants.'

Chapter Eleven

The woman known to her friends as Judith, and to the nation as Jayjay, came towards them. 'At last!' she said furiously. 'I've been sitting here for *hours.*'

'I thought you were working all weekend,' said Thea. 'That's what Millie said.'

'They changed the schedule. The weather's not right. Besides, I'm too upset to work.'

'So, what can we do for you?' Drew asked.

'Who's this?' asked the actress rudely.

'Drew Slocombe,' said Drew, holding out his hand. 'I've come up for the weekend. It was all thanks to me that Thea got this job in the first place.'

'He's *dead*,' Judith burst out, ignoring his proffered hand. 'And *you* found him.' She stared intently from face to face. 'Why do you look so *normal?*'

'Come in,' said Thea. 'Let's talk properly.'

She led the way up to the front door, feeling a fraud at behaving like a hostess in a house that was in no way hers. Hepzie ran ahead, showing no such qualms.

They went into the living room and stood awkwardly for a minute. 'Shall I make coffee?' Thea asked tiredly.

'I never drink coffee,' said Judith scathingly, as if this was the most obvious fact imaginable.

'Tea, then.'

'Why are you here?' Drew interrupted. 'What's it all about? We're packing up and going in a little while. We saw Millie this morning. She's got the dogs back, but she thinks they can go to your house.'

'Your *mansion*,' Thea corrected. 'With permanent staff who won't object to taking care of two sheepdogs.'

'I'd love to have them. I'm very fond of them. And they're all that's left of Richard.' Without warning, the floodgates opened and with tears

169

coursing down her face, she also poured out a torrent of words. 'Listen, will you. Richard was the sweetest man. So natural and normal, not at all fazed by the media and all that stuff that follows me everywhere I go. I can't *believe* I'll never see him again.'

Drew and Thea met each other's eyes, full of helpless questions. Neither said anything. Judith clasped her hands together and walked the length of the room and back. It occurred to Thea that this was the sort of thing an actor learnt to do as a matter of routine. Ordinary people almost never behaved in such a way.

'Listen,' Judith said again. 'You *saw* him – lying there in that barn. How did he look? How exactly did he die? I know it sounds ghoulish, but I *have* to know.'

'It's not ghoulish,' said Drew. 'It's quite natural to want to know the whole story. But we probably can't give you all the answers. There were no signs of suffering. He hadn't moved at all after he landed. So it must have been quick.' He reached out a hand to her, which she flinched sideways to avoid. Her face was a picture of misery, the corners of her mouth drooping and bags appearing under her eyes. All suggestion of acting abruptly vanished.

'Poor Ricky!' she choked. 'The poor man. He must have fallen off the edge by accident. He would never have done it on purpose. That's what they think, isn't it? I bet he saw a cat or something up there and went to rescue it. He was quite an awkward person, you know. His balance wasn't very good.'

'An accident,' echoed Thea slowly. That possibility had apparently not occurred to anybody. 'You think that's likely?'

'I don't know. I just can't believe he did it deliberately. He had such a lot to live for. He was making plans for retirement, travelling and so forth. He talked to me about it, because Millie was never interested. I really loved the way he talked. Millie says he was quite unfriendly with most people, always looking for a reason to take offence, but he was fine with me. He said I was a breath of fresh air.' Thea made a mental comparison between this agonised performance and the monosyllabic sidekick who had come to the house with Millie on Friday morning. It was disorientating.

'I'm sure you did each other a lot of good,' said Thea stiltedly.

'We did,' said Judith, her eyes shining. 'It was a beautiful friendship. And Millie was pleased that we got along so well. She laughed at us, but she liked it really.'

'It all sounds very ... rewarding. An escape from all the celebrity stuff.'

Judith gave a little shiver. 'I hate it, you know. There's never any end to it. People think it's the best thing that can happen, landing a part like this, but it's murder, honestly. My life isn't my own. It's like being wrapped in silver foil all the time – all people see is the shiny celebrity and nothing of the person inside.' The demeanour had changed again. Now the young woman was being bravely confiding, setting right the general assumptions surrounding her way of life. The

171

tears had dried completely, Thea noted.

'The money must be good, though,' she said. Then she caught a look from Drew, which made her cringe inwardly. *Thick-skinned*, she remembered. That's what he'd called her. He appeared to be thinking it again. And yet it was a perfectly reasonable comment, as far as she could see.

'The money is amazing,' said Judith with a sigh. 'I should probably have said *gold* foil. I'm a walking lump of gold. And you know what? It doesn't help. You still have to *live*. You have to get up, and eat and talk and *do* things. And you can't trust people when they say they like you. They mostly want to sell you things, or get you to invest in their stupid projects. It's ridiculous, when you think about it.' She leant against the back of a chair, her head drooping. 'I can't see how I can go on without Rick. He kept me grounded. He never demanded anything from me, never wanted anything to do with my working life. He would never come to the clubs with me, never met all the other actors and that. We had our own special little world, away from all that rubbish. I'd be hooked on drugs by now without him. That's what'll happen now. I know it will.' The first words of this speech had felt quite genuine to Thea, but the rapid decline into self-pitying melodrama made her doubt her own impressions.

'Sit down and I'll make tea,' said Drew, cutting through the little scene. 'Then we'll have to start getting ready to go. I have to be home by six.'

'Home?'

'I live in Somerset.'

172

'You're both going?' Judith looked around the room. 'Just walking away, leaving everything in a mess here?'

The living room wasn't the least bit messy, thought Thea resentfully. But upstairs was. Upstairs there were heaps of clothes, open drawers, boxes of papers and piles of books. 'I haven't been asked to stay,' she defended. 'I think Millie's going to have to deal with it from here on.'

'Or the cousin,' said Drew, from the doorway.

'Who?' Judith looked blank.

'You tell her,' said Drew to Thea, and disappeared into the kitchen.

'He was at the home this morning. He's called Teasdale. He was visiting Mrs Wilshire.'

'Whose cousin is he? I've never heard of him.'

'He's Richard's first cousin – the son of Rita's sister. He's quite old. Lived in Saudi Arabia or somewhere until recently. He's very jolly. The woman in charge at the home thinks he's wonderful. They were going to tell the old lady about her son, together. They'll have done it by now.'

'She didn't know? Where was Millie? What's she playing at?'

'She'd gone by then. They didn't let her see her gran because she was playing bridge.' Thea felt uneasy about conveying any further information. She had a strong sense of walking on thin ice, beneath which lay murky relationships. Judith and Richard; Richard and Millie; Millie and her celebrity friend – the triangle was all too obviously fraught with dark emotions. Questions began to pop up like mushrooms. Was Millie secretly jealous of her friend's relationship with her father? Was Richard embarrassed about it, or just star-struck by the girl's fame and fortune? Did Judith fully understand the implications? Had she really never heard of the cousin? What did any of them stand to gain from the others? When she finally caught up with her own thoughts, Thea realised she had become inescapably drawn in. She was hooked by the revelations of the day – not just Judith's unlikely affection for a man with little charm or appeal, but the appearance of a long-lost cousin, and the delay in telling Mrs Wilshire the tragic news. *Drat!* she said loudly to herself. It no longer felt possible to just bundle her dog into the car and drive away. And one reason for this was that she found herself rather admiring Judith! Jayjay, the celebrity. There was also the thrill of enjoying a one-to-one conversation with a person almost everyone in the country knew by sight. It would be something she could boast about, once the Chedworth business was concluded. Even if the entire encounter had been phony, a counterfeit performance laid on by a skilled actor, it had felt exciting and revelatory. There was a lurking implication of a self-deluded girl stalking an older man who had no feelings for her at all. The damaged celebrity in search of normality and protection. It would make a very neat reversal of the usual pattern, where the sad lonely man persuaded himself that the lovely actress fancied him.

But Judith wasn't finished. 'I only met her

once – Richard's mum, that is. I came here with Millie, ages ago now. Mill thought her gran might let me look at some of the old clothes she's got, in case they'd be good as costumes, but she didn't want us touching them. Said she'd kept them in perfect condition for seventy years, and she didn't want people messing about with them.'

'I've messed about with them,' said Thea, feeling guilty. 'I could never get them back as they were. I hope she doesn't find out. Or perhaps Millie could gently tell her what's been happening, and ask her what she wants done with all the things here.'

Drew came in then with a tray, holding a teapot, three cups and a plate of biscuits. 'Where did you find those?' Thea asked. 'Have they been in a tin for months?'

He laughed. 'No. I had them in the car. I bought a few things yesterday, on the assumption there'd be no food in the house. I only just remembered.'

Judith gave a loud dramatic sigh. 'She is still alive, you know. Everything still belongs to Richard's mum. Don't you feel it's all rather yukky, going through her stuff like this?'

'I assumed that was why Richard asked me to do it – keeping his own hands clean, as it were.'

Drew spluttered over his tea at this, but Judith merely nodded. 'That's exactly right. I said the same thing to him. But actually, it's mainly Millie's fault. She's the obvious person to do it. She's been all over the place ever since her gran went into the home. Screaming at poor Rick one

175

minute, and then asking if she could borrow money against this house the next. She's been a good friend to me, so I shouldn't speak against her, but to be honest, she is a bit of a taker. Expects it all to be handed to her on a plate. She won't put the graft in, like I did.'

There was not a lot to say to this. At barely twenty-five, it was difficult to believe that the girl had spent long hard years stacking supermarket shelves while attending hundreds of auditions, as the general pattern seemed to go. It had to be at least two years since she joined the cast of the soap opera. Many might think she had enjoyed a solid-gold career with plenty of extremely good years ahead of her. She was, as far as Thea was aware, a reasonably talented actor, and her looks were distinctive enough to carry her well into her thirties. Long faces like hers were highly regarded in the fickle eyes of the general public, rather to Thea's chagrin. She blamed the woman in *Sex in the City* – Sarah Jessica Parker – and a gaggle of younger lookalikes.

'Your chauffeur not working today, then?' Thea said, after a pause.

Judith snorted. 'You make me sound like royalty. It's just a driver – different men every time, pretty much. It's a not-very-subtle way of making sure we actually turn up when we're supposed to. They treat us like naughty schoolchildren. One of these days, they'll fix tracker devices on us, or implant microchips, so they can always find us. It's a massive cast, you know. They talk as if they're organising an army, half the time.'

'A different world,' murmured Drew. Then he

worked his shoulders manfully. 'I've got half an hour, max,' he announced, addressing Thea. 'What are you going to do?'

'Good question,' she said. 'An hour ago, I'd have followed you back to North Staverton, but now – well, it doesn't feel right to just abandon things here.'

He tilted his head at her, saying nothing. Then he looked at Judith, who looked right back at him.

Thea agonised, thinking aloud. 'I expect I *could* leave it all to Millie. The house is her responsibility, not mine. I don't imagine I'll even get paid for the days I've done. But there are so many loose ends. You see that, don't you? You'd stay as well, if you could.'

Judith gave a snorting little laugh. 'You two!' she said. 'What are you like?' It was funny, even if it came from a line of TV dialogue. She went on, 'The big "loose end", as you put it, is that Richard did *not* kill himself. The idea is insane. There's nothing about him that could make that a sensible idea.'

'Have you ever been in that barn?' Drew asked her. 'Do you know how high the upper part is?'

'I have, actually,' she admitted. 'Richard took me there a couple of times. He had a thing about it. Did I tell you he took the dogs there quite often?'

'Millie mentioned it. Did he know who owns it?'

Judith shrugged. 'He must have done. But he said he'd been going there all his life, so nobody's bothered about it, obviously. We used to climb in

177

from the field next to it. The road gate's kept locked with a chain and a padlock.'

'Why hasn't anybody converted it into a house?' Drew asked. 'You never see an old barn like that, left as it was originally.'

'I can think of lots of reasons,' said Judith vaguely. 'It's too high for a house, for one thing. It'd be like living in a cathedral.'

'But it's a place he might go if he was feeling ... low or worried, or something,' Drew pursued. 'To go and think, maybe. Like a cathedral,' he finished thoughtfully. 'There is a sort of holy feeling to it, somehow.'

The two women gave him sceptical looks. 'Holy?' said Thea. Judith gave one of her snorts, which served to remind Thea that this really was the same person she'd met on Friday. Up to then, there had been few points of similarity.

Drew stuck to his point. 'You know what I mean. A big empty space, with sunbeams filtering in, and nothing to distract you.'

'Richard didn't see it like that,' said Judith. 'He just liked the way it has survived, in an area that doesn't care very much about agriculture or industrial history or anything like that. He loved the way it'd been built, with that fantastic roof. I think he'd have bought it if he'd had the money, just to keep it safe.'

'It'd cost a fortune,' said Drew.

'But *you* could have afforded it,' said Thea slowly. 'Did he ask you to buy it for him?' That might be at least part of an explanation for the man entering into a relationship with her, she supposed. Again, it suggested a reversal of the

178

expected scenario – although rich young women had certainly been pursued by older men in need of some cash, from time to time.

Judith's eyes filled again. 'I would have done, in a heartbeat, if he'd let me. But he was far too proud for that. No – we did joke about going to live in my Chipping Norton house, so I could look after him when he's old. He never really liked Chedworth, you see. Said it had painful associations.'

'But he grew up here, didn't he?' said Thea.

'So? His childhood wasn't very happy, by all accounts.'

'There are things from his boyhood still in one of the rooms upstairs.' Thea was trying to reconcile the idea of an unhappy childhood with the man's manner on Thursday evening. It did fit reasonably well, she concluded.

'Are there?' Judith sniffed back the tears. 'Can I see them?'

Thea shrugged. 'I can't stop you, can I? I've got no authority over the house and what happens in it.' She frowned. 'I don't seem to be answerable to anybody, really.'

'It's a shambles,' said Judith. 'Richard was the lynchpin. Everything went through him. Now he's left a great black hole and nobody knows what to do.'

The words reflected Thea's feelings quite accurately. Every time she tried to find an answer or a decision, her instinct to consult Richard Wilshire was thwarted. He had juggled his mother, daughter and girlfriend – and perhaps even the newly arrived cousin. Not to mention the irascible

179

woman across the road. His dogs depended on him, too. Without him there was a sort of implosion. Everyone was scrambling to understand what had happened, assembling scattered bits of information to no particular effect.

'I see what you mean,' she said weakly. 'So, nobody knows what comes next?'

'I'll get on to Millie and insist she makes some proper decisions,' said Judith. 'I can't stop now. I'll come back one day and have a look at the stuff he's left. Millie might want to come as well.'

'Good,' said Drew approvingly. 'Sounds the best course.'

They all lost patience at the same moment. Judith zipped up her smart jacket and headed for the door. Drew swept up the teacups and took them to the kitchen. Thea did nothing, but her thoughts were all on the stacks of clothes and other things upstairs.

Four o'clock was upon them, and Drew was going to leave, whatever happened. Thea was almost glad. The indecisive standing about had got thoroughly on her nerves, the whole day had been a frustrating waste of time. If Richard Wilshire had fallen off the barn loft by accident, then there was no more to be said. If he had done it on purpose, that raised questions, but they hardly concerned her.

That only left one other possibility, and nobody appeared to be seriously considering that.

Except one person, it seemed. When Judith pulled the front door open, rooting in her pocket for car keys, and staring at the ground, she almost collided with a man. 'Hey!' he shouted. 'I know you.'

Judith's loud sigh could be heard at the far end of the hallway. Drew came out of the kitchen at a trot, alarmed at the aggressive tone.

'Who's that?' he asked.

Nobody replied at first. The man had one foot over the threshold, his eyes fixed on Judith's face. 'Who are you?' Drew said again.

'Brendan Teasdale,' came the reply, as if this should mean something.

'Teasdale?' Thea joined Drew, blocking the way into the house. 'A relation of the cousin we met this morning, then?'

'My father is Mrs Wilshire's nephew. We used to come here now and then, when we were small.'

'Ah!' Cogs clicked into place and pennies dropped. 'Millie said something about that. You're older than her, though.'

The man was perhaps in his early thirties, his dark hair close-cropped, and he had a fleshy mouth looking as if it smiled much of the time. He showed signs of finding himself both outnumbered and outmanoeuvred. He threw repeated glances at Judith, as if she was the one who really mattered to him.

'How can we help you?' asked Drew, in his usual polite fashion.

'I've come to find proof that Richard was murdered,' he said with a scowl.

181

Chapter Twelve

As a bombshell, it worked fairly well. Certainly it was a conversation-stopper. Judith stammered, 'Murdered?' but otherwise there was silence.

Brendan Teasdale pushed himself further into the house, and closed the door behind himself. Hepzie trotted up to him, clearly intending to jump up at his knees, but then thought better of it. Yet another disappointing encounter, she was plainly thinking.

'Auntie Rita sent me an email, and forwarded one that Richard wrote a while ago.'

'When?' asked Thea.

'When what?'

'When did she send the email? Surely she must be far too upset this afternoon to bother with anything like that.'

'You don't know my aunt,' he said, with a hint of pride. 'She sent it just after three o'clock, saying I should come right over here and have a good look in the attic, because there could be items that proved Richard was murdered.' The man continued to glance repeatedly at Judith, his face flushed.

'But it doesn't name the killer,' Drew persisted, his face not quite straight. 'How very frustrating.'

'You can't name people as murderers, in writing. That's libel.'

'Not if it's true,' said Thea, her head spinning.

Drew's scepticism was almost funny – and yet here was a relative of the dead man making the most serious claim imaginable. He had a stubble-strewn chin, and slightly crumpled clothes, and yet looked well-muscled and healthy. His skin was tanned. His accent was classless. It was impossible to draw any reliable conclusions about him.

'I don't have to explain anything to you,' he said stiffly.

'It sounds like something in a story,' said Judith, who was showing no sign of following through her intention of leaving. 'Or a television play.'

'It is a bit like something from Agatha Christie,' Thea agreed. She looked with something like kindness at the man. 'We don't altogether believe you, you see.'

'You would if you knew this family,' he said, pushing his face towards her. 'With our history, you'd worry about what might happen, as well.'

'Are you saying others have been murdered?' Thea looked at Judith, who might be expected to have some knowledge of the Wilshire background. But all she got was a blank look.

'Nothing proved,' said Brendan Teasdale. 'But people have died without warning. That's what happened to my grandmother. She was twenty-two, with a young baby, and she just dropped down dead. Completely out of the blue. Everything to live for.'

'And you think somebody – what? Poisoned her or something?'

'There were rumours,' he said darkly.

'I've not heard that story,' said Thea. 'But it

sounds like natural causes to me. A brain aneurysm or something like that.'

The man shook his head, more in confusion than denial. He had still not recovered from the shock of seeing a famous TV star in the flesh. And now she thought about it, that struck Thea as surprising in itself. Wouldn't he have been aware that his cousin had such a friend? Wouldn't it be hot family gossip? But Brendan was still following the thread raised by his dead grandmother. 'The family never got over it,' he said. 'Auntie Rita kept all her sister's things. I suppose you've seen them.'

'Yes. Richard employed me to sift through it, and make an inventory of it all,' said Thea impatiently. She had been forced to give this same account of herself a few too many times. 'So what?'

'Have you sifted through things in the attic?'

'Not yet.' Thea was suddenly reminded of another attic in another Cotswolds house. Cold Aston, it had been, and the attic had harboured some real surprises.

'Good. I'll go up there now and see what I can find.'

Judith stirred at last. 'Have you told Millie about all this? Shouldn't she be here – or at least kept in the loop?'

'I haven't seen Millie since she was five years old. Why would I talk to her now?'

'For one thing, her father's just died, and you might want to offer her your condolences,' Judith shot back. 'If you really are part of the family, of course. How do we know you're not

184

some sneak thief coming to check the place for antiques?'

The man's colour grew even darker at this. 'Ask me anything about the family, then. I know it all. I've been doing my research for a while now.'

'So why haven't you seen Millie?' asked Thea. 'That sounds very odd.'

'I was in Dubai with my father until a couple of months ago. We met Richard and Auntie Rita a few days after we got back. Millie was never around.'

'I don't think I can let you just barge up to the attic,' Thea worried. 'We ought to check with Mrs Wilshire's solicitor or somebody, first.'

Drew caught her eye and mouthed *We?* with raised eyebrows. She gave a rueful little shrug in response. 'And if it *was* murder,' she went on, 'we ought to inform the police. Show them the email and let them look for this so-called proof.' She heard herself with mild surprise. Brendan Teasdale was agitated, jiggling his hands and working his lips all the time. He seemed to have no idea of his next move, but to be working from some fixed idea that was not going to adapt itself to unexpected situations. He was so obviously thrown by the presence of Judith, even after she had spoken to him like an ordinary human being, that any credibility he might have had was leaking away.

Then Judith shook herself and made an abrupt departure, saying very little. Drew watched her enviously. He could not leave so easily. The Teasdale man was an impediment to fond farewells. And nothing had been decided as to where Thea would spend the coming night. His wish had been that she would pack up her dog and follow him down to North Staverton. Now that seemed to be a receding hope.

'The police won't listen until we have something concrete to show them,' said the man, who had let Judith go without protest. His single-track purpose was at least uncomplicated. Interestingly, he showed no sign of fear or guilt at the mention of the police. 'I'm going upstairs now. You can't stop me.'

'At least I can go with you and see what you get up to,' said Thea, feeling brave.

'Why would you do that?' The man seemed genuinely puzzled.

'Let him do it by himself,' said Drew. 'We've got no grounds to stop him.' *Mind your own business,* was the plain subtext to his words.

She was reproaching herself for her timidity concerning the attic. If she hadn't been such a fool about spiders, she would have gone up there on the first day, and perhaps found the whatever-it-was that showed Richard Wilshire was in danger. Exactly what it might be was impossible to guess. She wanted to see it for herself, if it existed. Drew had made no secret of his wholesale scepticism over the story, but it did at least appear that Brendan expected to find something. And that was enough for Thea. Besides, attics, as she had already been thinking, could be magically amazing at times.

'I want to,' she said stubbornly. A new thought occurred. 'After all, Richard expected me to go up there. It was part of the job. He and I talked about it on Thursday. I just hadn't got around to it. I suppose he wanted *me* to find this mysterious evidence. Otherwise, he'd have just told you or your father about it.' Her eyes narrowed. 'He didn't trust either of you – that must be it.'

'Thea!' Drew was making the same horrified face she had seen before when she overstepped a mark.

'He hadn't seen me for twenty-five years,' said Brendan Teasdale. 'I doubt if he even remembered my name. Or my sisters'. He certainly never sent us any cards at Christmas or birthdays. And he didn't have much time for my dad, either. That doesn't mean he thinks we can't be trusted.'

'Sisters?' Thea was intent on getting the full picture.

'Older than me. Linda and Carol. I don't see them much. They've both got families. One lives in Kent. She came up a month or so ago to visit Auntie Rita. The other one's been in Panama for the past three years. We're rather a nomadic lot, I suppose.' He seemed to find this a melancholy thought.

Thea entertained a picture of a burgeoning family tree, spreading in all directions with unsuspected offshoots. 'Have you got a mother?' she asked.

'Of course I have. She lives in France most of the time.' Despite his desire to go up to the attic, he evidently felt compelled to answer her questions. She did have that effect on people much of the time and had no qualms about exploiting it.

'Not with your father?'

He gave a scornful little laugh. 'She's on her third husband, and I wouldn't put money on him lasting much longer.'

'Your poor father must think women will always abandon him,' she said. 'With his mother dying as she did.'

'He was far too young to remember that. Auntie Rita took care of him for a while. Then he went away to school and she had Richard. Not much fun for him, I imagine, but he wasn't the only one.'

'Sounds rather Victorian to me.'

'So, let's go, then,' said Drew, surprisingly. 'I can see we'll just be standing here all night, otherwise.'

As if a switch had been flicked, they trooped upstairs, the dog taking up the rear. Drew pulled down the metal ladder that cleverly unfolded itself as it dropped. 'Is there a light up there?' Drew asked.

'No idea,' said Brendan Teasdale. 'It's been changed a lot since I last saw it. We had to use a stepladder to get into it in my day.'

'Yes, there's a window,' said Thea. 'A Velux, I think.'

Drew rubbed his face, as if to dispel annoying thoughts. 'It amazes me that Mrs Wilshire could send emails only a couple of hours after hearing her only son has died. It seems incredible.'

'It's not,' said Brendan. 'I can't pretend to know her very well, but it didn't take long to work out she's made of stern stuff. It's a family thing. They don't waste much time on sentiment.'

188

'Was your father there with her when she was emailing?' asked Thea.

'Probably. I haven't heard from him. But she'll have been glad to have him there. She always preferred him to Richard, apparently. That was one reason Dad went off abroad for most of his life. He wanted to leave the field clear for Richard to get his due from her. He's a generous chap, my dad.'

The whole family was still an enigma to Thea, and this young man in particular confused her. First he burst into the house, only to be pole-axed by the sight of a famous celebrity. Then he let himself be delayed and diverted by a welter of questions. Protective of his father, dismissive of Millie and in no way impatient to report an apparent murder to the police, he seemed to be following some great imperative that made as little sense to him as it did to anybody else. 'Did somebody *tell* you to come here?' she asked. 'Have you any idea what you're looking for?'

'Auntie Rita,' he repeated. 'She said I should come.'

There was something childlike about the use of 'Auntie'. Didn't most people revert to 'aunt' when they reached their twenties? Like 'Mum' and 'Dad' instead of 'Mummy' and 'Daddy'. But then, Brendan had said he had two older sisters. He was the baby of the family, still spoilt and patronised. She was searching for clues to his character, she realised, wanting to know as much as she could about these Wilshires and Teasdales and the past hundred years of their history.

But at the same time she was distracted by the

189

continued presence of Drew, who should have left for home ten minutes ago, at the latest. Drew had moved away from her in some alarming way, during the day. He had turned slippery and detached, his mood impossible to read. She glanced behind her, where he was waiting at the foot of the steps. She was sandwiched between two men, both of them with minds focused somewhere she could not grasp.

'When did she come to this house?' she asked.

'When my grandmother died – obviously.' His voice was muffled as the upper part of his body vanished into the attic.

'Why obviously?' she demanded. 'How is it obvious?'

'Because this was *her* house. My gran's, that is. When she died, her sister inherited it.'

'But–' It was an awkward position from which to conduct a conversation. 'Didn't she have a husband? Wouldn't he have got it? Why a sister?'

'Whew!'

'What?'

Brendan was in the attic, and Thea scrambled up the last steps and onto the bare floorboards beside him. It was full of light, thanks to the centrally positioned window on the rear side, looking over the garden at the back. The roof was just high enough for a person to stand upright in the middle.

At first it seemed disappointingly ordinary. Three or four tea chests were tucked as far as they would go under the sloping roof beams; a brown trunk beside them; a stack of framed pictures leant against the back wall, beside a

190

chimney breast; countless cardboard boxes; several rolled-up rugs; a standard lamp. It was like a rather poorly stocked junk shop. Drew pushed up beside her.

'So?' he said.

'Drew – why are you still here?' Thea demanded. 'You're going to be terribly late.'

'I've already phoned Pandora and asked her to hold the fort until I get home. It'll be okay,' he said absently. 'I did it while we were still downstairs. You never noticed.' He scanned the attic with an air of disappointment. 'Looks fairly unexciting to me.'

Brendan was darting from side to side, pulling at boxes and then bending over the pictures.

'How can there be anything to prove Richard was murdered?' Thea asked. 'It's a ridiculous idea. If he knew somebody was going to kill him, why didn't he go to the police?'

'He didn't *know*. He was scared it *might* happen. So he left a suggestion as to where we might look to understand why. Isn't that it?' It was Drew, addressing Brendan, putting words into his mouth. 'As a kind of insurance.'

'Something like that,' Brendan agreed. He was still inspecting the pictures, turning them round one at a time. They had been stacked with their backs to the middle of the attic. Some of them were quite large. 'Landscapes and a couple of portraits,' he muttered.

'Ancestors?' Thea asked.

'No idea. Never seen them before. What else is there, then?' He moved away, stepping over the carpet and opening another cardboard box.

191

'Stamps!' He sounded excited. 'The famous stamp collection. I thought it must have got sold or stolen ages ago. They were my great-grandmother's, originally. Auntie Rita's mother. She was born in 1888. Everybody collected stamps then, apparently.'

He extracted a single album from the box, and began to carefully open its pages. 'I can get them valued.'

'Is there just the one album?' Thea asked.

He nodded.

'Not worth killing somebody for, then,' said Drew, trying to keep them to the point. 'Unless she's got a penny black, I suppose.'

'Your grandmother was called Dawn – is that right?' Thea asked, checking the family tree she was holding firmly in her head.

'Yes. Apparently that's when she was born, and her father was a poetical sort of chap, the First World War was going on at the time.'

'Was he a soldier?'

'Uh-huh.'

'Did he survive?'

'Just about. Lost a leg and a thumb, at Passchendaele. He and his wife lived to very ripe old age, both of them.'

'You're very well informed, for a young man,' Drew observed. 'I haven't the slightest idea what my great-grandparents were like. Couldn't even tell you their names.'

'We're all obsessed,' said Brendan. 'My elder sister, Carol, the one in Kent, has it all written out in fancy copperplate script and hung on the wall, with pictures of everybody. Lucky nobody

192

had twelve kids, is all I can say. It fits on quite a small sheet of paper.'

Thea gave a confident summary: 'So when Dawn died, possibly under suspicious circumstances, her sister – your Great-Aunt Rita – inherited the house, and had her nephew, your father, living here with her. She later had a son of her own, who was Richard, recently deceased. Your father's cousin. But there's – what? Twelve or fifteen years age difference? So they'd never have been boyhood chums. And where were the husbands? Mr Teasdale Senior, and ditto Mr Wilshire?'

'You amaze me,' said Drew. 'I'd got the generations in a complete muddle.'

'I can give the whole story,' said Brendan Teasdale, with a hint of competitiveness. 'Dawn was born during the First War, Rita in the early twenties. When Dawn died, her sister was only eighteen, so the house was kept in trust for her until she reached twenty-one.'

'Where was Martin's father?' Thea persisted. 'The widower.'

'He went to pieces and drifted out of the picture, never to be seen again, as far as I know. He came from a very well-to-do family. Titled. He was a youngest son out of several sons. But he was always all right for money, so he never laid a claim to the house. I still need to do more research on him. He probably joined the armed services during the war. He'd have had no reason to be exempted.'

'But didn't he want to see his little boy? Where did he go?'

'Precisely what I'd like to find out. My father says he doesn't remember ever meeting him.'

Thea found herself more and more sympathetic with the young Martin and his miserable childhood. Even his Aunt Rita had replaced him with a child of her own, once he'd gone off to boarding school.

They were flipping idly through the contents of the tea chests, Thea cautiously watching out for angry spiders. Old magazines, books, childhood games, school exercise books were all muddled in together. 'There are a lot of gaps to the story,' Thea mused. 'How did Dawn come to own such a big house at such a young age? And how come she made a will so early? And why wasn't your father the beneficiary?'

'I can't explain all that now. It's fairly logical, given the times they lived in. Men were in short supply and there were a lot of complications. My father says he can remember regular visits from the family solicitor, to change a will or revalue something or other. But it did add to the rumours about her being murdered, of course. Carol has a few things to say about it.' The man was holding a green schoolbook, with a ragged front cover scribbled all over with typical childhood doodles. 'My dad's classwork book,' he murmured. 'That's what they called it. The one you made notes in, that you never had to show anybody.' He flipped through it, and then clapped it shut. 'No time for that now.'

'Come on, then,' urged Drew. 'We can't stay up here all night. I have to be somewhere. We're not going to find anything.'

194

'Okay,' said Brendan, surprisingly docile. 'Let me just take a few bits and bobs.' He tucked the exercise book under his arm, and clasped the stamp album to his chest. 'And it would be good to take one of the pictures, if one of you could help me.'

He one-handedly selected a large framed painting. Drew lifted it for him, and held it up to the window for a look. Thea edged closer. It showed two girls sitting shoulder to shoulder. One was about six or eight, the other a nubile teenager with wavy brown hair. It flowed unrestrictedly down to her breasts, drawing attention to them under a thin gauzy garment. The younger girl was fingering a lock of hair, with a sly smile. 'Blimey!' said Thea. 'Isn't it a bit ... suggestive?'

'Downright erotic,' said Drew.

'Are these the sisters? Rita and Dawn? It's got a sort of thirties feel to it, so that would fit.'

'It must be them,' said Brendan. 'I've heard about this picture – always wanted to see it for myself. There was a worry that Rita was going to have it destroyed, but Richard must have hidden it up here until she forgot about it.'

'How did you know about it?' Thea asked. She was putting all her efforts into maintaining a grasp of the many facts Brendan had disclosed. If he could be believed, the Wilshires and the Teasdales had had virtually no contact for decades.

'My father always loved it. It was in his bedroom when he was a little boy here. It is his mother, after all. He talked about it a lot.'

'Why would Rita destroy it?'

'Look at it,' said Brendan simply. 'Would you want such a picture of yourself to be stared at by all and sundry?'

'Still not enough to kill somebody for, if that's what you've been thinking,' said Drew. 'Though it might be worth a bit. Who's the artist?' He tried to decipher a tiny signature at the bottom.

'Some young chap, apparently. He died in 1940. An airman or something. Never had time to make a name for himself.'

The careless words did not deceive Thea. 'Did he know your grandfather, do you think?' she asked. 'There sounds to be some sort of connection to me.'

'This isn't what I was looking for,' Brendan told her. 'How could it be? How could a picture prove anything about a murder?'

'But you appear to have got what you wanted,' said Drew mildly. 'I wonder what that is.' He eyed the stamp album thoughtfully, and Brendan gripped it more closely to his chest.

'I've got the only things I can find that could possibly throw some light on it all,' said Brendan. 'I'll take them to Auntie and see what she makes of them.'

By common consent, they descended the flimsy stairs to the lower regions of the house. Brendan took custody of the picture, with Thea feeling a nagging guilt at allowing him to disappear with items that belonged to his great-aunt, and which might be valuable. There was no certainty that he really would take them to her. She tried to convey her worry to Drew, nudging him with her elbow.

'What?' he asked.

She braced herself. 'It's okay, do you think, for him to just go off with things like this?'

Brendan heard her, loud and clear. 'You've got no authority to stop me.'

'I know. It's just—'

'Leave it,' said Drew. 'We've seen what he's taken. We can testify about it, if it ever comes to that.'

'Fine,' she shrugged. 'Nice to meet you,' she said to Brendan, with a blatant lack of sincerity.

'Thanks,' he said distractedly and was gone.

'Drew, I really think you need to go and relieve Pandora. The kids'll be wanting to see you.'

'I had to stay and protect you from that man.'

'What do you mean? He wasn't going to hurt me.'

'You don't know that. Everything he said was a complete pack of lies.'

She just stared at him, waiting for an explanation.

Chapter Thirteen

'All that nonsense about an email,' Drew said. 'It couldn't possibly be true. He concocted it as a ruse to get into the attic. I suppose he wanted the stamps, but it might have been the picture.'

She closed her eyes against the new layer of complication. 'I'm not so sure. Don't you find it's the far-fetched stories that often turn out to

197

be the true ones? I thought it rang true, on the whole.'

'Well it didn't to me,' he said irritably.

'All right. So, why would he raise the idea that Richard was murdered at all? Wasn't that taking an awful risk? It could so easily blow up in his face.'

'My guess is that he knows your reputation for getting involved in murder investigations, and thought it would be a good way to convince you to let him do what he wanted.'

'Oh Lord, that's an awful idea,' she objected. 'When did you think of that?'

'Just now, to be honest. And I still can't believe Rita would be able to summon her thoughts enough to send an email that could persuade her great-nephew to drop everything and rush up here like that.'

'He lives in Cheltenham, doesn't he? Isn't that what Mr Teasdale said this morning?'

'Yes, that's right.' Drew was still preoccupied with the effort to make sense of it all. 'Maybe I'm wrong, after all,' he said. 'Mrs Wilshire really is a strong-minded woman. If they told her that Richard killed himself, and she was certain he would never do such a thing, she might go straight for any proof she can find that he didn't.' He sighed. 'I can't think straight, with so much going on.'

'I'm just as bad,' she said. 'But I think you've got the old lady wrong. I've heard you say that people can be amazingly capable and coherent, right after hearing the most shocking news. They adapt like lightning, sometimes. They need explanations – a narrative, to use the jargon –

that make it easier to cope with. Isn't Mrs Wilshire likely to be that sort of person?'

'Quite likely, yes.'

'Okay, then. And you don't doubt that Brendan really is her great-nephew, do you? He knew so much about the family, he must have been.'

Drew nodded. 'It was what he said on the doorstep that set me against him. You don't start shouting about murder like that, if you're genuine.'

'It was odd,' she agreed. 'But he'll have had a shock as well. He expected to get to know Richard better, and catch up with Millie, and now it's all changed. Then he gets an email from his aunt that he probably doesn't really understand. I think I believe him, you know.'

'Well...'

'It is very confusing for everybody,' she sighed. '*Was* Richard murdered, do you think? Is that what we've decided?'

'Oh yes – I've thought so all along,' said Drew. 'The story doesn't hold water, otherwise. The loft isn't high enough for suicide. And if he died close by and was quickly moved into the barn, there wouldn't be much evidence to show what happened.'

Thea was deeply impressed that he had worked so much out with no external signs to suggest his thought processes. She struggled to keep up. 'You think he was bashed in some way that made it look as if he fell?'

'I don't know. We have no idea what the post-mortem might show tomorrow. They're bound to be doing it then, even if they don't believe he was murdered.'

She grimaced. 'What if he fell off some other high place that killed him, and was then moved – would that be obvious from the post mortem? There'd be the wrong amount of blood in the barn. Broken bones would be displaced. Have you been working all this out since yesterday?'

'I did go through it in my head quite a few times,' he admitted. 'I've been thinking quite hard for more than twenty-four hours.'

She paused. 'I wondered what the matter was. I thought it was something to do with me.' A tension she had been almost unaware of was falling away. 'I thought I'd upset you somehow.'

'Sorry, love.' He pulled her to him. 'You mustn't be so unsure of me. You're my number one priority, you know. Nothing's going to change that.'

She still wasn't entirely able to accept this. 'What about the children? And the new business? And Maggs? I don't want to come before them. That's too much responsibility.'

'I meant, at the moment. I can't go and leave you with all this mess. Pandora understands. Oh, and she says Maggs wants to speak to me, but didn't like to phone in case she disturbed us.'

Thea flapped a hand at his phone. 'Call her, then.'

He did so, his face expressionless. 'Maggs – hi. How's Meredith?... Good. Lovely. I gather you wanted me...'

The one-sided conversation enhanced a wholly uncalled-for exasperation in Thea. She wanted to go outside and run somewhere, to stop her brain crashing about in helpless circles. There was guilt looming ever more adamantly, at all her stupid, inappropriate responses to everything Drew said or did. He was doing his best to rescue her from a complicated situation, which he had landed her in to begin with. He was sad and worried about old Mrs Wilshire. He wanted the truth to be found concerning how the woman's son had died. And he probably also wanted the house to be left neat and tidy, with everything listed and labelled and sorted and stacked.

Meredith. She repeated the name to herself. Wasn't it Welsh? Or was that only when the accent was on the second syllable, which was not how Drew had said it. Meredith Cooper. It had a certain ring to it, she thought. Better than the name Kim, which her brother Damien and his wife had given to their new daughter. The family had expected Hope or Theodora or Christiana – but Kim had no associations that anybody could discover. That baby had been born a month early, its startled and biologically elderly parents hopelessly intimidated by the whole experience. Thea's (and Damien's) mother had marched to the rescue, as grandmothers routinely did, and as a result was intensely in love with the infant, who showed every sign of reciprocating.

Not a bit like the family she had been learning about that afternoon, then. The Johnstones had their shameful secrets, it was true, but nobody had died before their time, or bequeathed each other houses that were full of ancient possessions. Or not quite, anyway, she amended, thinking of Drew's inheritance in Broad Campden.

He was listening intently to whatever Maggs was saying. 'Yes,' he muttered a few times, and other monosyllables that told Thea nothing. 'If you're really sure,' he then said. 'All right, Maggs. That's very sporting of you.'

His vocabulary could be that of a schoolboy at times. He fell into it when dealing with elderly bereaved customers, from a vague instinct that it would reassure and console them. He was probably right about that. He and Maggs would say 'smashing' and 'lawks' now and then, as if they'd just been reading an old *Beano* comic.

So Maggs was being sporting. Thea experienced the pang of being on the furthest angle of the triangle, the two others united in a small conspiracy, however benign it might be. She wanted to snatch the phone and demand to know what they were planning. Ten seconds later, she was being conscientiously updated.

'She says I should stay here another night. She'll go into the office tomorrow, with the baby, and help Pandora, who's happy to babysit my kids between now and then. She can get them off to school in the morning. They can cope so long as I'm back in plenty of time for the funeral on Tuesday.'

'She knows about clothes, breakfast, and all that?' Another pang assaulted her; this time laced with jealousy. Drew's domestic arrangements were surely *her* business more than they were Pandora's.

'Stephanie will talk her through it. She's very

202

capable. Nine, going on sixteen, as Maggs would say.'

'They've worked it all out, behind your back.'

'They want me to be with you. They think you're the answer to bigger problems than getting the kids off to school. I'm marrying a rich widow, who will set the business straight and settle me down into contented middle age. They all think that's an outcome profoundly to be desired.'

'Hmm. Rich widow, eh?'

'Rich enough to keep things afloat. Although I have been thinking it might be an idea to rent your Witney house out, rather than selling it. You'd get seven hundred pounds a month for it, at least. That would cover pretty much all the bills. Food, fuel, electric, anyway.' He sighed as if such a situation would be nothing short of heaven. 'And quicker than going through all the hassle of selling it.'

'Drew – this isn't the moment to start talking about all that. We're in the middle of a serious mess here. Don't you think we should try to phone Millie, at the very least? We should ask her if she really has got a cousin called Brendan. I seem to remember Norah Cookham mentioned him on Friday, so I suppose that clinches it.'

'Why does it matter?'

'I suppose it doesn't. Even if he is a relative, we could still report a theft of items from the attic.' She stopped. 'Ignore me. I'm just trying to make everything even more complicated, aren't I?'

'Oh well.' He drifted into the living room, rubbing his head. 'So, what are we doing now? It occurs to me that I'm extremely hungry. We've hardly eaten all day.'

'Oh, Lord. There's still no food in the house. We can go to the pub, I suppose. It's about three minutes' walk away, after all.'

'Right. So be it.'

She hesitated. 'It's lovely that you're staying. But I'm not really sure *why* you are. What are you protecting me from? I'd be happy just to lock up here and get the hell out.'

'Leaving Dodge to stew in its own juices.' His attempt at an American accent was ludicrous and she laughed.

'Seriously,' she reproached him.

'Call it a hunch. A lot's happened today, and we ought to sit down and sift through it. It was only yesterday that we found Richard, after all. We need to give ourselves space to get over that.'

'But you see dead bodies all the time, and I've seen my share of them, these past few years.'

'It's never easy when it's sudden and violent. We owe it to Richard to stop and reflect. It's all been far too much of a scramble with all these people accosting us.'

'And the rest,' said Thea, thinking of decisions about the future, and the demands of their lives, here and now. 'But I'd be very happy to stop and reflect, if that's what you suggest. Can it be done in a pub, do you think?'

'Doubtful. Especially if people guess who we are. There'll be more accosting, if we're not careful.'

'The only real escape would be to leave.' She was still unclear as to exactly why he was finding that such a bad idea. 'We can give Richard all due attention, wherever we are.'

'We can't find out who killed him, though. We have to be on the spot for that. And I quite fancy the pub.'

She gave him a long look, aware that his thought processes had far outrun her own. 'Did you tell Maggs there was a probable murder here? If so, when?'

'I texted her this morning, just with a few basics. You know how she likes to be kept informed.'

'I'd have thought she had enough to occupy her for the time being.'

'Apparently not. She said just now that the baby sleeps half the time, and it's all a bit boring. She refuses to become one of those mothers who can't think of anything else but the baby. I'm her route into the wider world, she says.'

'Babies *are* rather boring,' Thea remembered. 'I always thought so.'

They saw no reason to delay going to the pub, except that poor Hepzie had enjoyed no exercise whatsoever all day, and Thea insisted on a fifteen-minute session in the field at the end of the road. Drew went too, on the grounds that he also needed to give his legs something to do. It still seemed to Thea that he had made a much greater sacrifice than was actually called for, in neglecting his children for another night. The sense of a small conspiracy between Pandora and Maggs – and possibly Stephanie, too – was unsettling. Thea Osborne was a woman who had always disliked behind-the-back secrets, thanks to growing up in a large family where information was often used as currency. She wanted everything open and honest and forthright. So she said, 'What's really going on back home? Why is everybody so concerned for you to stay here with me? Do they think I can't look after myself?'

He kicked at a tuft of brown grass and nibbled his lower lip for a moment. 'I think they might think you'll resent it if I go back to them and leave you on your own. They don't want you to be annoyed with me.'

'They're scared I'll dump you? Suddenly I'm a Good Thing after all? I can remember a time when Maggs regarded me as little short of a witch, stealing you away from your natural obligations.'

'That was when Karen was still alive. She's changed completely since then. As well you know.'

They watched the spaniel roaming across the field, nose down, following trails left by numerous other dogs. 'I suppose Hepzie might miss the house-sitting,' said Thea doubtfully. 'She's always been very adaptable in all those strange houses. And the various animals mostly tolerated her pretty well.' She thought back over the many cats, dogs, poultry, sheep and other beasts that she and Hepzie had been entrusted with. 'I'm not sure I could have done it without her. It's a lonely business, and often terribly dull.'

'She can be entertainment for my kids, from now on,' he said. 'Because you're never going to be lonely again.'

It would be mawkish coming from anyone else, but he meant it as a statement of fact. It was also a warning that Hepzie could expect to be relegated to second place in Thea's affections from here on. For Thea, this came with a twinge of guilt at the betrayal. The faithful little dog should not suffer because her mistress had a boyfriend – or husband, as he insisted he would soon become.

Drew did his best, but he would never be entirely comfortable with the idea of a dog in bed with its people. It was all down to a person's upbringing, Thea supposed. Whilst the Johnstones had not been an especially doggy family, there had been a scruffy mongrel throughout much of Thea's childhood, which she had insisted was mostly hers. She had invited it to share her bed on weekend mornings when she lazed under the blankets with a book, and the habit had returned after Carl's death. She made no secret of the consolation she derived from the soft presence in the night.

'Love me, love my dog,' she said lightly. It was rapidly becoming a mantra.

'I'll do my best,' he promised.

Walking back, to the point where the field ended and the cul de sac began, Drew's head went up. 'There's a car,' he said. 'Outside the house.'

'It might not be for us.'

'What's the betting?'

He was right. A few more yards and they could both see Millie Wilshire standing close to the car with a man. 'Who's that?' asked Drew.

'Never seen him before.'

They approached at a brisk walk, with Hepzie still running free. She ignored the people and went to the front door of the house as if she'd always lived there.

'Millie,' said Thea. 'Are you waiting for us?'

The girl looked drained and miserable – far worse than when they'd seen her that morning. 'This is Andrew Emerson, the farmer I told you about. The one who was waiting for Dad on Friday, for the TB test on his cows.'

Andrew Emerson also looked exhausted, his face deeply lined. He barely smiled as he nodded a greeting. At first glance, he appeared to be something over sixty, but Thea had a suspicion he was rather younger than he looked. His hair was a lightish brown, similar to Drew's, and his small eyes a murky greeny-hazel. There was a groove between his eyes, and more around his mouth. He conjured an impression of a struggling settler in the American Dust Bowl, the weather and fate implacably against him.

'The police have had me in for questioning,' he said in a deep voice. 'Trying to trace Richard's last movements.'

'Oh!' Thea was about to ask *Do they think he was murdered, after all?* when a nudge from Drew silenced her. 'So what can we do for you?' she said instead.

'You should probably talk to each other,' said Millie reluctantly. 'You both saw Dad more recently than I did, and everybody seems to assume I'm the most unobservant person in the world – so perhaps you can find an explanation

208

between you for what happened to him.'

Thea frowned at this idea. 'Do you have a cousin called Brendan?' she asked.

'What? What's he got to do with anything?'

'He came here today. He really is your cousin, then?'

'Sort of. His father is my father's cousin.'

'Right. That's what we thought,' said Drew. Thea realised he was interrupting her on purpose, worried that she would say something upsetting. 'I know about cousins. It means you have the same great-grandmother,' Drew went on. 'Making you and Brendan second cousins, strictly speaking.'

'Right,' said Millie, with a glance at the farmer. 'So – can you talk to Andrew or not?'

'We were just off to the pub. Why don't you come as well?' Drew invited. 'We've hardly eaten anything all day.'

Andrew Emerson and Millie both seemed doubtful about this suggestion. 'People might recognise us,' said Millie.

'Does that matter?' asked Thea. 'I can understand why your friend Judith might find that a nuisance, but it's different for you, surely?'

'They'll know about my dad dying by now. They'll be embarrassed. And they might think it's wrong for me to be out drinking at a time like this.'

'I don't drink,' said the gravel-voiced farmer. 'I don't go into pubs, if I can help it.' He sighed. 'And I am definitely in no mood for it tonight.'

'What happened with your cows?' Thea asked him. 'Did someone else test them?'

He nodded. 'Came yesterday afternoon. Four reactors. That's the end of us now. We can't keep on like this.' He rubbed a hand across his face, fingers splayed, as if using an invisible wash cloth. 'You have no idea what it's like,' he muttered. 'Like being kicked in the face every time you dare to hope it might be getting better.'

'So...' Thea's hunger was, to her shame, the dominant consideration.

'He talked a lot about you,' the farmer told Drew. 'When he came for the first part of the test. Said you'd got life pretty well sorted. Facing facts, talking straight about dying. He liked that. You helped him decide about his old mum.'

Thea tried to visualise the conversation conducted over the wretched cows and their incipient TB. She knew enough about the subject to be aware that perfectly healthy-seeming animals could show up positive on the test that was rigorously enforced by the authorities. And a positive result meant certain death. A farmer and a vet might well discuss dying and associated matters in such circumstances. 'Do you think he killed himself, then?' she asked.

'Of course he didn't. It wouldn't even enter his mind. What possible reason could he have for doing such a thing?'

'Did you say that to the police?'

He nodded. 'They said it just might have been an accident, but that came to much the same thing, as far as they're concerned.'

'They weren't seeing you as a murder suspect, then?' Thea said, tactlessly. She was more or less thinking aloud, without considering the effect of the words. At her elbow, Drew uttered an exasperated sigh.

'What?' the farmer almost shouted.

She held her ground. 'Well, if it wasn't suicide, and an accident seems unlikely, then what else is there?'

He subsided quickly. 'All right.' He looked at Millie. 'You were right,' he said. 'She is scary.'

'Who? Me?' Thea was astonished. 'Scary?'

'Accusing a man you've never met before of murder. Richard was my *friend*. He told me all kinds of things. He said so much about you–' addressing Drew '–that I had to come and see you for myself. Plus, I was hoping maybe you could fill me in on how he looked. You found him, in that barn. Nobody else can put my mind easy on how it must have been.'

Drew pulled a face and glanced at Thea. She understood his difficulty: only by professional straight talking could he give a satisfactory answer, and sometimes that could be straighter than people might like. He was regularly reproaching her for saying too much, getting too graphic, forcing people to face truths they preferred to avoid – but his own instincts were not so different from hers.

'It's impossible to say,' he began. 'A dead body relaxes completely. The face always looks bland and unemotional afterwards. Nobody dies with their last expression still permanently on their face, like you read in stories. As far as we could tell, he hadn't moved at all. The ground underneath him wasn't churned up or anything.'

'But – what exactly *killed* him?'

211

'I think his skull cracked. And possibly his neck was broken. We didn't move him, obviously – although the dogs did nudge him a bit before we pulled them away.' A sound from Millie reminded him that there was a listener even less likely to want gruesome details. 'Sorry,' he said. 'But as the next of kin, you'll be able to ask the Coroner's officer for the cause of death – tomorrow, probably. It'll be on the death certificate, anyway.'

'Okay,' she said thickly. She raised her face to look at him. 'A week ago, I would never have dreamt any of this. I couldn't even bring myself to come here, knowing Gran was never coming back.'

'Did something happen?' Thea suddenly asked. 'I mean, before your father died? Why did you come here on Friday, when you were so against the whole thing?' She tried to remember what had been said. 'You were angry with your father for clearing the house. You asked me if I was his girlfriend, when surely you knew–' She stopped, wondering, as so often before, just who knew what.

'What? What should I have known?'

'Well – your friend Judith says she was very close to him.'

'Close? She liked him, if that's what you mean. He treated her like an ordinary person. That's all it was.'

In a murder investigation, the police would have explored in detail every movement made by Millie, Judith, Andrew Emerson and others on the day Richard Wilshire died, as well as any un-

212

usual circumstances in the days before that. They would have asked about arguments, sudden changes, impressions. Some of their findings might have filtered through to Thea in her meetings with Higgins and perhaps one or two other officers. As it was, virtually none of these enquiries had been made, because nobody openly asserted that there had been a murder at all. Andrew Emerson had been asked a few questions, apparently, to get an idea of the timings, but nothing more than that.

'*Did* something happen?' Drew also asked her.

'Sort of.' Millie swung one foot to and fro like a small girl. 'Martin showed up, out of the blue, for one thing.'

'Martin?'

'My dad's cousin. Martin Teasdale. I thought you saw him at the home. When I phoned this afternoon, that's what Mrs Goodison said.'

'Oh – yes, we met him.'

Millie shrugged. 'Well, he and two of his children are living back here in the UK now, and they've started taking an interest in what Gran can tell them about family history. Brendan's obsessed with it.'

'So we noticed,' said Thea. 'Although he said it was his sister Carol as much as him. He took some things away,' she added conscientiously.

'What do you mean?'

'From the attic.' Thea pointed at the house with her thumb. 'Listen – I don't want to be rude, but I'm starving hungry. It's six o'clock, and we need something to eat. If there's nowhere else, we'll have to go to the pub. There's no food

213

in the house.'

'Brendan took things from the attic?' Millie spoke slowly, stressing every syllable, as if checking a statement that was too terrible to be true. 'What things?'

'A stamp album and a picture, and an old schoolbook.'

'Hmm. That doesn't sound too bad. He can have the stamps for all I care.'

'Thank goodness for that.'

'We shouldn't hold you up,' said Andrew, who had been fondling Hepzie for the past few minutes. 'I should get back.' He turned to Millie. 'Richard's dogs,' he said. 'Are you sure they'll be all right?'

Millie nodded. 'I'm taking them over to Judith's place now. She's thrilled to have them.'

'I know, but – they need to *work*. At least be amongst cattle or sheep, free to run about. I ought to take them, but...' An agonised expression crossed his face. 'I can't guarantee them a future, the way things are.'

'They'll be all right,' said Millie, putting a hand on the farmer's arm. 'You've got other things to worry about.' She turned to Drew and Thea. 'Andrew's got a sick wife, as well,' she told them. 'And his daughter's gone off to America.'

'Celia's on the mend,' said the man bravely. 'She was up most of yesterday.'

'What's wrong with her?' asked Thea.

'A really nasty bout of shingles. We had no idea it could be so debilitating. I've had to hire in some help to cover for her.'

'Sounds grim,' said Drew with just the right

214

note of sympathy. 'But you won't really give up farming, will you? Isn't that awfully drastic?'

Andrew's mouth twisted in a show of pained inevitability. 'After what's happened to Richard, it doesn't seem worth carrying on. Life's too short for constant worry, working all hours for nothing. We still have a bit of equity if we sell up now – enough for a little house and garden. I can do odd jobs.' He looked straight at Drew. 'Actually, that's another reason I wanted to see you.' He hesitated and his colour heightened like an embarrassed teenager. 'This burial business of yours. As I said, I like the sound of it. I was wondering if you might be needing another pair of hands. Digging graves, carrying coffins, driving – all that side of things?'

Drew put a hand up, half-warning, half-making a grab for something that felt like a very good offer. 'Hold on – I haven't got it running over here yet. Not by a long way. Although – there is a deadline not too far off now. Ask me again in six months' time and I might well have a place for you. Assuming we can agree details, and get along together.'

'How do I find you?'

Drew felt in an inside pocket and located a business card. He handed it to the man, who read aloud: "Drew Slocombe, Peaceful Repose Green Burial Ground." Sounds great.'

'Thanks. I warn you, there's not a lot of money in it.'

'More than there is in farming,' said Andrew.

'Drew...' said Thea, putting a hand to her middle.

'Food?'

'Yes, yes, you get on,' Andrew said quickly. Then he had a thought. 'Just one more thing. If we're thinking somebody might have deliberately killed Richard, I'd look no further than Bloody Norah.' He said the name in a whisper, with a meaningful glance at the house just behind them. 'Everybody knows they had a big fight over the dogs and her cat.'

Millie uttered a brief giggle. 'Bloody Norah,' she repeated.

Thea also laughed. 'My father used to say that,' she remembered. Then her face grew serious. 'But it couldn't really have been her – could it?'

Chapter Fourteen

It was well past six when Drew and Thea finally got to the Seven Tuns and ordered a meal. 'Whatever's quickest,' said Thea shamelessly to the woman at the bar.

They sat in the largest room, set out as an informal dining area at the back of the building. Windows looked out onto a deserted garden and patio. They could see two other bars, revealing what a large hostelry it was, and had always been. 'Must be costly to maintain,' muttered Drew. 'No wonder it was out of business for so long.'

'Was it? How do you know that?'

'Heard it somewhere,' he said. 'I've been doing

216

lots of research into Cotswold society, you know. I need to understand my market, for the new business.'

'Right.' The meal wasn't coming nearly as quickly as she would have liked, but the beer she gulped down did a lot to assuage the hunger pangs. 'What a day!' she sighed.

'It's not over yet.'

'It's almost dark,' she pointed out. 'I call that the end of the day.'

There were very few other customers in the pub. An October Sunday evening was hardly the most popular time for drinking, they supposed. 'There are seven mirrors in here,' Thea noted idly. 'Is that meant to be lucky, do you think?'

He smiled. 'I doubt it. They've just gathered up as many characterful old artefacts as they could, and hung them on the walls. Must have been fun to do.'

'I like Chedworth,' said Thea. 'I didn't think I would at first. It's so much bigger than I expected, I wish I'd given myself more time to explore it.'

'You can stay a bit longer,' he said. 'You don't have to be anywhere, after all.'

She shivered. 'That's not a very nice feeling. I shouldn't be so uncommitted. It's like being in limbo, waiting for a decision. Why didn't we just go back to your place this afternoon?'

'We'd have missed Andrew Emerson, and I am very pleased to have met him. He could be the answer to a prayer.'

'You mean God told us to stay, so you could meet him?'

'If you like.' He smiled. 'More likely an old pagan deity who wants my burial practices to catch on. Getting back to pre-Christian times and all that.'

'I miss Higgins,' she realised. 'Or Gladwin. Some police person to talk to. Poor Richard, swept away and ignored because it's convenient to assume he killed himself. If he was murdered, the person who did it must be very pleased with himself.'

'That's part of why we're still here,' Drew said. 'The poor man deserves better.'

'He wasn't particularly nice, though. A bit of a coward, actually, getting me to do the house sorting instead of facing it himself.'

Drew nibbled his lip. 'That Judith seemed to like him.'

'Did you believe her? I thought it might have been a bit of self-dramatising, the grieving girl-friend role, sort of thing.'

'She never said that, exactly. Just that he was a welcome change from the people she usually mixes with.'

Thea sighed. 'I've got very sceptical in my old age,' she admitted. 'I wasn't entirely sure I could trust that Mrs Goodison, either.'

Drew nodded. 'I know about women like her, remember. They value their reputation above everything. Nothing's allowed to sully their precious home. If she had any inkling that Richard was murdered, she'd do all she could to distance herself from that.'

'Especially if it looked as if his mother was involved.'

He snorted in amusement. 'Like – she killed him?'

'No, of course not. I meant, if it had something to do with her house, or money, or something. After all, the usual motive for murder is to acquire something that the dead person has.'

'Is it?'

'Or to stop them from revealing something. Or because they've done something awful to you. Or because you lose all self-control and just keep bashing them. Or–'

'Stop it,' he begged. 'That's enough.'

'What's the matter? You usually don't mind murder talk.'

'I feel guilty,' he admitted. 'All this is my fault.'

'How is it your fault that Richard Wilshire's dead?' She was genuinely puzzled.

'Not that. I expect he'd be dead regardless of anything I've done. But I dragged you here, and I keep on dithering about Broad Campden and what happens next. I'm pathetic.'

'Don't be ridiculous. Look – this is what we'll do. We'll go back to the house, tidy up the worst of the mess in the bedrooms, leave the key under a stone at the back and be out of here first thing tomorrow. We're never going to be of any use hanging around like this. If Higgins and his boss persist in thinking it was suicide, then they won't have any time for us. We'd never be able to change their minds. Millie seems reconciled to that explanation, even if his mother isn't.'

'We don't know for sure what his mother thinks. I'm not sure I can just leave without another attempt to see her. I have an obligation to her.' He scratched his head. 'That's another thing that's making me feel guilty.' Then his phone warbled in his pocket. He scrabbled for it and peered at the screen. 'Must be Pandora,' he said.

It wasn't Pandora, but young Stephanie. Drew's voice became warm and gentle, listening to a long story, his responses giving Thea no clue as to its import. 'I was going to phone you,' he said, pulling a face at Thea that suggested he had actually forgotten any promise to do so. 'It's been very busy here. You'll have to find Timmy some clean pants and socks for school, okay?... Yes, I know. But it's just for a day or so, sweetheart. You can manage perfectly well. It's character-forming.' Listening to this, Thea deduced that he had used a catchphrase that would reassure his little girl. He laughed lightly. 'Don't worry about me, darling. I'm perfectly all right. Thea sends her love. We'll be back soon. I'm not promising, Stephanie. You know I never make promises. Can I talk to Timmy?'

A pause, in which nobody spoke. Then, 'Hi, Tim. How's it going?... Good! Great! Pandora might read to you if you ask her nicely. You can tell me what happens in the next chapter, when I get back. I know, son. But everything's okay. Be good at school and I'll see you soon. No fighting with Stephanie, right?'

The difference in his tone when addressing his two children was almost painful. It was an aspect of him that Thea was still getting to grips with. She had gathered some scraps of information about the early years, with Tim's conception a surprise and his arrival not quite the cause for delight that Stephanie's had been. Then Karen's injury and eventual death had been made much worse by the existence of a small dependent boy. Timmy had a look that made a person wince. A brave, vulnerable, quiet child. Drew could try harder, Thea concluded, but she lacked the nerve to say anything.

The call ended, Drew continued to play with the phone. 'I took photos of that barn,' he said. 'Just before you and the dogs found Richard. I wanted to capture its size, and the odd constructions in front of it.' He skimmed through a few pictures. 'They're not very good.'

'Let's see.' She took it from him. 'They're not bad. You should have done black and white. Then they'd be like something by Ansel Adams. The sky's lovely. And these blocks of stone or whatever they are look good in the foreground.'

'You're an art critic,' he smiled.

'Not at all. But I understand a bit about composition. What *are* these stones? They look like paving slabs, stacked in a pile.'

He peered over the table, seeing the little picture upside down. 'No idea,' he admitted.

'They're quite close to the barn door. Something like a foot square. Maybe somebody was planning to make a hardstanding for tractors, or a path.'

'Seems unlikely. They'd just spread a layer of concrete, surely?'

'It doesn't matter.' She went on looking at the picture.

'Um ... Drew. Have we finished here? Can we

221

go back to the house and do a bit of brain-storming?'

'Brainstorming?'

'Yes.' She was emphatic, and just a bit excited. Little ideas were springing up like seedlings. Then she looked through the pub window at the sky outside. Her brain had done quite a lot of storming in the past two seconds, rendering superfluous any need for more. 'It's not quite dark yet. I think we should go to the barn, not the house.'

'Now?'

'Yes. Now. We might already be too late.'

'Thea, it's ten past seven. The sun set half an hour ago, at least. It's much too dark to do anything useful. Besides, the police have probably taped it all off.' He resisted the urge to point out that he had no idea what she was thinking.

'No, they won't have. Not for a suicide. Why would they? I've got a good torch in the car. It's only a few minutes from here.'

'I can't stop you,' he said, with a hint of irritation. 'And I suppose you'll explain at some point.'

'It's a wild theory, that's all. It'll probably turn out to be complete nonsense, but we should go and have a look, just in case.'

He stood up without another word. The meal had served its purpose, paid for jointly. Two more people had come in while they were eating, but the pub was still very quiet. Mindful that it had been closed for some time in recent years, it struck him that survival was far from guaranteed, even now it had reopened.

'I need you to explain,' he pleaded. 'Somewhere I seem to have missed a major step in the logic.'

She had begun the walk back to the house, at a brisk pace. 'In the car,' she threw back at him.

Six minutes later they were negotiating the sharp steep bend in the road to Yanworth, and Thea was taking Drew through her thoughts. 'What if he was murdered by somebody who had planned it all in advance? The person knew about the barn and its high platform, and decided it would be a good place for a suicide. But just pushing him off might not kill him – so they hit him in such a way as to make it look like an injury inflicted by a fall. It would have to be a flat thing, because the floor's flat. Now do you see?'

'Sort of. But those slabs must be too heavy to hold with one hand. How would the killer keep Richard still while they hit him in just the right place? Especially as the injury was mainly at the front of his head. How would you manage that?'

She pondered for a moment. 'Perhaps he was already unconscious. Or stooping down for some reason, looking at the floor. That would work rather well, don't you think? There are any number of possible explanations.' She waved an airy hand.

'We don't know that he died from the damage to his head, of course. That might have been inflicted simply to make it look like a fall. If I'm right that his neck was broken, that'll be the cause of death. And that is much more likely to be the result of a fall. And what about other bones? He would need to be covered in bruises

223

and impact injuries to make it look convincing.'

She made a little sound of resistance. 'I guess it would be possible to whack him in a few places – hips, back, shoulders – the places he'd be likely to land on.'

'Horrible thought. I wonder sometimes about your imagination,' he admitted. Then he said, 'But if he was already dead, there wouldn't be bruises, as such. Just the usual pooling of blood – and that would give the police grounds for suspecting foul play.'

They had arrived at the straight stretch of road just before the barn. 'Here we are,' Thea announced. 'And it's still not really dark.'

'Too dark to find the sort of evidence you've got in mind.'

She stopped the car beside the gate directly in front of the barn. 'We can't go through there,' said Drew. 'It's chained shut, look.'

'So it is. We'll have to go through that field gate, like we did before.'

'Thea – I know this is what you always do, and so far you've come through more or less intact, but really I must just say it's not the way civilised people behave. You ought to go to the police with your idea, and leave it to them.'

'They'd fob me off and not do anything. Regulations would require a full SOCO team, forensics, reports – all the stuff they've decided to leave out, for some reason.'

'Finances, presumably.'

'Or another case they think is more important. Illegal immigrants or somebody looking at websites that tell you how to make a bomb.'

Thea led the way through the uneven terrain, across a ditch onto the concrete forecourt of the barn. The sky was growing darker by the minute.

'They're still there, look,' she said, her voice suddenly loud. The torch in her hand was directed at the small pile of square stone slabs, scanning the surface of the top one. 'Hmm – it looks fairly clean.'

Drew bent over it, without touching. 'You think he would just put it back where he found it? Isn't it more likely to be chucked into a thicket of nettles?'

'If it was all as carefully planned as I think, he'd definitely put it back.' She peered closely, pressed against Drew's shoulder. 'But you're right – there's no blood or anything on it.'

She straightened, and idly swept the torch beam left and right. 'I was thinking, you see, that a person falling from a height has different injuries from any other cause. No sharp edges, or punctures.'

'Yes, I understand.' He sounded somewhat tetchy. 'But the idea that he was hit a fatal blow with a slab of stone is very far-fetched, don't you think?'

'Probably. It made sense when I first thought of it. But now I don't know. Would you land face down, if you deliberately jumped? You would if you were pushed from behind. And then you wouldn't crack your skull open, would you?'

'Thea...' he begged. 'This is all very graphic. I know I wouldn't like you to be all girly and squeamish, but this is rather the other extreme.'

'Sorry,' she said crossly. 'But if the police aren't going to ask these questions, then *somebody* should. And we found him – we owe him some sort of attention.'

'I know.' He made a visible effort. 'Well, he was lying partly on his side when we found him, wasn't he? That fits with a fall. And his head was at a very unnatural angle. That fits as well. But the severity of the impact seemed excessive, given the height. Your theories are sensible, from that point of view. It's been going round and round my head ever since yesterday, that it's a highly unlikely suicide.'

'It is,' she agreed. 'Very unlikely.'

'And I can see that the only thing we can hope to do is find some hard evidence to take to the police and get them to open a proper murder enquiry. But I have to get home tomorrow. Stephanie sounded very bereft. And there'll be work mounting up. There could be a new funeral at any moment. And I'll really have to be there in time for the funeral on Tuesday.' Anxiety was thick in his voice.

'Okay,' she pacified him. 'If we can't find anything now, we'll have to give up.'

'It's too dark,' he complained. 'We'll never find anything in this light, even with your torch.'

'Think – we have to think,' she urged. 'What if there were *two* people, determined to kill Richard? Then one could hold him and the other crack his skull.'

'There'd be signs of a struggle.'

'No, but if there were two, they could have carried him into the barn and arranged the body to look like a suicide. There might be signs of a struggle out here somewhere, if we knew where to look.'

'He was big,' said Drew. 'Heavy, but not especially strong.' He sighed. 'It's no good. The more we guess, the less persuasive any of it seems.'

'Lateral thinking,' she said, mindful of a death she had been involved with where conclusions were drawn very prematurely. 'We have to drop all our assumptions and start again.'

'Is this when the brainstorming starts? I think we missed that part.'

'The main thing we need is *evidence*. Until then, the police won't listen to us. We can bang on about gut feelings and logical probabilities as much as we like, and they'll take no notice at all. So we need a weapon, most of all.'

'They must do some sort of post mortem,' Drew said. 'It was a sudden unexplained death. There always has to be a post mortem in that situation.'

'Do they do them on Sundays?' She already knew the answer, but had a feeling that Drew needed to feel as if he was the one in control, for the moment. Any more suggestions from her might well prove counterproductive.

'Hardly ever,' he told her. 'It'll be tomorrow at the soonest. And they're not going to go into much detail. Cause of death; nature of his injuries; general condition.' He laughed ruefully. 'Actually, I don't know exactly what they do.'

'Neither do I, except for what I've seen on *Silent Witness*. But we should start by assuming he was murdered and see if we can construct a scenario that fits – with evidence.'

'Oh, Thea. We're playing at detectives here, aren't we? Following our old game, because we both love it. I think it's time we grew out of it.'

She could not see his expression in the vanishing light. 'I can't help it,' she admitted. 'Now we're here, and we both knew Richard Wilshire, and we've met so many of his family, and he's *dead*.' She spluttered incoherently, with unexpected images of her own husband Carl intruding. 'I know most people manage to let it all go and get on with ordinary lives. I know it's peculiar, the way I go rushing in to confront anybody I think might have done something terrible. It's something in my character, I suppose. A stupid need to get stories straight and stop people from getting it all wrong. I hate it when a myth gets established and perpetuated, based on wishful thinking and lies and secrets. I *hate* that.'

'Okay,' he said gently. 'I get it. I suppose I've got the same thing in my character, more or less.'

'You have. Yes. So if Millie Wilshire truly believes her father killed himself, and he really didn't, that's the story that'll go down the generations, and nobody will challenge it. And that's so horribly *wrong*. Isn't it?'

'Of course. Nobody would disagree with that.'

'Except perhaps the person who killed him.'

She swung the torch again, following the beam intently. 'What's that?' she said suddenly.

'Where?'

'Leaning against the barn, look.' She kept the light on a thick plank of wood that nobody would

228

look at twice, in normal circumstances. About four feet in length, and ten or twelve inches wide, it had no obvious purpose. Thea went towards it.

'That can't be a murder weapon,' Drew objected. 'Not left in plain view like that. Nobody would be so ... blatant.'

Thea was examining the plank without touching it. 'It looks clean, the same as the stone,' she said disappointedly.

'Turn it over,' said Drew, with a hint of agitation in his voice. 'Use a hanky or something.'

'I haven't got a hanky.'

But Drew had. He took an old-fashioned square of cotton from his trouser pocket, and wrapped it around his hand. Gingerly, he gripped the top of the wood and pulled it towards himself. It leant away from the barn, so they could see the underside. At first it looked as bland and insignificant as the top side, but Thea shone the beam on a smudge near the bottom. In the artificial light it looked dark brown. 'It *could* be blood,' said Drew doubtfully.

'It's exactly the right shape for the purpose, don't you think? And there might not have been any blood left on it.'

'Heads always bleed.'

'Yes, but not instantly. If you whacked someone with this and then pulled it away, it wouldn't have to get bloody.'

Drew inhaled slowly, steadying himself. 'You're describing a very brutal attack on a defenceless man. Defenceless and probably totally unsuspecting. A monstrous thing to do.'

'All the more so for being planned, and made

to look like suicide. Could that Andrew chap have done it, do you think?'

'On first impressions – which are entirely unreliable – I'd say he might have lashed out in a rage, but not covered it up very well afterwards. And there's still the small problem of how the killer managed to keep Richard still while he whacked him.'

'He did look rather *ravaged*,' mused Thea, not properly listening. 'Maybe that was guilt, and not misery over his cows after all.'

'I would venture to suggest it had to be someone quite tall and strong. This plank's heavy, and you'd need some force to lift it and crack a skull with it.'

'We don't know it was this, for sure,' she reminded him. 'We're jumping to conclusions.'

'I think it's likely enough for us to tell the police.'

She couldn't hide her excitement. 'Oh, good!' she said.

Then Drew's phone went again, and he carefully replaced the length of wood before answering it. 'All right,' he said, after listening for a few moments. He took it from his ear, and said to Thea, 'Mrs Wilshire wants to speak to me. That was the woman at the nursing home... Yes, hello Mrs Wilshire. What can I do for you?'

Thea had never before heard his undertaker's voice, but here it most unmistakably was: gentle, patient, professional and dependable. She wasn't altogether sure she liked it.

Chapter Fifteen

He was quiet after the call ended. Thea had gleaned little from his side of the conversation except that he had promised to go back to Stratford to see old Mrs Wilshire, the next morning. 'Is it about Richard's funeral?' she asked.

'Not really. She said she has to talk to somebody and I'm the only one who she can trust.'

'Can *we* trust *her?*'

'I don't think we have anything to fear.' The very mildness of his tone felt like a reproach.

'I didn't think we had, personally. But we've already decided that people must be telling lies.'

'Thea, she's very old, and I've already got a relationship with her. She's a bright, brave lady who faces the inevitable a lot better than most people do.'

'Old people tell lies just as much as anybody else.' She knew this from personal experience, she wanted to add. 'And she's clearly a bit peculiar, keeping all that stuff in the house, preserved for no sensible reason.'

He merely nodded. 'Let's get back,' he said after a pause. 'We can't do any more here.'

'And I need to rescue my poor dog. She doesn't like being alone in a strange house.'

They got into the car, turned it round and returned down the steep twisting lane into Chedworth. Thea's mood was jangled. She was irritated with herself and by extension with Drew for witnessing yet again her less appealing side. They wanted the same things, she insisted to herself. Not just to resolve the mystery of Richard Wilshire's death, but to be together, a contented couple with enough money to live on and a joint purpose in life. The goal was clear, but the getting there seemed to be increasingly fraught.

The house was in darkness. It was anything but welcoming, even with the enthusiastic greeting they were given by the spaniel. It was not long after eight o'clock, the evening still ahead of them. A sharp panic gripped Thea at the prospect of having to entertain Drew for at least two hours before they could decently go to bed. The panic increased as she acknowledged how wrong this worry was for somebody meant to be in a loving committed relationship. She had forgotten what couples did together. Watching television felt like a failure. There were no games anywhere – and she was fairly sure Drew disliked anything as banal as Scrabble or Canasta, anyway. She must have asked him at some point, she thought – and now could not recall his answer.

What had she done with Carl? It felt shameful to even ask herself the question, but equally it was impossible to avoid. She had been half of a couple with him – everything she knew on the subject inevitably included him.

'I'll make some coffee, shall I?' she said.

'If you like.' He was standing with his back to the living room window. A memory stirred in which Thea had been in a room when a missile came crashing through a window, sending shards of glass everywhere. Memories like this were popping up repeatedly, she realised. Episodes from her many house-sitting commissions, where there had been violence and complexities of every sort. Temple Guiting, she remembered. Fifteen minutes earlier she had been reliving her time in Blockley. Cold Aston – where she'd been in a house with an attic – and Lower Slaughter had both woven themselves into her thoughts during the day. It was a troublesome kaleido-scope of recollections, making it difficult to con-centrate on this amorphous Chedworth mystery. Perhaps it was only her experience of the past few years that made her think Richard had been murdered in the first place. Murder was what she had come to expect. In Frampton Mansell an apparent suicide had soon turned out to be a killing, after all. Likewise in at least two other places. But there had also been the opposite, where a presumed murder proved to have been accidental. The police had quickly acquired a habit of consulting the inquisitive house-sitter who had few inhibitions about speaking to strangers and asking them questions that were close to rude at times. People had objected – in Cranham and Temple Guiting especially. But Thea Osborne had been undeniably helpful. An accidental sleuth in many ways, she had seldom solved the case all on her own; but now and then she had. Drew, too, had played his part, especially in Broad Campden and Snowshill.

She groaned softly, recalling all these many adventures and how gruelling some of them had been. She had forgotten the intention of making coffee, standing in the doorway, watching her fiancé.

'What's the matter?' Drew asked.

'Just thinking. Remembering. Feeling a bit tired and middle-aged about everything.'

He was instantly only an inch away from her, then pulling her close, resting his chin on the top of her head. Drew wasn't tall, but Thea was definitely short. They fitted neatly together. He rubbed her back, and swayed her gently from side to side. 'Poor old love,' he crooned. 'We can't go on like this, can we? It has to change. Tomorrow.' He said it with determination. 'Tomorrow will be the first day of the rest of our lives, and we're going to get it right. We're going to leave this place with our heads high and our consciences clear.'

'Huh?' She barely heard his words, but there was something not entirely comforting in the tone.

'We'll go to Stratford first thing tomorrow, and after that we'll tell your DI Higgins everything.'

'Everything?'

'Including our wildest guesses and groundless suspicions. We dump it all on him and go.'

'Right,' she said, thinking that Drew didn't know Higgins, if he thought that was a workable plan. But just to have a plan that put her at its centre was reassuring. It told her that everything was probably all right, at least in the essentials.

Nothing else happened all evening. It wasn't necessary to entertain Drew, she discovered. They could simply be together, cuddled on the sofa, talking sporadically about every sort of trivia. By

234

unspoken consent they shelved the whole business of the Wilshires. The brainstorming, such as it was, could wait. They had worn themselves out, driving around the countryside meeting people and following hunches. Nobody could survive such a day without collapsing at its end.

Hepzie was on Thea's other side, inconspicuously staking her own claim to a cuddle. It seemed to Thea that the presence of her pet was a given, just as Drew's children were. It didn't need to be spoken aloud. Banishing the spaniel from the bed when Drew was in it seemed to her concession enough.

Then it was Monday, and they were back to obligations and focus; Mrs Wilshire expected, and Drew was again conscientious and caring. 'Will you say anything about Richard probably being murdered?' Thea wondered.

'I imagine she'll say it herself. I'm assuming that's what she wants to talk about.'

'If that's so, why us? Why not the police?'

He made his usual open-handed gesture that doubled as a shrug of ignorance. 'Obvious reasons, I'd guess. They wouldn't listen to her, would they? Even less than they listen to us.'

'I woke up thinking about the family history,' she said. 'Those two sisters, and the cousins. Brendan's dad, what's his name, must be over seventy. Richard and he can't have been much company for each other, with such a big age difference.'

'So?'

'Nothing, really, except I've been trying to

imagine what it was like. And where are their fathers?'

'Maybe the old lady will tell us. People often reminisce after a death. They have a compulsion to tell the whole story, sometimes.' He gave a rueful sigh. 'All part of my job to listen to it, of course. It can take hours.'

'The home won't be too happy to have us there right after breakfast, I bet. They'll be trying to do cleaning and all that.'

This time Drew gave a real shrug. 'I often think *home* is the wrong word for it. There's no way the inmates can carry on as if it was really their home. It's much more like being in prison, when you think about it.'

She shuddered. 'Don't spoil my illusions. I had to reassure Richard that there was a lot about it that was positive. Getting all your cooking and washing done, for example. And always being nice and warm. And the setting is gorgeous.'

Drew was suddenly alert. 'Did you discuss it, then?'

'I told you – he was feeling horribly guilty. I wanted to make him see it was the best thing to have done. When we found his body, my first thought was that the guilt overwhelmed him so he couldn't bear it any more. I did think he'd killed himself.'

'We must go over it again in the car. Leaving in five minutes, okay? We'll take mine.'

'So long as Hepzie can come.'

'She'll have to go between the baby seats, then.'

'You don't still call them that, do you? The kids must love that.'

'They don't mind,' he said irritably. 'They think it's funny.'

In the car, he was acutely focused, behaving almost like a police detective on a case. 'It makes no sense for Richard to have felt so guilty. His mother was more than ready to make the move. Her legs were letting her down and the stairs were a real hazard. She'd dropped a pan of boiling water recently and knew she couldn't trust herself with cooking any more. And she's such a *philosophical* person. She faces up to things. That's obvious, I suppose, from the way she planned her own funeral. So Richard didn't have anything to reproach himself with.'

'Well, he thought he did. He was miserable with it. All sort of crumpled inside, if you see what I mean. You know how a person's face goes when they feel guilty.'

He gave this some thought. 'I'm not sure I do,' he admitted.

'I can't describe it, but you'd recognise it if you saw it. As if there's a lump of something you can't bear to touch or think about, somewhere in your chest.'

'This is getting whimsical. Especially from a woman who I have never thought of as having a troublesome conscience.'

At first she took this as an implied criticism. But before flying to her own defence, she paused. 'I do feel a bit bad about keeping you from your responsibilities,' she said lightly. 'But on the whole I suppose I think guilt is rather self-indulgent. If you parade to the world how guilty you feel, that implies that you're a good person, admitting your faults. Unselfish and all that. And it also carries a hint of control.'

'Does it?'

'I think so. If a person feels guilty at their mother growing old and needing more attention and help, that suggests the guilty one thinks they ought to have somehow prevented the inevitable. They believe, somewhere inside, that they can control nature.'

'Or perhaps they're just ashamed of how little they want to do about it. Or how poorly they manage things, getting into a situation where they haven't got time or resources to give the old person what she needs.'

'And you think that's closer to how Richard was?'

'I do. Except ... I still don't understand why he would think she was unhappy or uncomfortable, or blaming him in any way.' He gave a little laugh. 'In fact, in this particular instance, I have a hunch that your assessment might be closer to the truth than mine. My first impression was that they were a very devoted mother and son. Now I think that needs some modifying.'

'Or we might both be wrong, and he had something else entirely to feel guilty about.'

He drove for another half-mile before replying. 'Lateral thinking,' he said then.

'Brainstorming.'

'You think he did something awful, and was killed for it?'

'It's a hypothesis,' she said. 'That fits the facts, as far as they go.'

'Which isn't very far,' he said with a sigh.

It was ten past nine when they got to the care home. The front door was firmly closed, and the car park sparsely occupied. 'Even the cleaners aren't here yet,' said Drew.

They rang the bell, and were mildly surprised when Mrs Goodison herself admitted them. Even more surprisingly, she was all smiles. 'Oh, you've made good time,' she approved. 'Come in. It's chilly today, isn't it?'

She led them purposefully along a corridor and around a corner to a door on which she knocked. Without waiting for a response, she slowly opened it. 'Rita?' she said in a tone half-deferential and half-brisk. 'Mr Slocombe's here.'

Inside, the old lady was sitting in a big arm-chair beside the window. There was a bed and a table against one wall, with another chair, book-case and chest of drawers distributed around the room. On the table was a laptop, with its lid up. Mrs Wilshire looked up without a smile, and said, 'Yes, I saw them arrive.' Her window looked across a lawn and through a fence to one side of the car parking area. She could only have glimpsed the pair before they disappeared from view. 'It's good of you to come,' she added.

Drew took her hand, and then waved Thea forward. 'I hope you don't mind my bringing her with me? We did try to visit you yesterday, but your nephew took prior claim.'

'So I understand. That must have been annoying for you. But I'm pleased to see you now,' said the old lady, bowing her head. 'It was good of you to go to the trouble. I hope you won't feel

I'm wasting your time. The thing is, you see, I suspect you might turn out to be useful.'

Thea had taken a step forward, but went no closer.

'I'll get another chair,' said the matron, or whatever title she gave herself. Thea glimpsed a touch of reproach at her presence. Drew was supposed to come by himself. Perhaps her being there was a potential spanner in the works. And yet, the doorstep greeting had seemed genuine and Mrs Wilshire herself showed no sign of resenting the appearance of an extra person.

The chair was quickly supplied, and Mrs Goodison made a dignified retreat. If she had any worries or anything to hide she covered it very well. Thea felt a thrill of anticipation at the conversation to come. There could hardly fail to be revelations of some description.

'I am really so sorry about your son,' said Drew. 'It was a great shock.'

'Thank you.' There were signs of tears in her eyelashes. She did not wear spectacles, Thea noted. Her gaze was clear and her hearing evidently more than adequate. But her hands were shaking and her ankles looked swollen inside a pair of blue socks. She wore trousers and a sweatshirt, clearly comfortable with them both. 'I have to make a great effort to believe it.' She looked straight at Drew. 'The temptation to fall back on fading memory and an exaggerated senility is surprisingly strong. It would be an acceptable way of avoiding the pain, after all.'

Drew made a quick snort of understanding.

'I suspect they thought I would do just that,'

she went on. 'Retreat into addled wits and refuse to accept what they were telling me. That would have made it easier for us all. For perhaps an hour I almost gave in. And then I remembered you, and all you had seen of Richard and myself. I remembered how reliable and straight talking you were when we met. Added to that, you – by some extraordinary chance – found my son's dead body. I could hardly pretend to be senile, knowing that, could I?'

People didn't say 'senile' any more, Thea thought idly. She had not quite followed the logic of the last remark, but trusted that it had one. There was nothing illogical about this old lady.

'I'd hate to think you let me influence you,' Drew said uneasily.

'That's not what I mean. All I'm saying is that you gave me courage when I needed it. My reaction was all my own – a fierce refusal to believe what they were telling me and a determination to prove them wrong. That's the part I fancy you might help me with.'

Thea felt a stab of pride hearing this, understanding better than before that Drew held a position of great privilege with newly bereaved people, never trying to divert them from the embarrassing fact of death or assuring them that everything would be all right.

'I'll do what I can,' he said.

'So please give me the whole picture, from the start.'

'All right. Well, it was really his dogs who found him. We stopped at the barn for a look, because it was so ... picturesque and the dogs

241

got very excited.'

'I remember it vividly. Richard used to go there with his little friends, when he was a boy. The farmer was forever chasing them away, but they always went back.' Her eyes misted, less with grief than a sort of frustrated rage. 'There is no way at all that he would kill himself there,' she said with loud emphasis. 'It has nothing but happy associations.'

'You mean, he wouldn't spoil that for you?' asked Drew.

'Or himself. Suicide is never a *happy* thing, is it?'

'No.' Drew shook his head. 'Not unless the person was insane.'

Thea entertained a brief image of a lunatic launching delightedly into the void, arms outstretched, from the high barn platform. That most definitely was not Richard Wilshire.

'So ... you don't believe it could have been an accident?' Drew asked carefully.

'Of course not. I know he wasn't a boy any longer, but he was in good health and fit enough. No dizzy spells or wonky legs. You know,' she went on, 'I never had much sympathy for relatives who insisted so adamantly on knowing the exact circumstances of their loved one's death. What did it matter? I thought. Dead is dead, however it comes about. And now I'm one of them. I can't tell you how important it is to me that the world should have the right facts about how Richard died. I can't allow him to be remembered as a suicide. Even his daughter doesn't seem to fully understand how much it matters.'

To Thea, as she listened, this carried echoes of the conversation she and Drew had had the evening before.

'We've met Millie several times since Friday,' said Drew. 'Have you seen her since they told you about Richard?'

'She telephoned me at six o'clock last night. There didn't seem to be much for either of us to say. We were quite unable to console each other. I have a horrid feeling we each think our loss is greater than the other's.' She smiled wanly. 'And that odd Judith girl, of course. She battened onto Richard like a leech.'

The old lady's grasp of the current situation seemed almost miraculous to Thea. She thought of another aged woman, in Blockley, whose wits had wavered alarmingly. People varied, obviously, and stereotypes were always a mistake; but for someone so very old to keep abreast of relationships and emotions in others was definitely impressive.

'But, do you know – and I can say this to you, and nobody else – the pain is actually more bearable than you'd expect. Perhaps I'm a monstrously insensitive creature, or it could yet be too early to say, but I am a lot more concerned to have the truth revealed than I am with nursing my misery. The police tell me he didn't suffer, which helps a lot. And I am very sad about his dogs. They were devoted to him, you know. But he had no wife. That is, he has an ex-wife, who will certainly feel shock and sentiment, but she wasn't dependent on him. Nobody was. That makes a big difference, I find.' Her face contracted for a moment, giving the lie to some of her brave words.

Drew leant towards her, but did not touch her. 'I've heard the same sort of thing before,' he said. 'It's the thing I most value in the British. No false emotion. The stiff upper lip is very underrated. And when a person genuinely is annihilated by the loss, it's all right for them to show that, too.'

'Authenticity,' Mrs Wilshire nodded. 'I've always liked that concept.' She smiled again. 'Would you believe I studied Jean-Paul Sartre in some depth, back in the sixties? I thought he was the most brilliant man alive. I still find that Existentialism is the best explanation available for the human condition.'

'Wow!' said Drew.

'Well, never mind all that. I asked you here to help me discover the truth of what happened to my son.' She looked at Thea, almost for the first time. 'I hope you can stomach some direct remarks?' she said. 'I'm too old for euphemisms and evasions.'

Thea smiled. 'I don't think you need worry about me. This isn't the first time I've been involved with violent and sudden deaths.'

'So, please continue,' the old lady urged Drew. He gave her a brief but honest account of finding her son's body, his apparent injuries, and the arrival of the police.

'It did seem from the start that they thought it was suicide,' he concluded.

'I thought so as well, at that point,' offered Thea. 'It did fit the way everything looked.'

'I will not entertain that idea for a minute,'

244

said Rita Wilshire. 'Not for a *minute.*'

'No. Well...' said Thea.

The woman regarded her for a moment. 'What did you say your name was?' she said then.

'Thea Osborne.'

Mrs Wilshire's eyes turned inward, where she searched her memory. 'The house-sitter,' she concluded. 'I have a good friend in Snowshill, who spoke of you a lot last year. Such a tragic thing, that was. My friend was deeply upset by it. I must say I feel rather privileged to meet you.'

Thea felt herself flush. Her burgeoning reputation was one reason for no longer wanting to carry on as a house-sitter. It was increasingly uncomfortable, forcing her to defend herself more and more often. 'I'm sure the stories have been exaggerated,' she said, refraining from asking the identity of the friend. It was not relevant to the case in hand, after all. She quailed at the knowledge that Mrs Wilshire had no idea that Thea was sleeping on her feather mattress and rifling through her possessions.

'I hope not. I'm relying on you to solve this mystery for me.'

Drew produced a small notebook and pencil. 'We should make notes,' he said.

'Of course.'

He found a clean page and poised the pencil over it. 'There are a great many questions,' he said. 'For example, you say Richard knew the barn, and I wonder whether that's of crucial importance.'

'He didn't have the dogs with him on Friday,' said Thea, before the old lady could speak. 'Was that unusual? And there seems to be no sign of his car. How far is the barn from the farm where he was supposed to be testing cattle? Would he have walked from one to the other? Have the police asked all this?' Suddenly she realised how scrappy and inadequate all their discussions had been thus far. Every time they seemed to be getting somewhere there had been an interruption or diversion. The car was a major element they had barely even considered.

'Very good,' Mrs Wilshire approved with a smile. 'I can see you have a very clear mind.'

'You don't know the answers, do you?' Thea said.

'I'm afraid not. Nobody expected me to think about details like these, moments after being told my son had died.'

'And they were right,' said Drew. 'Have you lain awake all night, thinking about it?'

'Half the night,' she admitted. 'They gave me a pill that knocked me out until about three am.'

'So write down what we need to ask the police,' Thea told Drew, going over the same points again. 'Where was his car?' She paused. 'The dogs were still here at his Stratford place on Thursday evening. Millie told me that. She was surprised he hadn't taken them with him to work, as he usually did.'

Drew sighed. 'That will have added weight to the suicide theory. They'll think he planned it all along, which is why he didn't take the dogs.'

'But he might have been asked to meet somebody there,' said Mrs Wilshire. 'Some local farmer, perhaps, who had evil intentions. He wasn't very popular, I know that, bringing such dreadful news about their animals.'

'And the woman over the road from your house,' Thea said. 'Norah Cookham.'

'Bloody Norah,' smiled the old lady. 'We all called her that. You've met her, then?'

'She told me the dogs killed her cat.'

'I'm afraid they did. One of those sudden fits of madness that can happen to any dog.'

Thea nodded. 'Even my spaniel has had her moments. She was absolutely awful at Christmas, suddenly attacking a dog four times her size.'

'Norah isn't really so bad. She's had a sad life and it's embittered her rather. She's done a remarkable job on herself, you know. Now she's all alone in that great house, a bit like me. We go back a long way and we've always got along well enough, provided Richard kept out of her way. She wasn't hostile to me as long as he kept the dogs away. She visits me here now and then, which I appreciate.'

Thea had a sense of a logjam shifting, the pent-up waters ready to flow freely again. The waters of explanation and information, concerning family history, village relationships and reasons why Richard Wilshire might have given someone cause to commit murder. She settled back in her plastic chair and anticipated a flood of useful disclosures. 'So, can we get one thing straight?' she asked. 'Was coming to live here your own idea, or did Richard persuade you?'

'Thea!' Drew protested. 'What does that have to do with anything?'

She glared at him. 'It would settle the con-

247

fusion about what was making him feel so guilty.'

'Guilty? Richard was feeling guilty?' Mrs Wilshire leant forward.

'He told me he was,' Thea confirmed. 'And you could see it on his face.'

Drew sighed, but said nothing.

'Well, whatever he felt guilty about, it couldn't have been me,' she said firmly. 'I was quite ready to move here. I had no illusions about it. There are many disadvantages, of course, but nothing in life is ever perfect. We make the best of it. I worry about all the things left behind, I admit. They were entrusted to me, and I've done my best, all these years, to keep everything safe and in good condition.' Then she frowned. 'When did you see Richard, then?'

'On Thursday.' Too late, she remembered that Mrs Wilshire knew nothing about Richard's decision to open up the various boxes and drawers in the house and list their contents. That, perhaps, was the source of his guilt feelings. Hadn't Millie said something to that effect, on Friday? Or was that just a hunch on Thea's part? In any case, the cat had escaped from the bag. 'There *are* a lot of things,' she said.

The old lady was quick to understand. 'You've seen them?'

'Yes I have. I've seen almost everything.'

'You've been in my house?'

'Yes. I've slept there the past few nights. Your son was employing me to make an inventory of everything that you have.'

Mrs Wilshire slumped back in her chair. 'Why in the world would he do that? There was

248

nothing that could interest him. And if there was, all he had to do was to ask me about it.' She looked dazedly at Thea. 'An *inventory?* Is that what he called it?'

'I think so. A list, with descriptions of it all. I am most terribly sorry. I feel awful now.'

'And so you should. Did it not occur to you to ask whether he had my permission to do such a thing?'

'I'm afraid not.' She swallowed. 'And it gets worse.'

'How could it get worse?'

'Well, yesterday, your nephew – *great*-nephew, I mean – came to the house and asked if he could go up to the attic. We didn't see how we could stop him, but we did go with him. He seemed to think there was something up there that would prove Richard was murdered. He said you'd got an email that Richard wrote, saying something about being worried he might be killed. We didn't really believe him, but we still didn't see how we could stop him going up there. He took a few things away with him.'

Mrs Wilshire's jaw tightened alarmingly.

'Just tell me he didn't take the stamps,' she said.

Chapter Sixteen

There followed a confused fifteen minutes, with Mrs Wilshire manifesting a depth of feeling that exceeded anything Thea could recall. Okay – old women were very often angry or bitter or resentful, but this was something more. This one was speechless at first, her face suffused with a deep red. Drew was clearly concerned for her health; a heart attack seemed only too likely. He fetched a glass of water from a carafe beside the bed, and nothing much was said for a while. When she did regain her equilibrium, she seemed inclined to blame Thea in particular for being so gullible as to allow Brendan into the attic.

'I was there, too,' Drew told her. 'There was nothing we could do. We didn't have the authority to prevent him.'

'I *knew* I should have brought the stamps here with me. I wanted them to go to Carol – Martin's daughter. She's a good girl. She emails me at least twice a week with all the news. She has a daughter who's a valuer for an auction house. She collects all sorts of things, including stamps. But Brendan has always had his eye on them. He's what we used to call a spiv, years ago. No proper job – just wheeling and dealing. It was that ludicrous school they sent him to, in my opinion. Never taught him proper self-discipline.' She was still enraged, but her colour was better. A glance at Drew told Thea that they were back on more predictable ground.

On the assumption that it might be therapeutic to encourage her to talk, Thea prompted, 'School?'

'Oh, it was one of those throwbacks to the sixties. No rules or exams. Little more than childminders. By the time his father saw sense, it was far too late.'

'Mr Teasdale,' said Thea softly to herself, simply in order to keep track.

Mrs Wilshire, in spite of herself, was equally anxious to keep things straight, it seemed. She nodded. 'Martin Teasdale, my sister's son. I raised him as my own, as they say, after his mother died. A long time ago now, of course. Then he swanned off to Abu Dhabi or wherever it was, when he was twenty-four and I was heartbroken all over again. Even worse than when he went to boarding school. But he never stopped writing and phoning. And now he's back again, which is lovely. He's going to be such a consolation to me now ... I mean, with Richard gone.'

'He seems a nice man,' said Drew. 'And Brendan isn't all bad, I'm sure.'

She gave him a knowing look that to Thea seemed almost cunning. 'Oh yes, Martin's been very attentive, I must say, and of course he's the same person he always was. You never entirely lose that bond, I suppose, even after over half a lifetime. He was such a darling little boy.' She glanced at her laptop. 'But the *stamps*,' she burst out. 'You have to get them back. Brendan doesn't care about them – he'll sell them for a pittance. I *knew* I should have brought them here with me. I did so love them when I was young.' She wrapped her arms around herself, rocking in a much more obvious anguish than she had shown over her dead son. Thea had obscure thoughts about displaced pain and how this must be an example.

'Should we ask his father?' Drew suggested. 'He must be the best person to retrieve them.'

'I suppose so.' She looked round, as if expecting Martin Teasdale to materialise. It was the first hint of confusion that Thea had seen. 'I think he's coming again today.' She frowned. 'Did he take anything else?'

Drew took a steadying breath. 'Well, yes. A picture. He said it was of you and your sister as young girls. And a schoolbook. Just a nostalgic bit of rubbish, really. But it's a good picture. I imagine it might have some value.'

'Schoolbook? That can't have been his. We've never kept anything from Brendan's schooldays. Why would we? What possible connection would they have with me?'

'Well, that's what he said.'

'No,' Thea corrected. 'He said it was his *father's,* not his.'

'That would make more sense,' said Mrs Wilshire, as if an important point had been settled. Thea and Drew both waited in vain for a reaction to the removal of the picture. Instead, Mrs Wilshire stuck to the subject of the book. 'But I think it must have been Richard's. Did it have a green cover? Scribbled on? I remember

252

him putting it up there, saying it still had lots of blank pages, and he might use it one day.'

'That sounds like it,' said Drew.

All three appeared to realise at the same moment that they had drifted off the subject of how Richard had died, and what should be done about it. Mrs Wilshire gave herself a little shake, as if to force herself back to the main point. 'Where were we?' she asked.

'We should tell you what happened yesterday evening,' said Thea. She understood that Drew had a professional resistance to going into excessive detail as to the precise cause of a person's loved one's death, but she had little doubt that the old lady could cope better than most. Especially as there was nothing unduly gory about it and very little sign of suffering. 'We went back to the barn last night,' she said. 'We were there when you phoned, in fact.'

'Oh? Looking for clues?'

'Actually, yes.'

'Did you find anything?'

'We're not sure. It was dark.'

The old lady looked to Drew. 'You didn't say anything on the phone,' she reproached.

'There was nothing *to* say. We thought it would be soon enough to tell you this morning. After all,' he went on, slightly desperately, 'you were only told of his death yesterday afternoon. I didn't want to overburden you with anything else.'

'What day did you find him? Remind me.'

'Saturday afternoon.'

'Do they know exactly when he died?'

'They haven't said anything to us, but I know about these things, of course. I'd say he died quite early on Saturday. And that's curious, because nobody seems to have seen him or heard from him all day Friday – and he never went home on Thursday night.'

'So he wasn't lying there all broken for very long, then. That's a slight comfort, I suppose. I was afraid he'd been there since Thursday, prey to animals and weather – horrible thoughts.' She shivered. Then she spoke with a visible effort, her gaze on the floor. 'And today they'll be performing an autopsy on him.'

'That's right. And they might find evidence that's been missed so far.'

'Evidence that he was attacked?' She looked doubtful. 'If that's what you mean, I fear you have more trust in our criminal investigators than I do. Especially as I imagine it would suit them for it to have been suicide.' Her face crumpled for a moment, and then cleared. 'What other explanations could there be for his death? I can tell the two of you have been thinking about it.'

'We have,' said Thea. 'And there are several odd aspects to the whole business. For a start, the *height*. It's true that it is very high, and nobody would want to fall off that platform, but you wouldn't really expect it to kill you.' She glanced at Drew, half-expecting a signal that she was being too plain-spoken. But he just nodded. 'The thing is, as I understand it, a person seriously intent on killing himself will want to be as sure as possible that he really will die. The

254

worst outcome is a horrible injury that makes you dependent on other people, but isn't fatal. That's what stops so many people from taking overdoses. They're not sure it'll work. Wouldn't it be the same if you decided to jump off a high place? I mean – you'd choose the Clifton Suspension Bridge or the top of a skyscraper, wouldn't you?'

Drew and Mrs Wilshire both shuddered at being forced to consider something so visceral. Then Drew said, 'She's right, isn't she?'

'The police appear to disagree. They told me in no uncertain terms that they did not suspect foul play.'

'I know they did. For them it's largely a matter of evidence.'

'But they never looked properly for evidence,' Thea protested. 'They took the whole thing at face value.'

'They're trained to keep it simple, as far as possible. They saw a high place, a broken body, no trace of anybody else and nothing they perceived as a weapon. We told them the man was feeling very guilty, and the nature of his work was essentially depressing. With their limited interest in psychology, that would be more than enough to confirm suicide.'

'But the autopsy?' said Mrs Wilshire.

'I'm afraid it won't be very comprehensive. I don't know a lot about it, but I suspect they'll do a blood test for toxins, as well as matching his injuries to the known effects of striking a level surface at speed. If they found a wound made by a sharp edge or pointed object, they would have to think again. But I very much doubt that's going to happen.'

'Do you know precisely what caused him to die? Was it a broken head?'

'Well, his skull was definitely damaged. But I think it must have been his neck. I think perhaps he fell awkwardly, head first.' He grimaced, obviously reluctant to say any more. 'A lot will depend on that, of course. I mean – which it was.'

'Oh dear.' She bowed her head again. 'I keep remembering him as a baby. Isn't that foolish? *That* Richard had disappeared long ago, so why does it feel as if I've only just lost him? What a silly thing the brain is – as if I believed I could one day rediscover that sweet little thing, if only he stayed alive. Ridiculous.'

'I can't explain it,' said Drew. 'But it does seem to be human nature.'

A short silence fell, and then Thea spoke. 'I think we ought to focus on the mystery of how he got there in the first place, and why, don't you? The police don't seem to have followed up on that at all.'

'We don't know that,' reproved Drew. 'They will want to find out who saw him last and what his frame of mind was at that time. They have to try to account for his last day, for their own records.'

'He was perfectly all right on Wednesday,' said the old lady. 'He spent an hour here in the evening, before going home.'

'And he never said anything about hiring me to go through your things?'

'Not a word. I don't expect I'll ever forgive him

for that.'

'But you were very close? He visited you a lot?' Drew was instinctively trying to soften her fury. As an undertaker, he never wanted his mourners to be unduly angry with their loved ones. It made for an uncomfortable funeral.

Mrs Wilshire gave him a long look. 'Mothers and sons,' she said. 'A very fraught business, as I'm sure you are aware. We were quite typical, I imagine. A lot of pretence involved, following the usual pattern expected by society. He visited me and we chatted about the weather or politics or food. We seldom strayed into anything personal. With one big exception, of course.' She held her gaze on Drew's face. 'My funeral. He tried to put me off, you know. Said it was morbid. Said I could trust him to follow my wishes without making it a formal agreement with an undertaker. Ha!' She almost spat. 'I don't think so. I have always found trust to be a very insecure business. Where would I be now, with my son dead before me, if I didn't have the arrangements made already?'

'Your granddaughter might take it on. Or your nephew,' Drew suggested.

'They might. But they wouldn't want to. All they want is to ransack my house and rewrite the family's history.'

'I was thinking,' began Thea, 'you were sure to find out about me being at the house eventually. How did Richard know that Drew wouldn't say anything to you? And Millie knew I was there because she and Judith came to see me on Friday.'

257

'A remote risk. I had no plans to meet Mr Slocombe again, until he came to collect me feet first, as they say. And Millie was very probably told to remain quiet.'

'She *was* very angry about it,' Thea remembered. 'At first, anyway.'

'But not angry enough to come to me and help me to put a stop to it.'

A rap on the door silenced them. Mrs Goodison came in, followed by a girl of about eighteen in a white uniform. 'Time for coffee,' the woman almost sang. 'You must be parched from talking so long.' She made way for the girl, who was carrying a tray. There were three mugs on it, as well as a jug of milk, bowl of sugar and a plate of biscuits. *Presumptuous*, thought Thea. What made them think she and Drew both drank coffee?

'What time is it?' Drew wondered.

'Eleven o'clock. You've been here for quite a time. Rita must be worn out.' The accusation was no less real for being veiled with a smile.

'I am nothing of the sort,' said Mrs Wilshire.

'That's lucky, because Mr Teasdale telephoned just now and said he would be along shortly. He said he would be happy to take you out to lunch, if you were up to it.'

'There won't be anywhere open on a Monday,' said the old lady. 'Not in October, anyway.'

'Plenty of places are,' the matron argued. 'As I'm sure you know.' She smiled approvingly at her charge's robust manner. All very right and British, she was plainly thinking.

Thea and Drew sipped their coffees and

signalled to each other that they would be more than pleased to stay and meet Martin Teasdale, if it could be arranged. If for no other reason, there was the potential disagreement about the stamp collection and the part Brendan had played so far. The matron and her minion withdrew, with some reluctance.

'We still have a lot to talk about,' said Thea. 'We haven't come to any kind of a decision about what to do next.'

Mrs Wilshire appeared to be revived by the coffee. She spoke to Drew, 'I had little idea what to expect from you, other than a listening ear. You have given me that handsomely and I'm grateful. My sole purpose is to discover exactly what happened to my son.' Then she looked at Thea. 'You mentioned his car once or twice. Is that not a significant clue as to what his intentions were? Is it hidden somewhere? Have the police perhaps found it and failed to inform us?'

'Very likely,' said Drew. 'They have no reason to keep me or Thea informed, and as I understand it, they still haven't spoken to you directly.'

'They're afraid I'll drop dead on them, I suppose. I must say I had not quite bargained for the way a person becomes less than human once inside a place like this. You're no longer regarded as a person with abilities and faculties and opinions. The only thing I lack is functioning feet and legs. The rest of me works well enough.'

'We should ask about the car,' said Drew. 'It must be somewhere.'

'I think we should report that plank of wood, as well,' said Thea.

'Wood?' Mrs Wilshire's head lifted sharply.

'That's right. Last night we were looking for something that might have been used as a weapon. Something that was wider than a man's head, so there'd be no marks left by an edge. We started with the theory that it was a deliberate attack, made to look as if he'd landed on the floor from a great height, but really he was hit.'

'Yes, yes. I understand perfectly. What did you find?'

'A wide piece of wood. It was propped up against the barn wall, quite inconspicuously. We couldn't examine it properly in the dark, but it might have had a bloodstain on it.'

'Where is it now?'

'We left it where it was. Nobody's going to touch it.'

The old woman gave her a scornful look. 'Except perhaps the murderer, waiting for the police to get out of the way. He could easily go back and take it away and burn it.'

'Why not do that on Friday, if they were going to? I think it's safer just to leave it where it is.'

'Why didn't you tell the police about it right away?'

Thea sighed. 'I suppose we'd just had enough for one day. And we didn't think they'd take much notice, especially on a Sunday evening. They'd tell us off for going back there, probably.' It sounded feeble, even to her own ears and she looked at Drew to see if he felt the same.

'The police will take a lot of persuading, I expect. They're going to look incompetent if it does turn out to be murder after all.'

The conversation was going round the same circle again, Thea realised. Try as they might, it was difficult to focus on a single point when there was so little hard fact available. 'It would be nice to meet your nephew properly,' she said. 'We didn't get a chance to talk to him yesterday.'

Mrs Wilshire grimaced. 'He was relieved when he realised you were an undertaker. He thought you were a solicitor helping me to rewrite my will.'

'Why would that worry him?' Thea asked.

'My dear, everyone is worried where their old relative's will is concerned. The spectre of the cat's home nags at them constantly.'

'But a granddaughter trumps a nephew, surely?' A barely audible sigh from Drew told her that yet again she had overstepped a mark.

The old lady showed no sign of offence, however. 'I agree with you. Martin has had a good deal from me, all his life. Not so much money as time, attention, encouragement. I set him back on track when his mother died, and made sure he always did his homework. I was a darn good aunt, by any standards.'

'I'm sure you were,' said Drew.

'I even delayed having a child of my own, thinking it would upset him to have a rival. He was twelve when Richard was born.'

Again the question of fathers arose in Thea's mind. But she could see it was not the moment to introduce the subject. Before she could yield to the temptation, another tap came on the door. The man with the big oval head appeared, smiling like a frog. He approached his aunt with

261

arms outspread. 'Here I am again,' he said, bending over his aunt for an affectionate kiss. 'Did you miss me?'

Chapter Seventeen

Thea and Drew held their ground, although Drew had risen from his chair. Martin Teasdale seemed to notice them rather belatedly, doing a dramatic double take. 'The undertaker and ... friend,' he said. 'Again.'

'I asked them to come,' said Mrs Wilshire. 'We've been having a very long chat.'

Long it had certainly been, thought Thea. The entire morning had got away from them as a result. The nephew raised his scanty eyebrows and pushed out his lips. 'That's nice,' he said unconvincingly.

'Brendan has stolen my stamps,' said the old lady, as if this was the single most urgent detail in the whole mass of material they had talked about. 'I want you to get them back from him. If I can't trust any of my relatives, I shall have to ask Mr Slocombe to take custody of them for me.'

'Er...' said Drew worriedly. Nobody paid any attention to him.

'Nonsense,' scoffed Teasdale. 'He hasn't stolen them at all. He's keeping them safe, because the house is standing empty and anything could happen. Fire. Flood. Theft – anything.'

'The house,' repeated his aunt, with a frown. She put a hand to her head. 'The house. You know...' she looked at Drew, her voice faint, 'this is all a bit too much. I seem to have drained all my reserves. I'm sorry.'

Drew was at her side in an instant, reminding Thea that he had once been a nurse. 'You should lie down,' he said. 'You're giddy, aren't you?'

Don't die on us, pleaded Thea silently. Martin Teasdale tried to interpose his bulky self between Drew and the old lady, claiming a familial authority. 'Get away,' Thea told him sharply. 'Drew knows what to do.'

'I think I need food, that's all,' said the patient. 'I didn't eat anything at breakfast. Please don't worry yourself over me. Perhaps, some air – the room does seem rather *full.*' Her voice had strengthened, and the look she gave Teasdale made Thea snort in amusement.

This did not sit well with the man, whose eyes bulged in indignation. He spluttered, but said nothing coherent. He was himself no chicken, of course. Over seventy, well fed and fond of a drink, by the look of him. Did that fit with living in the Middle East, Thea wondered idly. Presumably the ban on alcohol could be circumvented by Western businessmen who chose to ignore rules that didn't suit them. Even to her non-medical eye, the man looked to have high blood pressure. There were little veins visible on his nose and cheeks. His eyes were already protuberant, even before emotion enlarged them further. She watched him with interest, trying to recall all the information she had gleaned about him from his son. Father of three; successful in his career, whatever it was; recently returned to England in retirement – and cousin to the dead Richard. Cousin, yes, but more like a brother in fact, raised by the same woman.

Drew had taken charge, manifesting a natural authority that he normally kept concealed. First he opened the door and looked out. A faint clatter of crockery could be heard, suggesting that preparations for lunch might be under way. 'Mr Teasdale,' he said, with polite formality, 'perhaps you could go and find a sandwich or something? You know your way around better than we do.'

'A *sandwich?*' The man stared as if he had been asked to locate a live lobster. 'This isn't a hospital with a canteen, you know. They don't sell *sandwiches.*'

'All right. Well, anything, then. Just to tide your aunt over until lunch. Surely that isn't much to ask?' With a toss of his head, the man went off down the corridor, muttering to himself.

'I'm afraid it is a lot to ask,' said Mrs Wilshire. 'It's a strange thing, when you can't get hold of food when you feel like it.'

It made Thea question again the word 'home' for the establishment. So many daily necessities you just took for granted in your own house were unavailable here. For anyone with their own habits and interests – probably including the collecting of stamps – there would be constant tidying up by staff, inadequate space to set everything out, interruptions and well-meant remarks of incomprehension. And all so very

264

well intentioned. 'Just ask,' they would say. 'This is Freedom Hall – just carry on the same as before.' And they would mean it, not understanding how hollow and frustrating their words sounded to anyone with a strong character and active mind.

'Don't you keep a small stash of food in your room?' she asked. 'For when you want something between meals?'

'I did at first,' nodded Mrs Wilshire. 'But when it was all gone, I couldn't get any more. Shopping is a distant memory for me now.' She smiled bravely. 'Not that I ever enjoyed it very much.'

Fresh implications were flooding in. How did you get new clothes? Books? Birthday cards for friends and relations? Unless you had a willing son or daughter, with time to drive you into town and patience to go round shops with you, you were presumably stuffed. Or was there a faithful band of volunteers somewhere who performed this role for inmates of residential homes? Sporadically, was the most likely answer. Women with time on their hands, who might easily be distracted by events within their own family, or deterred by aching knees and backs as they crossed the line into old age themselves.

She came within a whisker of offering the service herself, before remembering that she lived in Witney most of the time, and had no idea how busy or otherwise she was going to be in the coming months.

Perhaps Nephew Teasdale would do it from here on, anyway. Or one of his daughters. Perhaps he was genuinely devoted and conscientious and motivated by a wish to repay his aunt for her ministrations when he was a child.

Mrs Wilshire went on, 'The thing I really miss is the travelling. I've been to every continent in the world, you know.'

'Yes,' said Thea. 'I saw your brochures and leaflets. I was very impressed.'

'It seems a long time ago now. I spent the whole of my sixties seeing the world.' She giggled girlishly. 'My husband died, you see, so I was free to do as I liked.'

'Must have been expensive,' said Thea.

'Oh, that was all taken care of.' She clamped her lips shut, in a parody of a child with a secret.

All three of them remained quiet until Teasdale came back, carrying a plate. It held a slice of ham and egg pie and a small pile of mashed potato. 'Success!' he crowed. 'I barged into the kitchen and made our wishes known. They were actually thoroughly accommodating. Asked if you'd like a drink as well, and if so what.'

From his breast pocket he produced a fork, for good measure. 'Enjoy, Auntie,' he said.

Mrs Wilshire took the plate hesitantly, unsure how to balance it on her lap. Drew busied himself with moving the bedside table to a point in front of her chair. To Thea, watching it all, there was an element of farce. The food was completely wrong for the situation; a Mars bar would have served the purpose far better. 'Is this what we're having for lunch, then?' Mrs Wilshire asked.

'Along with salad, pickles – all that sort of thing. And some rather attractive-looking bread. I saw two big soft brown loaves that made me feel quite peckish myself.'

By some unspoken consensus, Drew and Thea understood that the time for their departure had arrived. They were both standing already and it seemed as if a force was moving them towards the door. 'We should go,' said Drew.

Mrs Wilshire looked up. 'Thank you so much for coming. I'm not quite sure what we've established, but I know I can trust you to take it further – on my behalf.' She flicked an almost imperceptible glance towards Teasdale, with a tiny frown. 'We will be in touch about Richard's funeral, of course, as soon as we know something.'

Drew quickly took her lead. 'Yes, of course. The Coroner's officer will contact you when we're free to proceed.'

The old lady sighed. 'I imagine Mrs Goodison will pass any messages on to me, in her own good time.'

Her nephew tutted softly. 'Now, Auntie, don't be like that.'

'I don't expect you to understand, but I really do find it very offensive that I was kept in ignorance for almost a whole day. As if I am too unimportant to be told the news immediately.'

'I would feel just the same,' said Thea.

'We had your best interests at heart,' defended Martin. 'Mrs G. thought there should be a supportive relative present when you heard the tragic news.'

His aunt thrust a forkful of pie into her mouth and was still chewing when Drew and Thea finally took their leave.

Hepzie was beyond reproachful when they finally let her out of the car. She squatted for a large wee inches from Thea's feet, and then trotted off towards the well-kept lawn without looking back. 'Come here!' called her mistress. 'We've got to go.'

'Poor thing,' Drew sympathised. 'All day in the car isn't much fun for her.'

'I can't remember when she last had anything resembling fun,' Thea said guiltily. 'There's usually another dog for company, even if she doesn't really play with them.'

'Bring her back to mine tonight and the kids'll cheer her up.'

'We're leaving now, are we?'

He gave her a startled look. 'Not *yet*, no. We've got to go all the way back to Cirencester and tell Officer Higgins what we've discovered.'

'Which is what, exactly?'

'That piece of wood, mainly. And ... um ... the fact that his mother is in no doubt that he was deliberately killed. And to ask what they think happened to his car. We might persuade him to divulge some of the findings from the post mortem, as well.'

'Funny the way Mrs Wilshire called it an autopsy. Isn't that American?'

'She probably watches *The Wire* or *Sopranos*. I told you, didn't I, that she was a great character. I love old ladies like her.' His face beamed approval and relish. 'So honest and brave. It's the best thing about my job, meeting people like that.'

'I thought she was great,' said Thea sincerely. 'Although I did think she might have shown just a bit more grief over Richard. I mean – she's had him for nearly sixty years. She's bound to miss him.'

'Oh, she will. It's early days. But she's chosen to focus on how he died, and until she's satisfied about that, she'll hold up very well. I must say she's unusual in staying so single-minded. Everything else is pushed aside for the time being.'

'Hepzie, we can't hang about here,' Thea shouted to her disobedient dog. 'Come on.'

It was necessary to haul the animal back onto the back seat, where she slumped with a dramatic flourish and closed her eyes. 'I really hate to say it,' Thea told Drew, 'but I'm hungry. It's yesterday all over again.'

'You never learn,' he sighed. 'Why didn't you pack some sandwiches or something, before we set out?'

'Why didn't *you?*'

'I don't have these sudden drastic urges to eat. I suppose we could pay a quick visit to the farm shop in Chedworth and buy another snack, the same as yesterday. It's on the way.'

'Perfect,' she said meekly.

They proceeded to follow this plan, with Drew showing increasing signs of stress at any delay. 'I can't leave the kids for another night,' he said more than once.

'You'll have to bring me back here,' she reminded him. 'I'll have to clean up the kitchen and turn things off. Should I get my car and follow you down to Cirencester? Then you can go straight off from there. It'll save you at least an hour.'

'Seems a bit convoluted,' he worried. 'But quicker in the long run, I suppose.'

'Much.'

They were waiting to pay for their sausage rolls and organic elderflower juice as they spoke. The shop was thinly occupied, with a handful of people sitting at tables in a separate section. As Drew fingered the sparse contents of his wallet, someone came through from the cafe and recognised him and Thea.

'Hello!' It was Millie. 'Why are you here?' she asked.

In some moods, Drew would have made some jokey reply about cosmic dust or reallocation of atoms, but on this occasion he simply sighed. Thea experienced a painful inner conflict, whereby part of her simply wanted to shake off the whole matter of Richard Wilshire's death and leave Chedworth, while another part noted immediately that his daughter was highly agitated and therefore interesting. It was not the shocked appearance of a newly bereaved person, but something more fearful or alarmed.

'What's happened?' she asked.

'They've taken Andrew Emerson in for questioning.'

Drew calmly paid for their purchases before saying anything. Thea led the girl outside, where she hoped the conversation might not be overheard. 'Judith's still in the cafe,' said Millie. 'I'll have to go back to her in a minute.'

'So the police do think it was murder, after all?' said Thea, quickly. 'Is that right?'

'I suppose it must be.'

'How do you know about Andrew?' As always, Thea needed to establish the extent of the spread of information. Who knew what could very often provide a helpful chain of communication that solved many a tricky mystery. The fact of a person assumed to be unconnected knowing more than they should was often an important clue. She struggled to articulate this to herself, as she waited for Millie's answer.

'Brendan told me,' came the gratifying revelation.

'And how did *he* know?'

'He was at the police station when they brought Andrew in.'

'Did he know who he was? I mean – surely they've never met each other?'

Drew had joined them, but manifested much less curiosity than Thea did. In fact, his level of detachment was beginning to cause her some concern. At this rate, he might well change his mind about going to the Cirencester police station at all. When his phone began to demand attention in his pocket, this risk was only increased. Thea held her breath, ignoring Millie, while he answered it.

'I can't be back before three,' he said. 'Probably closer to four.'

The sense of abandonment caught Thea by surprise. The whole weekend had been a jumble of unresolved issues and uncertain priorities, none of which had become much clearer with the arrival of Monday. Every time she thought they had agreed on a plan, the whole thing changed. She had a picture in her head of a train falling off its track, and then running blindly across a landscape with no sense of direction. The tracks that led to a future with Drew and his children, pausing along the way to set up a new home and business in Broad Campden, had somehow come unbuckled, because there might or might not have been a murder of a man they barely knew in a village they need never visit again.

And now Drew was returning to his own territory, where people needed him. He had a circle of family and associates that was willing to accommodate Thea, largely on its own terms. She had no such circle of her own. There was nobody needing her; nobody wanted to know what time she could be with them. Without Drew she was adrift, a train without a track. And yet, she was compelled by what Millie had just told her and the questions that gave rise to.

'Brendan knows everybody,' said Millie carelessly.

'But hasn't he only just come here?' Thea tried to remember everything the man had told her. 'I thought he lived abroad until recently.'

'Who told you that? His *father* was abroad, not him. He stayed here with his mother. He's hardly ever been out of the country, as far as I know.'

'He told me he'd lived in the Middle East for years.'

'He probably thought it would impress you. He's not very truthful.' Millie sounded as if this was no great defect in a person.

272

Thea swallowed it with some difficulty, before asking, 'What does he do for a living?'

'Buys and sells stuff. Auctions, boot sales – all that. He knows what things are worth.'

Thea nodded. 'So why was he at the police station?'

'I don't know.' Millie's voice was shrill. 'Why am I even *talking* to you, anyway? None of this is your business.' She looked at Drew. 'Your boyfriend's got the right idea. Sounds as if he's going back where he belongs. Why don't you just go with him?'

In a quiet way it was something of a crisis. Ignoring Millie, Thea focused on Drew. Was he thinking they could leave everything to the police, now they seemed to have reconsidered Richard's cause of death? Did he think it was all over? It would be perfectly logical to take that view, she supposed – and in failing to do so, she was very likely showing herself to be deeply irrational. But from his estimated time of arrival back home, it would appear that he still intended to go to Cirencester and talk to the police, which was reassuring.

'We've spent all morning with your grandmother,' she told Millie, making no attempt to conceal the accusation in her tone. 'She's a very remarkable person. So strong and sharp-witted.'

'Yeah,' muttered the girl. 'Tell me about it.'

'What does that mean?'

'You should try living with her. She never stops criticising, nagging, belittling. My dad mostly, of course, but anybody who comes near her is fair game. Nobody's ever good enough.

Nobody but her has any sense. You know why we didn't tell her about Dad on Saturday? Because she'd have said it was all somebody's fault – mine or Martin's or even yours. Yes, she probably blames you as much as anyone.'

'She doesn't. She was very grateful for our interest. She needed somebody to talk it through with. And how come you've changed your tune so much? You were all on her side when I saw you on Friday.' Millie's abrupt alterations of view were unsettling. She seemed to utter random statements as to her opinions and feelings with no concern for consistency.

'My father has died,' said Millie with considerable emphasis. 'I have no idea what happened to him, or what happens next. I've been trying to make sense of it, thinking it all through – the same as Gran's been doing, by the sound of it. If he killed himself, then he must have been feeling guilty about something, don't you think? And if another person pushed him and killed him, that's totally different. How am I *supposed* to feel, not knowing which is true? Should I be sorry for him or angry with him? The police are useless. Brendan only wants to get his hands on Gran's stuff. If I didn't have Judith, I think I'd go mad. And now here you are, muddling everything up.'

'Go back to your friend,' said Thea crossly. 'We'll be out of your way after today.'

'All right.' But she didn't go back into the shop immediately. Drew was watching them, his phone call ended. Millie turned to him. 'Sorry if I was rude,' she said. 'It's just all so horrendous.

I don't know what I'm saying half the time.'

'You weren't rude to me,' he said mildly. 'And of course you're in a state. Anybody would be.'

Millie's eyes filled with tears and she stumbled back to where Judith was presumably sitting patiently waiting for her.

'You were too nice to her,' said Thea. 'She was fine when she was cross.'

He merely rolled his eyes, and took her by the arm. 'Come on. We're in a hurry, remember.'

Chapter Eighteen

They drove to Cirencester in two cars, after Thea had returned to the house and quickly removed perishables from the fridge, checked that lights were off and doors locked. She collected her own possessions, and left the key under a rather obvious stone. Then she led the way, because she was more sure of the route to the police station and Drew's TomTom required an address or postcode, apparently. She missed being able to chat in the car, her dog still sulking on the back seat and in no mood for sympathetic listening. As they yet again navigated the length of Chedworth, seeing nobody, admiring the old stone houses on either side, Thea was forced to acknowledge the special beauty of the place. The very silence was appealing. The old lane that must have meandered parallel to the little River Churn for millennia still seemed to have its own independent existence, regardless of the human erections that had sprung up along its length. There were sections that remained pure countryside, between the sporadic clusters of buildings. Three of these clusters were distinctive enough to have their own names – Middle and Lower, as well as actual Chedworth with the church and pub to give it superiority. Pushing aside thoughts and worries about murder and misery, the history of the place made itself felt. Thea was a natural historian, anyway. She felt the presence of past populations, identified their traces in old walls and lanes. And Chedworth offered a good deal more than most, with its Roman villa and ancient woodland. She was sorry to be leaving, in a way. There might have been some real enjoyment to be had, if things had gone differently.

She regretted the missed walks, the closer inspections of gardens. She hadn't even seen the villa for which Chedworth was famous. Speeding down the A429 yet again, she had a sense of endings and omissions. She was not going to be a house-sitter any more. She would never again be dropped into an unknown village, to discover crimes and secrets and unexpected characters. In many ways, she was glad. But she would miss the adventure, the feeling of being a kind of pioneer pushing into the middle of a settlement and stirring it up. There had been times when she had forced people to take a closer look at themselves; to accept that there was a dark side to their idyll. Now she would be confronted by a very different challenge: building a solid relationship with Drew and his children. She would have to understand the nuances of his work, and be at his side in creating a viable business. And perhaps on idle days, they could revisit some of the memorable little places she had come to know over the past three years.

Cirencester was quiet, parking easy. Hearing a deep canine sigh from the back seat, Thea decided to show mercy and take the dog with her. 'Come on, then,' she said, fishing the lead from the pocket in her door. 'You've spent enough time in the car, poor old thing.' Hepzie wasn't old at all, but middle age was certainly upon her.

Drew gave the spaniel a quizzical look, but said nothing, as they assembled at the front of the building.

'I can't remember why we're here,' said Thea. 'I've been thinking about other things entirely.'

'We're representing Mrs Wilshire,' he said. 'Making the case that she's not satisfied with the conclusion that her son killed himself. And requesting that they keep her informed directly, and not through the Goodison woman.'

'Oh.' She blinked in admiration. 'That sounds very bold.'

'I haven't got time to mess about. They need me at home.'

'Let's hope Higgins is here, then. I doubt if anybody else would listen to us.'

'At least it's open. A lot of them have been shut down recently.'

'It brings back memories,' she said, looking up at the bland modern building. 'I came here quite often with Phil.'

'Does he still work here?'

'I think so. I never really understood how it was arranged as far as CID was concerned. Even Jessica gets confused about the way they share the facilities.' A pang accosted her at the realisation that she had not spoken to her daughter for at least two weeks, and not seen her for some months. Never a terribly attentive mother, she seemed to be in danger of letting Jess drift away completely, with her fixation on Drew.

'Well, come on, then.'

Detective Inspector Jeremy Higgins was in his office and willing to see them. He made no mention of the dog, which jumped up at his legs as if greeting its most favourite person in the world. He merely patted her head and pushed her down. 'Well, you were right,' he said heavily. 'It was murder.'

A sadness hung in the air. Higgins looked weary and depressed. Drew made a sound between annoyance and surprise. Thea pulled at her dog and wondered what happened next.

'The postmortem,' Higgins went on. 'The pathologist found splinters of wood in the man's scalp. And there was no wood anywhere on the floor of the barn.'

'In that case, we know where the murder weapon is,' said Thea. 'We found it last night. That's what we came here to tell you.'

'Have you arrested Andrew Emerson?' Drew interrupted.

'One at a time,' pleaded Higgins, making a pacifying gesture with both hands. He looked at Thea. 'Weapon?'

'A big plank of wood, propped against the wall of the barn. We left it where we found it, and hardly touched it. It might have blood on it.'

Higgins picked up a phone from his desk and thumbed it. When somebody responded, he gave brisk instructions for a search for the object. 'If you haven't found it already,' he added. He listened for a moment, and then said, 'Good. Keep everyone away from it, then.' Then he spoke again to his visitors. 'We've been searching the premises since eleven o'clock today. Your murder weapon had been noted but not examined, apparently. I'm told it's rather large.'

'If they knew a wooden object killed him, and there was the very thing sitting there, why didn't they put two and two together?' demanded Thea.

'They're proceeding cautiously, starting inside the barn. These things take time.'

'Well this will be welcome news for Mrs Wilshire,' said Drew.

'Really?' Higgins raised his eyebrows.

'She's very anxious to know what happened. And even though it's appalling to have your son murdered, I suspect it's marginally less terrible than to have him commit suicide. That would make her feel guilty about her showing as a mother. Don't you think?'

'I don't know. I can't see much comfort for her in this news, I must admit.'

'But poor Andrew Emerson!' said Thea. 'Surely you don't think he did it?'

'You know him?'

'Not really. We met him yesterday. We met just about everybody yesterday, actually. It was a very

279

busy day.'

'We haven't arrested him. He was here for questioning, but he's gone home now. A very unhappy man. Unhappy men do desperate things. But there were never any grounds for arresting him. Not until we get a lot more evidence.' He sighed. '*If* we ever do.'

'Well, I'm sure we can leave it in your capable hands now,' said Drew. 'I have to be getting home.' He looked at his watch. 'I might just make it in time to meet the children after school.'

'Who's doing it, if you don't?' Thea asked.

'Pandora, of course. And she's gone well beyond the call of duty already.'

That was very true, thought Thea. Pandora was a model of generosity. But then, a man left on his own with young children was never going to want for female solicitude. Drew in particular, with his soft nature, would have them flocking round. She would follow him to Staverton as quickly as she could, she resolved. *She* was his woman of choice, with nothing else to do for the foreseeable future but collect his kids from school and find something for them to eat.

'Well...' said Higgins, into the lull. 'If that's all...'

'You pulled the rug from under our feet,' said Drew. 'We thought we'd have to convince you there were reasons to suspect it was murder. As it turns out, we could have saved ourselves the trouble, and simply phoned you about the piece of wood.'

'It was good to see you,' Higgins said, obviously meaning Thea rather than Drew. 'Although

I'm not so sure about your dog.'

Hepzie was increasingly stir-crazy, roaming around the small room, sniffing the corners and eyeing the people impatiently. 'She needs a good long walk,' said Thea.

'Well, thank you for coming,' Higgins tried again. 'Now, if there's nothing else...'

'I feel I haven't done what Richard wanted me to,' said Thea sadly. 'All I did was leave the house far more untidy than I found it.'

'How come?' asked Higgins.

'I'm sure we told you. Richard was employing me to sort through his mother's things. He wanted to know what was there – three bedrooms and an attic all full of accumulated stuff. Clothes and papers, mainly, but all kinds of other things as well.'

'A stamp collection, for example,' said Drew.

Higgins was edging them towards the door like a subtle sheepdog. He reached around them and pulled it open. 'Bye, then,' he said absently. His tongue worked around his teeth as if chasing a thought. 'Stamps?' he said.

Neither Thea nor Drew answered. They were already moving down the short corridor to the front office.

'Did you say stamps?' Higgins asked again.

'Purely as an example,' said Drew, with a quick look of warning at Thea. 'People of Rita Wilshire's generation usually collected stamps, didn't they?'

'So you found a stamp collection in her attic?' He addressed Thea.

'That's right. So what?'

'Only that I noticed a message on the computer, earlier today, alerting everyone to an attempt to sell a valuable stamp last night. It was tagged, you see. Every stamp dealer in the UK had been asked to report it if it turned up. And it has. In Gloucester.'

'It can't be anything to do with these stamps,' said Drew firmly. 'You can't imagine that an old lady of ninety would be stealing rare stamps.'

'No, Drew, listen,' said Thea. 'What if she *reported* it missing?'

'When? She only knew they'd gone this morning.'

'Ah! So she did. You're right – it's nothing to do with the Wilshires.'

'Hmm,' said Higgins. 'I expect you're right. But it seems an odd coincidence, all the same.'

'Not at all. I wish I'd never mentioned it,' said Drew irritably. 'All this is down to me,' he suddenly burst out, standing in the middle of the police station's reception area. 'Everything is my fault. I brought Thea into this. I encouraged Richard to make an inventory of the house contents. I reassured him that his mother was perfectly happy in the home. I have interfered at every stage, and look where's it's got me.'

Everybody – including the man on the desk and a woman with a teenaged boy sitting against a wall obviously waiting to be seen – stared at him in dumb amazement.

'You didn't kill Mr Wilshire, did you?' said Higgins in a soft voice.

Drew laughed wildly. 'No, I didn't. But I wouldn't blame anybody for thinking I did. Without me, it might never have happened.'

'For heaven's sake!' Thea spoke sharply. 'Don't be such a fool. You were doing your job and helping me with mine. You haven't done a single thing to feel guilty about.'

'I have, though,' he said, giving her a tragic look.

'Stop it,' she ordered him. 'You were only doing what you were asked to. Richard wanted somebody to sort out his mother's house.' She threw up her hands in a gesture worthy of Jayjay Mason. 'We've said all this already. Everything we did was well intended.' She frowned, hearing herself. There didn't seem to be any new things to say, and the old clichés rang increasingly hollow, the more she used them.

Higgins himself seemed to be at a loss, hovering indecisively in the doorway. 'Let me check something,' he said, mainly to himself. 'Don't go for a minute.'

He went back to the computer on his desk and started tapping keys. 'Hmm,' he said, twice, and 'No, no.' Then he looked up. 'Can't see anything that helps. Look, you two, there's no need for you to hang about. I admit we were wrong, and you were right. You should be pleased with yourselves, not feeling guilty.'

Then a phone rang on his desk and he waved them away without further words.

'Well, that's it then, is it?' said Thea. 'Can we just go home and leave it to the cops?'

'Looks like it.' They were leaving the building as they conversed, the words coming slowly.

'Hepzie will be pleased, anyway.'

'Rita Wilshire wouldn't do anything illegal,' he

insisted. 'Why would she?'

'Forget it. Nobody would murder someone for a stamp.'

'They might.'

'Drew – they're onto it now. They'll do a proper examination and find all the clues they need to catch the killer. We can go.'

He sighed. 'You have no idea how much I want to. I've got commitments. Children. Work. Maggs. I can't be here any longer.' They were almost at their cars, parked together a few yards from the police station.

'Nobody's asking you to.'

His face was still the picture of misery. 'Who was it, Thea?' he almost shouted. 'Who did kill Richard Wilshire?'

She tried to calm him with a hand on his arm. 'Not his mother' she said. 'Or his daughter. Most likely it was somebody we've never even met, or heard of. A farmer who lost control of himself. Or was crazily plotting vengeance for something that happened years ago. We did everything we could. We've given up our time, trying to help. Let it go, sweetheart. Give yourself a break.'

Then his phone warbled and she dropped her hand, half-hoping, half-dreading that it was his family summoning him home immediately.

But it was quickly apparent that it was no such thing. 'Sorry? *Who* did you say?... But how did you find my number?... But the police... I really don't think... Yes, she's right here... If you really think... Yes, all right.' He handed the phone to Thea with a helpless expression. *Who is it?* she mouthed, but he gave no reply.

'Hello – who's that?' she said into the phone.

'Norah Cookham. Listen, I'm so sorry about this, but I thought you'd want to know. My brother-in-law – the one who never forgets a car – has seen Richard Wilshire's Honda in the woods, just a field away from that barn where you found him. It's not really hidden, but he thinks the police haven't noticed it.'

'Why hasn't he told them about it?'

'Well – he has his reasons. Neither of us is exactly popular with the local constabulary. I know it sounds ridiculous, but I'm worried about the effect it might have on Rita. I mean – doesn't it make it look as if he did kill himself? And I have no doubt that she refuses to believe any such thing.'

'Drew and I are here at the police station now.'

'Good God! Can they hear what you're saying?'

'No, actually they can't.'

'Thank goodness. Now listen,' she said again. 'I've heard quite a bit about you and your undertaker friend. And I've learnt from experience that a person should think very hard before rushing to the police with information. It can go very much against you in the future, you see. I thought perhaps you might understand that. You of all people.'

'Well...' said Thea, thinking of the way she had taken the law into her own hands more than once. Cold Aston, Stanton and a few other places came to mind. Afterwards, trying to give an account of her actions, all she could say was that she had followed an instinct, however perverse it

285

might look. The police could be glacially slow sometimes. They had to follow protocols and cover their backs and check for credibility – while criminals escaped or committed further violent acts. Thea simply dashed in and confronted them – generally with fairly satisfactory consequences.

It was as if Norah heard her thoughts. 'You see?' she said. 'Now, there's absolutely no need for you to do anything, if you don't want to. But the car will be found by someone else at any moment, and they might well report it. If you'd like to go and have a look, Derek will wait for you. Derek was fond of Richard, you know. It's personal for him as well.'

'Derek's your brother-in-law.'

'He is. A man of many talents.' She gave a sound part sigh, part chuckle. 'If you drive up towards the Roman villa, there's a little road on the left shortly before the car park. It looks like the approach to a stately home – very straight. It runs beside the river. Drive down there, and on the right you'll see an opening, not very far along. The car's in there. I'll tell Derek you're coming. You can't miss him. He wears a trilby hat and has very bushy eyebrows. And he's quite short.'

'It'll take us nearly half an hour. We'll probably get lost.'

'No you won't. Just go straight up the A429 and turn left at Fossebridge at the bottom of the hill. It's less than twenty minutes from Ciren-cester. You are in Cirencester, aren't you?'

'Yes. We've got two cars. And a dog.'

'Take one car. Quick as you can, dear. You won't be sorry.'

Drew was sitting in his car by the time the call had finished, fingering the ignition key. His guilt and despair had mutated into impatience and annoyance. He looked up at Thea with a deep frown. 'She's mad,' he said.

'I don't think so. I think she's quite clever. Where are you going?'

'Home, of course. Where do you think?'

'I think that phone call was sent to us by one of your pagan gods. I think it's exactly what you need – what you were praying for, if you'd only realised it.'

'You're as mad as she is.'

'Well, I'm going back to Chedworth. I'm going to speak to Derek-the-eyebrows and walk around Richard's car and think about what it means.'

'It's only a car, Thea. It doesn't mean anything. Do you expect the person who killed Richard to be quietly sitting in the passenger seat, waiting for you?'

'No. But we've gone on and on for days about that car. We saw it as the biggest clue to the whole story. Now we know where it is, and I want to go and see for myself. It's what I *do*, Drew. I can't explain it. People think it's bonkers of me, but here we go again. And I want you to come with me. Leave your car here and get in mine. That's an order.'

Without another word, he did as she told him. With only one wrong turn, she drove northwards out of the town and back onto the familiar A429. Only nine minutes later they were at the left turn and heading for the Roman villa. Drew sat with eyes closed and shoulders stiff.

Everything happened as Norah had said. Derek turned out to be younger than expected, which made his hat and eyebrows even more noticeable. The vehicle he pointed to, parked under a row of trees, was a large metallic-hued four-wheel drive. 'Haven't I seen that before?' Thea wondered.

'On Thursday,' said Derek.

'No, since then.' She stared at the tinted windows and chunky tyres. 'It's just like the one Judith was driving yesterday.' She nudged Drew. 'You saw it as well. Isn't it the same one?'

'I don't know,' said Drew. 'Does it matter?'

'Of course it does. If she was using it yesterday, she must have left it here. Why would she do that? Isn't it hugely suspicious?'

Derek cleared his throat. 'Who's Judith?' he asked.

'Millie's friend. Jayjay Mason, the actress. She was very fond of Richard, apparently.'

'Oh, right,' he nodded uncertainly. 'Not seen her myself. Famous, is she?'

'Very.'

'There was a girl driving a Nissan with tinted windows, the other day,' he said. 'Would that be her?'

'Probably. Isn't this a Nissan?'

'No, it's a Honda. And it's Wilshire's right enough. Look at all the stuff in the back.' He indicated a jumble of plastic boxes stacked in the back part of the car, filled with medical-looking packets and bottles, as well as a folded set of overalls and wellington boots. 'That's all his vet stuff.'

'So – what now?' demanded Drew, plainly in a

288

continuing bad mood.

Thea walked all round the car, trying to think of something that would give Drew a reason to stop feeling so cross. Something that would justify this foolish delay and give them some fresh idea as to what must have happened to Richard. She peered through the driver's window. 'It's got a satnav,' she observed. 'Would it tell us where he last went?'

'Only if he used it for directions,' said Drew. 'I mean – if he went somewhere he already knew, he wouldn't need it, would he?'

'But it would still register the destination he last used it for,' she persisted, trying to clarify her idea to herself as much as the others.

'It's locked,' said Derek. 'If we try to get into it, the alarm's going to scream blue murder. And the satnav's built in. It'll only work if the ignition's on.'

Drew was slowly showing interest. He went to the driver's door and bent down to feel underneath the car. Triumphantly he produced a small metal box, which he opened to reveal a car key.

'My God, Drew! How did you manage that?'

He explained quickly how Richard had shown him the system a month earlier. 'I thought it was rather a good idea at the time. Might do the same thing myself.'

'So now we have a look at the gadget, do we?' Derek asked. 'Never used one myself. Wouldn't have the first idea.'

This came as a surprise to Thea, who had assumed she was the last person in Britain to adopt the habit. 'Well...' she began, when Drew unlocked the car, opened the driver's door and climbed in. There followed a lengthy process of trial and error, with Thea peering uncomprehendingly across his chest at the little screen.

'There are loads of places stored in the addresses,' Drew finally announced. 'But most of them are farms. There's also the nursing home in Stratford, which says "Mum"; somewhere in Chipping Norton; his own home – that says "home"; and a street in Gloucester labelled "Martin". It doesn't say which he went to most recently.'

'What's the Chipping Norton one, then?' asked Thea.

'No idea. Maybe we should make a note of the address. It says Wychwood Road.'

She found a much-used notebook in the bottom of her bag, and wrote the addresses in it. 'We ought to have the Martin one as well,' she said. 'Just for good measure.'

'So, what do we think?' asked Derek, looking as if he'd been uncomfortably upstaged. 'No signs of a struggle, or anything, is there?'

Drew got out of the car and locked it again. 'My fingerprints are all over it now, damn it. I should have thought of that before.' He heaved a great sigh. 'Why am I here? This is ridiculous. Why didn't we just tell the police the car was here and leave it all up to them?'

'Derek and Norah didn't want us to. *I* didn't want to. We've been handed this final chance to get the whole horrible business put straight, and it would have been all wrong to just ignore it.'

'How do we know we can trust this man?

What's in it for him?' He gave Derek a hard look, which was calmly received.

'Bit late to worry about that, mate,' he said. 'Our Norah isn't often wrong about anything. When I called her and said I'd spotted the motor, she knew, quick as a flash, what we should do about it. "Call that house-sitter woman and her boyfriend," she said. "They'll take it out of our hands." "Call them yourself," I told her, so she did, and here you are.'

'Take it out of your hands.'

'That's it. We don't want our names mentioned to the cops at all, if you'd be so kind.'

'So how will we explain being here, and just stumbling on the car? A car neither of us has seen before. Or not enough to remember and recognise,' Thea wondered.

'That's your problem. Maybe not say anything about it. Just use the information you've got from that whatnot, and see where it leads.'

Everything seemed to stand still for a while. 'What time is it?' Thea asked worriedly, before looking at her watch. 'Not quite half past two. That's good, isn't it? We've still got a little while to think about what to do.'

'I should be halfway home by now,' Drew said with an unnerving calm. 'I should have gone home twenty-four hours ago, to be exact. I'm now stranded here, with my car in Cirencester. I hope,' he finished with great severity, 'we are not intending to hurtle off to either Gloucester or Chipping Norton? Because that would very probably stretch my patience to breaking point.'

'Oh, Drew. I'm as confused as you are. But

remember what we were saying, just before Norah phoned. We didn't want to just leave everything in a mess here, did we? The police have let the trail go cold, doing nothing since Saturday. Now we've got a couple of possible clues, handed us by this kind man. We'd never forgive ourselves if we didn't do something about it. After all, it really is important. We're not just playing silly games, even if it feels like that at the moment.' She took a breath, trying to order several thoughts all at once. 'And *how* did Norah get your phone number, anyway?'

'She asked Rita,' said Drew simply.

'Of course she did.' This small fact did something in her brain, like setting a clockwork motor going after it had run down. Cogs turned and ratchets connected. She opened her mouth to put some of these connections into words, and then stopped. 'You'd better go,' she said to Derek. 'Because we're about to make some wild guesses and accusations. You'd be wise not to hear them, in case DI Higgins decides to torture the truth out of you at some stage.'

'Righty-ho,' said the man cheerfully, and went sauntering away towards the woods.

'Was he a real person or a leprechaun?' asked Drew.

Chapter Nineteen

Thea ran the scraps of theory past Drew, while he sat in her car and played with Hepzie's ears. The spaniel had jumped from the back and was on his lap. There seemed to be a newly formed bond between them, built of frustration towards Thea and her implacable determination to drag them around the countryside, in a quest to do good of some kind.

'Norah must have a hunch about who killed Richard. She might even have got the brother-in-law to hunt for the car. Which suggests one or both of them had an idea of where to look, and what might have happened. After all, she has known the family for ages.'

'So why didn't she go to the police?'

'She said she's learnt from experience that it can be a bad idea. She's got an impression of me as an amateur detective, apparently, so opted to get me to do the dirty work.'

'Which you did with enthusiasm.'

'I haven't done anything yet. The satnav was your idea. A very good one,' she added with a smile. 'So now we have at least a clue as to where Richard might have been on Friday.'

'Have we? Those addresses don't have dates on them. We have no idea when he last visited any of them.'

'Hmm, that's true. Well, it wouldn't have been

his mother. There's no way he was at the care home all day. And he wasn't at his own flat. Which leaves Chipping Norton or Gloucester. It says the Gloucester street is where Martin lives. That doesn't seem very likely, does it? Wasn't Martin in Stratford on Friday?'

'Saturday,' Drew corrected her. 'We don't know where anybody was on Friday, except Millie and Judith.'

'Brendan probably lives at the Gloucester address as well.'

'I thought he was Cheltenham.'

'That's what he said. But Millie says he tells lies all the time. I don't know. Cheltenham and Gloucester are pretty close to each other. I think we should go there and see if we can get it straight, and maybe even talk to them.'

'Thea!' He almost howled. 'You can't just accost people like that, with no reason. Besides,' he remembered, 'the police are probably there already, asking about those stamps. The Gloucester connection will give them cause to ask some questions.'

'So it will. I forgot about the stamps.'

'I'm sorry, love, but I'm not going anywhere but home. I might stay if I thought there was any sense in it, but as it is, we'd simply be interfering and casting aspersions with no basis. I'm needed elsewhere more urgently than you need me here. The police have everything in hand now. Phone them and tell them the car's here, and then take me back to Cirencester.'

'I can't. They'll want to know how we found the car, and I can't implicate Norah and Derek.'

'I seem to recall that Norah was an "enemy" on Saturday. How come she's suddenly flavour of the week?'

'She's intriguing. I thought she was just a rich and fairly brainless woman, with not much to show for her life. Some of that's true, I'm sure, but she's got hidden depths as well. All that business with the dogs and her cat. It sounds as if she really lost it, and made herself unpopular with the police. And now I'm wondering just what she does in that house all day. In any case, she knows Rita and Millie inside out, and that makes me wonder if she knows what happened to Richard as well.'

'If she does, she'll have to tell the police, eventually.'

'I think I'm going to go and talk to her. I'd also love to talk to Rita again. There are lots of things I should have asked her this morning and never did.'

'Phone her.'

'I could, I suppose. I could even send an email – she's got that laptop all set up, after all. I bet she spends half her time doing Facebook or a blog or something.'

'Thea, I'm not getting any real sense of a theory here. I mean – have you any idea who killed Richard?'

'Not exactly. But there's something about Judith that's niggling at me.'

'That would certainly hit the headlines. Now, I beg you to take me back to my car. You've got those addresses in your little book. That's all you can glean here, surely. *Please* let's go.' He gave her a pleading look, mirrored by the expression on Hepzibah's face.

'All right, then. It looks as if I'll be on my own for the rest of the day.' She gave a melodramatic sigh, which did not impress Drew at all.

'Your choice,' he said. 'Now get in.'

As they drove, he tried to explain himself more clearly. 'I do feel bad leaving you,' he began, 'but I just can't go around it all again. I don't want a repeat of yesterday. Don't make this my problem, okay. Now that the police have decided it is murder after all, we can leave it to them with a clear conscience. Our work is done. Don't you see that?'

'I do, of course. I absolutely do. I'm not criticising you. But I can't seem to pull myself free of it just yet, either. It's my failing. But it would be like leaving a film halfway through, having been completely enthralled by it. I've got to get answers to all these questions, or I'll never sleep. There's something big and bad in the family's past, and I want to know what it is.'

'Where does that come from? Not your obsession, but this thing about their past?'

'All those old clothes, kept so beautifully. The dead sister, Dawn. Even if that has nothing to do with the murder, I want to know the whole story. I think Brendan wanted to hook me in, telling me just enough, but not really explaining anything. I really would like to speak to Brendan again, as well,' she finished wistfully.

'You've no idea who killed Richard, have you?' He sounded faintly accusing.

'Not really. I'm pretty sure it wasn't Andrew

Emerson, which is lucky, if he's really going to work for you when you open the new burial ground. And I can't see how it could have been Millie or Rita. That leaves only a handful of people – amongst those we've met, anyway.'

'You can't really think it was Judith.'

'She might have been an accomplice. I do know we can't believe a word she's said. The truth might be the complete opposite of her story. Maybe Richard was stalking her and she wanted him out of her life. Maybe she's in love with Millie. Or Brendan.'

'Or nobody we know. Can you drive a bit faster, do you think?'

'Sorry.' She accelerated, passing the Hare and Hounds, thinking she might never come back to Chedworth again, and wondering whether she'd miss it. Her plans for speaking to Norah, Rita, Brendan – and whoever else might enlighten her – seemed somehow forlorn and futile, with Drew so implacable about it all. Stratford would involve a long drive back up the same road, taking until late in the afternoon. There was a growing sense of an ending. She was not going to do any more house-sitting. At some point in the past week that had become a firm decision. But she wasn't finished with the Cotswolds, it seemed. She and Drew really were going to settle down in Broad Campden and spread the message of natural burials and associated benefits.

But it wasn't ended yet. Knowing they would be returning to the area made it more urgent that this mystery of Richard Wilshire's death be confronted and solved, if humanly possible.

'I'm sorry,' she said again. 'About everything. We're out of sync, I suppose. I really hope you'll understand why I have to do it – at some point, if not now. I am going to talk to Rita again, in person. I think she's the key to it all.'

'I don't get it. You've got nothing like a coherent theory. You're just dashing about like a mad thing, asking random questions for your own gratification.'

'I'm not, Drew. I'm really not. At least – there's much more to it than that. My head's full of odd facts and things people have said. They all fit together somehow, and I need to know how.'

'That's what I said. It's all about you.'

'Don't be so vile. If I can get it straight for myself, that's good for the family as well. You heard Rita, how much it matters to her to understand it all.'

'I love you, Thea,' he said thickly. 'But I don't know if I can carry on like this.'

'You won't have to. Give me twenty-four hours. Absolute maximum. Have faith. After that, I'm all yours, for ever and ever.' She swallowed down the panic his words had evoked. One false word and it would all be over. She couldn't let him see how terrified she was. Her sense of self-sabotage was overwhelming, and she came to the brink of capitulating to his wishes. But something stopped her. She was Thea Osborne, not Mrs Drew Slocombe – yet. She had to follow her own urges, whatever the consequences.

'Twenty-four hours,' he repeated, with little sign of agreement. 'And then what?'

'I'll come down to you and tell you what's happened and we'll carry on as before.'

'Don't make promises. Do what you have to do. And I'll do the same.'

'Right,' she said, feeling as lonely as she did in the weeks following Carl's death. 'Well, here we are, then.' They were weaving their way through the northern outskirts of Cirencester, arriving at the police station within another few minutes.

'I'm very tempted to go and tell Higgins about that car,' Drew threatened. 'That would be the responsible thing to do.'

'They'll find it soon enough. And I don't expect it'll help them much. It just means that Richard probably went to the barn under his own steam. Voluntarily. Somebody persuaded him to meet them there.'

'Then hid his car, leaving flakes of skin and hairs and fingerprints and the rest of it, so the forensics people can identify them.'

She stared at him. 'When did you think of that?'

'About half an hour ago. Didn't you?'

She shook her head. 'Damn it, Drew. I don't know where I am with you. One minute you're washing your hands of it all, and the next you're practically giving the whole explanation of what happened to Richard.'

'I thought I was just stating the obvious.'

'Well, yes. But I hadn't thought about that aspect of it at all. I was thinking of the past and what motives people might have.'

'It needs both, I guess.'

She said nothing to that, but gave him a sad-

299

eyed look, hoping he could hear what he had just said. On his lap, Hepzie whined. 'She probably needs a pee,' said Drew. 'How many hours has she spent in the car today?'

'Too many. Again. Stop trying to get her on your side.'

Drew got out, carrying the dog. He set her down on the pavement, where she immediately squatted. 'Oh God, she's doing a great big poo,' said Thea. 'Right outside the police station. I'll have to pick it up. I hate doing that. I haven't got a bag or anything.'

Drew kicked the excrement into the gutter, where it was mostly hidden by the car. 'Sorted,' he said defiantly.

Thea giggled. 'Nice to see you can be antisocial when it suits you,' she said. He went to his own car, opened it and leant over to the back seat before straightening up with a folder in his hand. 'You might need this,' he said. 'It's got phone numbers in. Keep it safe, will you. I'll want it back.'

It was the prepaid funeral plan for Mrs Wilshire. Thea took it with a smile, but they exchanged no further words. She watched him go, her mind blank. Just how she proposed to solve a murder all on her own was the greatest mystery of all.

Chapter Twenty

Rita Wilshire possessed a mobile phone and an email address. Drew had noted them both down on the top sheet in the folder. It was all rather more businesslike than Thea would have expected. Eighteen hundred pounds had been paid already, to cover all expenses for the funeral, whether it took place in North Staverton or Broad Campden. That was also a slight surprise. She had assumed a natural burial to be significantly cheaper than that. Then she noticed the inclusion of a maple tree and the hire of a piper to play over the grave. Drew must have had to make a guess as to how much that might cost.

Email wouldn't do, so she telephoned Mrs Wilshire, with no real expectation of getting a response. But she was wrong. It was answered on the third trill. 'Hello?' came an exhausted-sounding voice.

'Mrs Wilshire? This is Thea Osborne, Drew Slocombe's fiancée. Would you mind if I asked you one or two questions?'

'You sound uncannily like a police officer. Are you doing this on their behalf?'

'No, not at all. But we have been to the police station this afternoon. I'm sure somebody's told you they are now treating your son's death as murder. Something in the post mortem changed their minds.'

'No. Nobody has told me. I expect they think it can wait.'

Recollections of other violent deaths surfaced in Thea's mind. Wasn't there always a family liaison officer holding the hand of the bereaved relatives? Didn't that person virtually move in and offer an almost smothering level of support? Just one more unforeseen consequence of living in a care home, she supposed. The FLO would be considered superfluous, in the circumstances. Mrs Goodison would be deemed a perfectly adequate substitute.

'That's very bad,' she said. 'Is anybody with you?'

'Not just now. I think they find me embarrassing. I'm afraid I gave in to emotion a little while ago, and they've tucked me into bed to get over it.'

But you kept your mobile on, and within reach, thought Thea. There was still plenty of life left in this old lady, then. And a lively interest in the world outside.

'This is going to sound strange,' she warned. 'And I can't altogether explain it myself, but Drew and I have been doing our own little bits of detective work. We've been involved all along, of course. It wouldn't be right to just drop it now and go home. So, can I ask you one or two things?' The inclusion of Drew was deliberate, but she felt bad about it. If she was dishonest with Rita, it would serve her right if the old lady repaid her in kind.

'Go on.'

'Right. Well, it's going to sound very intrusive,

I'm afraid. Do you know where Richard was when he disappeared that time? Millie told me about it on Friday, and it's been nagging at me ever since.'

There was a pause that seemed to last an unnaturally long time. 'He told me he was having a fling with a young woman. Said they went to Portugal for a summer of love. But it burnt itself out and he crawled back home again. Never told his wife or daughter where he'd been. But they guessed, close enough, and it was the end of the marriage.'

'It seems odd that he wouldn't tell his wife, though, after the event. Husbands usually do – don't they?'

'I know.' Something in the voice alerted Thea. 'But Richard has always been a very poor liar. He'd never have convinced her the story was true.'

'Because it wasn't.'

'Exactly. He never went to Portugal – just snatched it at random, for my benefit.'

'He kept in touch with you during those three months?'

'By email, yes. Made me promise not to tell Daphne. To my shame, I was rather proud of the fact that he put me above his wife. That he cared more for my distress and worry than hers. Of course, she had Millie for comfort.'

'So you believed the story at the time?'

'Most of it, yes. And then last week, he told me the truth of the matter. He had to, you see, because I was so close to discovering it for myself.'

With some impatience, Thea pressed on. The

303

slow convoluted disclosures were quite unnecessary, as far as she could see. 'So where was he?' she asked loudly.

'I'm not sure I should tell you. On the grounds that I might incriminate myself.' She gave a throaty little laugh, sounding as if the last of her energy was about to expire. 'It's not funny, of course. I am so irredeemably guilty, I fear it might kill me. Everything has been my fault, from the very start.'

'I'm sure that can't be true. You didn't kill Dawn, did you?'

'No.' A worryingly rasping breath filled the next two seconds. 'No, I didn't kill her. But I did things that were almost as bad.'

Thea found nothing to say, but the image of the painting from the attic, with the two seductive girls displaying themselves so shamelessly, came to mind. The younger one, smiling so knowingly, fingering her lip – that was Rita Wilshire.

'Well,' she began, with no idea of what she was going to say. 'I can't imagine that has anything to do with what happened to Richard.' Stupid, she chastised herself. Because it quite evidently did have everything to do with it.

'Thank you, dear. But you don't really think that, do you?'

'I'm sorry. I really didn't want to upset you. I'll leave you in peace now, and I hope...' What? That blissful oblivion came quickly, to soothe the guilt and distress that were evidently approaching rapidly? That some beloved relative – and it could only be Millie – turn up and offer consoling companionship?

'But I haven't answered your question, have I?' A querulous note now entered her voice, as if she had forgotten much of the conversation. 'You asked where Richard went, five years ago.'

'And you said it might incriminate you.'

'So it might. Well, it's only what I deserve. He went to see his father. Goodbye, dear.' And the phone went dead.

Which explained very little, at least at first sight. Okay, Rita was feeling guilty because her husband, Mr Wilshire Senior, had not been Richard's father, and had therefore probably been deceived. That wasn't good. It carried a lot of implications down the generations. Millie had a genetic inheritance other than the one she assumed.

Had Richard spent the lost three months living with the old man, getting to know him, hearing the full story from him? Or had much of the time been spent in tracking him down, following clues and hunches until the man himself was revealed? And why not tell people afterwards? Why keep it from his wife and wreck his marriage as a result?

Was there also an implication somewhere that Rita knew who had killed her son? And if so, was it somebody she wanted to protect? Brendan Teasdale came instantly to mind. Even if he had stolen her stamps, invading her attic and being generally obnoxious, he was her great-nephew and might therefore have earned some affection from her.

She sat in her car with the extremely disgruntled spaniel and tried to think. Drew had been right to accuse her of dwelling far too much on past history. More profitable, surely, to focus on exactly *how* the murder had been committed. The logistics of when and where would leave some sort of trail for the police to find. Weapon; tyre marks; hairs; phone calls; witnesses and alibis – it would all be keeping a dozen officers and more occupied all week. They would very likely assemble a picture of what must have happened to Richard Wilshire sometime early on Saturday morning. And from there they would construct a small pool of suspects to interview in the hope of catching them out and reaching a conclusion.

Yes, but... *Why?*

The answer to that question seemed to lie in the family's past. Without a scrap of clear evidence, Thea had arrived at this certainty. Not only Rita, but Millie and Brendan too – they had all reverted to old stories concerning Dawn and Martin and Richard's missing months. Somewhere in all this kaleidoscope of information, the answer must lie. She could almost taste it, just sitting there, an inch or two away. Now Rita's guilt seemed to contribute to the idea, as well.

But what to do about it? The two addresses in her notebook still felt significant. Richard had been in the habit of visiting his cousin Martin, it seemed. Or at least, he had done so once, and probably much more than that. An address saved in a satnav's memory must imply repeated visits. And that raised the question of just who lived in Wychwood Road, Chipping Norton.

'It's not far,' she said aloud to the dog. 'And we've got nothing else to do. Let's just give it a try.'

Hepzie expressed no opinion on the matter, other than a deep canine sigh.

Thea consulted her road atlas, muttering 'Up to Stow-on-the-Wold and turn right.' She was to find number 18 Wychwood Road, it seemed. And without a navigation system, it was liable to be a matter of trial and error. So be it. Chipping Norton was a small place. Ten minutes of driving around it should be more than enough. After all, she said to herself, it wouldn't be the first time.

It took a little under ten minutes, in the event. Wychwood Road was slightly outside the town, well supplied with trees and more contemporary than most of the other parts. Number 18, however, turned out to be not a private house, but a converted row of houses, so that it was in effect numbers 16 to 22. Obviously Richard's satnav hadn't been able to handle such a deviation from the norm. The resulting building was, to Thea's surprise, a residential home for the elderly.

This presented multiple difficulties. Who had Richard been visiting here? No other elderly relatives had been mentioned – except for the man's father, of course, and that had been five years ago. She parked inconspicuously opposite the main entrance with a sign outside and tried to think of a course of action. It was twenty to four. The inmates might be having tea and biscuits, or an afternoon nap. The weather was chilly, so nobody was likely to be sitting in the gardens at the back. She saw no pretext upon which she might go in and ask questions. What would she ask? *Is there anybody here who knows a*

Mr Richard Wilshire? That was the only one that made sense, but carried considerable risk. If there was somebody, who knew Richard was dead, there would be a lot of questions in the other direction.

At least she could get out and give the dog a breath of air. 'Come on, then,' she said, fastening lead to collar. 'Something might come to mind, I suppose.'

She walked herself and Hepzie to the furthest end of the road, admiring the glimpses of the old town, and trying not to think how close they were to her own home in Witney. Poor little cottage, so badly neglected in recent years. Initially she had been very glad to escape the associations with Carl and their violently truncated marriage. Before the first house-sitting commission she had been in a bad way, physically hurting herself to distract from the shocked and broken heart. The spaniel had been of some limited comfort, vastly better than nothing, but often rather overlooked, too. Just as she had been for the past two days, poor thing. In a paroxysm of guilt, Thea bent down and stroked the soft head. It was such a sweet creature, the long ears and large liquid eyes guaranteed to attract warm feelings. Her coat, untrimmed for many months, was luxuriously silky to the touch. In old age, Thea had been warned, this same coat would turn matted, especially around the leg joints and belly. But for now it was perfect. 'You're a good, lovely dog,' Thea said, with all sincerity. 'Whatever would I do without you?'

They turned back, just in time to see a small

group of people leaving the care home. Two of them looked familiar, and with no conscious thought, Thea ducked behind a convenient plane tree. The people had their backs to her, and were something like seventy yards away. She watched them cautiously, wishing she could hear what they were saying. There was an impression of drama in the way they huddled together, their expressions serious. But the very fact of their presence was really all the clue she required for her next move.

Because Martin and Brendan Teasdale could surely only be visiting a relative. The woman with them was dressed in a trim blue suit, and carried a briefcase. She had *solicitor* written all over her. Drew would have called it sheer guesswork, but Thea was convinced it was better than that. Deduction, she called it. The story was still full of gaps and contradictions, but essentially she could see the main picture. Essentially, she knew now who had killed Richard Wilshire and why. Answers that had been slowly coming into focus all day now formed in her mind, slotting into place with the facts she had accumulated in such quantity since Thursday evening. She remained tucked behind the tree, her dog pulled close to her legs until the three people had got into two separate cars and driven away.

'Lucky Derek-the-eyebrows isn't here,' she muttered. 'He'd have spotted my car right away.'

With profuse apologies she put the dog back in the car and marched through the front door of the care home. 'Is there a Mr Teasdale here?' she asked a woman in a blue nylon garment who happened to be in the entrance hall.

'What?' The accent was Spanish or Italian.

'Teasdale.'

'Oh, poor man. The ambulance is just gone. He has a heart attack. Poor man.' She shook her head. 'But he is so old.'

'Can I speak to someone about him?'

'Someone? Who?' The woman was not just having trouble with the language, thought Thea. She was also exasperatingly dim. Probably a cleaner or cook, she concluded.

'Someone in charge,' she suggested.

'Okay.' She was led up a flight of stairs to a room that looked over the street at the front. It had a bow window, and would have made a pleasant home for an old person to end their days in. 'Mrs Saunders – there is a lady,' the menial announced, and then withdrew.

Mrs Saunders had been standing at the window, and turned to see who the lady might be. 'I saw you in the street,' she said. She was about Thea's own age or slightly younger, stout, fair and flustered. 'Who are you?'

'I came to see Mr Teasdale,' she said boldly. 'But I gather he's been taken ill.'

'He probably won't survive the trip to hospital. I *knew* all this business would be too much for him. He's ninety-eight, after all, and very frail. It seems wrong. Who *are* you?' she said again.

'Well, nobody, really. I know Mr Martin Teasdale slightly. I saw him just now, outside. Why isn't he following the ambulance?'

'I expect he will. It's all been such a shock for him, you see. Everything happened at once.'

'How long has he been here, old Mr Teasdale, I mean?'

'Five years, more or less. He's always been very popular. Are you a relative? Or what?'

'It doesn't matter. I'm sorry to have come at such a bad time. I didn't see the ambulance.'

'It was half an hour ago now, at least. The solicitor woman wanted to check some paperwork. It did seem a bit insensitive, but she said she'd come quite a way and it made sense to do it now.'

'Did they speak to the old man? Was he well enough to see them?'

'Oh, yes. They were here right after lunch, and talked for an hour or so.' She frowned angrily. 'If you want to know my opinion, it was their fault that he collapsed. You could almost say they killed him – although you're not to quote me on that.' She shivered. 'Forget I ever said it. I don't know *what* I'm saying, to be honest. It was all so quick and upsetting.'

'I'm sorry to have bothered you,' said Thea. 'Terrible timing on my part. I'll go.' And she went, thinking she had done well not to reveal her name or reason for being there. With luck, Mrs Saunders would forget all about her in the turmoil of the afternoon's events.

There was only one imaginable place to drive to next. It wasn't far, heading north on the A3400, which was not a familiar route, and rather busy with end-of-day traffic. But it was well signed, and she had a groundless confidence that she would find the way mainly by instinct. Scrappy random thoughts filled her head, one of which was *Thank goodness I filled up with petrol on Saturday, with all this driving I'm doing.*

Chapter Twenty-One

Rita Wilshire was greatly changed since the morning. She had shrunk in size, for one thing, hunched in her chair with bowed head. Mrs Goodison warned Thea that she would be shocked. 'It happens like this sometimes,' the matron said. 'I'm not sure I should allow visitors, actually, but she did say she would see anybody who came. I think she had you in mind.'

'Really?'

'Just a hunch. I don't mind telling you this has been a very distressing few days for us all. It isn't often I have to deal with someone whose son has been murdered, as you might imagine.'

'I don't suppose it is,' said Thea, heading down the corridor unescorted.

The old lady revived slightly when she realised who had come into her room. 'You telephoned,' she said.

'I did. You told me the whole thing was your fault. I think I understand what you meant by that now.'

'Clever girl.' Her voice was weak, almost inaudible at times. But she put in a visible effort to speak her mind. 'It's strange, you know – I never felt a bit of guilt at the time. My husband was a

312

useless creature, always depressed or distracted. Martin came to us when Dawn died, like a ready-made son. It all seemed to fit so neatly.'

'Did you remain in touch with his father all along?'

'Oh, no. He was in the Forces, you see. Burma. Prison camps, that awful railway and malaria and all that. He came back a wreck. It's miraculous he's lived so long, after all that damage.'

'It's all so long ago,' murmured Thea, trying to grasp the fact that such ancient history was real personal experience for these old people.

'It has come much closer in the past few weeks. As if it was all just gone a short while ago. The memories are as clear as crystal. It's astonishing.'

'So Martin grew up with you, just like your own son. Did he call you Mum or Auntie?'

'I was always Auntie Rita. We made sure he knew who his mother had been. She was such a darling thing, you know. Everybody loved her. We kept her memory alive.'

'You kept all her clothes, and linens and other things.'

'There seemed to be no choice. In a way, the things were *her*, I suppose. I planned to hand them over to Martin's wife when he married, but she never wanted them. Just laughed at them. Said they were moth-eaten rubbish. Nasty bitch, she was.'

The revival was slowly continuing, the voice growing stronger. Thea had pulled up the second chair and was sitting knee-to-knee with the old lady, bending forward to catch every word.

'And then Richard was born,' she prompted.

'So he was. Martin's cousin, officially. And actually, of course. But also his half-brother. They looked uncannily alike. Still do. I mean, did, until...' She heaved a shuddering breath. 'Those foolish boys! What can they have been thinking? I never *dreamt* one of them could end up dead.'

'You had an affair with Martin's father. Mr Teasdale. What's his first name?'

'Neville. He's the younger son of an earl, you know. Well, a *much* younger son – three older brothers, poor chap. He never used his title. Could never see the point of it. But there's family money.'

'And he gave you some of it,' Thea guessed. 'Which you spent on ten years of exotic travels.' It was remarkably gratifying to have that little secret revealed.

'That's right. I had to put some pressure on him, but he paid up handsomely in the end.'

'But Martin's a legitimate son, and Richard wasn't – so he can't have had any claim on money. Is that what he hoped to get from making contact the way he did?'

'I told you about that, did I?'

Thea was focusing intently on the information flowing fitfully from the old lady. It was explaining a lot and yet still leaving a hundred questions to be answered. She also felt burdened by the knowledge that the ancient Neville Teasdale might be dying in an ambulance as they spoke. No way was she going to impart this news, but it felt wrong to withhold it. When the truth came out, Rita would feel manipulated and used. She

314

was never going to want to see Thea Osborne again.

'Did you love him?' she asked.

The sigh was like a tiny puff of warm air. 'I loved Martin. When he went away to school it was agony. I'm afraid I simply exploited Neville in the most outrageous fashion. I wanted another of his sons to love and raise, and it was easy enough to get him, as it turned out. Poor chap hardly knew what was happening. Of course everyone assumed it was John Wilshire's child. Even John himself seemed willing to believe it. I told him some rubbish about a drunken night of passion that he'd forgotten.'

'But Richard thought John was his father as well?'

'Until he met Brendan, who showed him pictures of Neville. Brendan does family history, the fool. Came to the house asking to see old photos and bringing some of his own. I could hardly refuse him, could I? Martin was there, as it happened, and I could see Richard getting thoughtful. Next we knew he'd disappeared in a puff of smoke, and his wife went off her head with worry.'

'But if he was simply getting to know his father, why did he keep it such a secret? Why would it matter?'

'Neville would have denied the whole thing. He's an old-fashioned Victorian, afraid for his reputation. He swore Richard to secrecy.' She managed a breathy little laugh. 'And yet he was so pleased about it, too. He and Richard formed a bond almost instantly. Richard was angry with me, of course, because it could all have been too late. There was this decrepit old man, deaf and rambling – they set about doing what they could to make up for lost time.'

'Who else knew about it?'

'Brendan guessed, but they would never confirm it to him. He talked about getting a DNA test done, but never did it, as far as I know. After all – it has nothing to do with him.'

Thea sat there, processing the story and following a number of implications, saying nothing. Eventually she asked, 'Was there really an email from Richard, saying he feared he might be killed? How else would Brendan know to go up into your attic?'

'You asked me that before.'

'I know I did. And I'm not sure I believe your answer.'

Rita Wilshire looked up, attempting to straighten her neck and back. 'My dear, look at it from my point of view. All I have now is Millie, and Martin. They're the only two who are going to come and see me. And Millie's liable to swan off to some foreign country at any time. Martin's got himself a place in Gloucester, which is not so far away. He's a cheering presence. And he emails me every day.' She smiled wistfully. 'I do love emails, always have. It felt as though they invented them just for me.'

'And you've always loved him.'

'That's right.'

'More than Richard?'

'You have a special place for the first one. To all intents and purposes, that's what he was.' A wash of sadness crossed the old woman's face, turning it grey. 'And now it's all at an end, isn't it. Richard has gone. Neville won't survive for long, once he's told the news. The family, such as it was, has all turned to ashes. And the whole thing is my fault.' She kept her eyes on Thea's face. 'It's a lesson that takes a lifetime to learn. Be sure your sins will find you out. A small selfish act, so very many years ago, will come back to bite you. But have mercy, my dear, if you can. I dare say quite a lot depends on you now.'

Thea drew in a deep breath, making calculations as she did so. What was the worst that could happen? What could she gain by doing what she planned? How was it her business, anyway?

Before she could say anything, the door of the room swung open and Millie burst in. 'Gran! Oh, Gran! How are you? What're *you* doing here?' she demanded of Thea. 'Aren't you ever going to go away and leave us alone?'

'Manners, dear,' reprimanded the old lady. 'This lady has our best interests at heart.'

'Does she? What makes you think that?'

'Well...'

It wasn't entirely true, thought Thea guiltily. It wasn't thoughtfulness or altruism that motivated her so much as a need to see the story to its conclusion and find answers to the many questions that had arisen. But now she had the main answers hovering an inch away from her nose, but was prevented from verifying them by the intrusion of this annoying girl.

'I've been at the police station for hours,' said

Millie angrily. 'They've got a mad idea about Brendan and some stamps. What's that about, anyway? They've arrested him by now, I expect. They didn't explain it at all, but as far as I can work out, they seem to think Brendan killed Dad because of some valuable stamps that were in the attic at Chedworth. How can that be possible?'

'It's not,' said Thea and Rita Wilshire in one breath.

Ten minutes later, Thea left the care home, having said little more to the old lady or her granddaughter. She suspected that Rita knew what she was thinking, and what she was going to have to do. She was cast in the role of Nemesis, which was far from comfortable. She could see no other course of action but to return to Cirencester and reveal her findings to DI Higgins. It felt slightly tame, and anticlimactic, but also inescapable.

And yet there were still unanswered questions. How much did Norah Cookham know? And Millie, who gave an impression of bewilderment, but always seemed to be on the spot when anything important was happening. And biggest question of them all – how had Richard actually been killed? She had a feeling she would be asking as much as answering, once she located Higgins.

Her phone trilled at her, just before she got to her car. Assuming it to be Drew, she did a double take when the screen said 'Caller Unknown'. It could be anyone, of course. Probably nothing to do with the business in hand. She answered warily.

'Mrs Osborne? Martin Teasdale here. Where are you?'

Her heart thumped. 'How did you get my number?'

'You gave it to Millie. She gave it to Brendan. We've all got it,' he said carelessly. 'Now please listen. Where are you?'

'In Stratford.'

'I see. Well, I'm in Oxford. My father died half an hour ago. I'm guessing you're with my aunt. If that's right, could you be kind enough to give her the news?'

'*What?* Why me? Of course I won't do that. It's not my place. She's lost everything, these past few days. I've no intention of adding to her distress.'

'No problem,' he said calmly. 'I only thought it might be the easiest thing. I'm not going to insist.'

'I'm leaving, anyway. Millie's with your aunt. You could phone her and ask her to do it. Not that I understand why it's so urgent. It was over twenty-four hours before anyone told her that her son had died.'

'That's why, of course. She'll not forgive such a delay again.'

'I think she's gone beyond all that now,' said Thea.

He was quiet for a few seconds. 'What did you mean, she's lost everything?'

Her heart thumped again. 'Well...' she said, 'the dreadful way her son died.' She emphasised the word *son*, from an obscure sense of wanting to keep Richard in the forefront.

'Listen,' he said. 'You and I should meet. I understand that you've been a kindly presence these past few days, you and your partner. I'd like to express my gratitude. Perhaps we could meet in Chedworth – say in an hour's time? At the house.'

'What for? I don't need any thanks. I wasn't going back there again. I've done all I can.' A thought struck her. Brendan could not have been arrested, as Millie supposed, because he had been in Chipping Norton with his father only ninety minutes earlier. 'Is Brendan with you?' she asked, without thinking.

'Why?'

'No reason. Just a thought.'

'Well, he is, as it happens. But I was going to take him home to Cheltenham before meeting up with you. He has things to do.'

'He stole your aunt's stamps,' she said. 'She's very upset about it.'

'Bullshit,' he said. 'That's just Auntie Rita's paranoia. Forget about it. The stamps aren't going anywhere.'

Thea said nothing. Martin Teasdale went on, 'So you'll meet me, will you?'

'Only because it's on my way,' she said. 'I can spare a few minutes, I suppose.'

'Lovely. Make it five-thirty, then. At the house.'

She was mad to agree, she decided. Totally insane. Not only could there be no conceivable gain to be made, but she had no desire whatever to see Chedworth again. Her thoughts and guesses concerning Martin Teasdale made him the last man on earth she should meet alone in a deserted village. And yet, the old enemy – curiosity – was controlling her. Here was a chance to anticipate the laborious police investigation and get answers directly.

'Sorry, Heps,' she said. 'But we're not finished yet.'

She was five minutes late, because she'd stopped at the same garage shop that she and Drew had used to refuel, and bought a bag full of food. The dog would be hungry, too, so she got some Winalot biscuits to tide her over. They had eaten as she drove, which did at least make her feel more energetic, and clearer in her thinking.

She parked a little way past the house, and resolved to conduct the ensuing conversation in the open air. Letting Hepzie out, to run free in the quiet cul de sac, she walked up to a car containing a man in the driving seat. Behind him there was a bulky rectangular parcel wrapped in black plastic.

'No Brendan, then?' she said.

'I told you I was dropping him off first.'

'I heard that he'd been arrested on suspicion of murder.'

'You heard wrong.'

'Well, it doesn't much matter. We can soon put them right, can't we?'

Only then did he open the car door and climb out. He was a solid man, with a sheen of prosperity and confidence. His eyes were clear and his cheeks well shaven. Of all the people Thea had met in the last few days, this one carried the least hint of guilt. He moved easily, obviously free from any of the joint pains that so often afflicted men of his age. Even his knees seemed to work perfectly. His features were disconcertingly similar to those of the dead Richard, his cousin and half-brother.

'Who would have guessed what a dangerous little thing you turned out to be?' he said with a smile. 'Brendan told me how you questioned him like any prosecution lawyer. All that stuff about our family, which is so very much not your business.'

'Does Brendan know what you've done?'

'Don't beat about the bush, dear. Call a spade a spade, why don't you?'

She was beginning to feel that this man was having no difficulty in disarming her. She was doubting some of her own perceptions and conclusions. But she wasn't done yet. 'That classwork book he found in the attic. It was yours, wasn't it?'

'Richard's, actually. Full of doodles and scrappy ideas. Funny the way he left it up there. I think it was deliberate, don't you?'

'Did he really leave an email predicting that he would be killed? Your aunt won't tell me.' It was a niggling detail that kept distracting her.

'Up to a point, yes. Brendan saw a printed-out email at Auntie Rita's. Richard was eaten up with all kinds of worries. Not just family stuff, but all those farmers who hated his guts. But he didn't expect to be murdered. He just hinted that there was something important in the attic that might explain a few things. Brendan always did overdramatise everything.'

322

'He's not the only one,' said Thea, thinking of Millie, and even old Mrs Wilshire herself.

'Well, they all got the family gene, I guess. It comes from my old grandma. Rita and Dawn's mother. But let's not get into that now.'

'I think I understand quite a bit of it already.'

'You do, do you?'

'I know that your father is also Richard's father. I imagine that had implications for inheritance of his estate. He's from a rich family, with titles and stately homes and all that.' She heard herself faltering. There was a glitch in her logic that she hadn't noticed. But she pressed on. 'And this house,' she said, waving at Rita's handsome Cotswold property. They were standing on the front path, neither showing any sign of wanting to go indoors. Thea had a feeling that Martin was deliberately remaining in the open as a gesture of reassurance. And for that, she found herself quite liking him.

'The house goes to Millie. There's no argument about that.'

'But there was an argument?'

'On a quite different level – yes, I'm afraid there was.'

She waited, aware that she had absolutely no claim to any knowledge of private family business, but equally aware that Martin had asked her to come and meet him. There must be *something* he wanted to say to her. He'd talked about gratitude for her kindness, on the phone. But he wasn't carrying a bunch of flowers and he had called her a dangerous little thing. All of which led to a loss of balance.

'We argued about our mothers, essentially. Neither of us knew Dawn; we both regarded Rita as central to our lives. Richard knew perfectly well that I would never have agreed to putting her in a home. He went ahead and did it without any consultation. But when I saw her there, I realised it was for the best. I made no objection. The same thing when I heard that he'd employed you to go through my mother's possessions. I was forced to concede that it was well past the time when they should be opened up and disposed of. I was annoyed when I finally got hold of the fact that he had approached our father some time ago, and wheedled his way into his affections, in these final years of his life. Bit by bit, I found Richard a thorn in my side on just about every level. He did his best to obstruct my visits to Auntie, as well. He turned his girl against me. He read all the emails I sent to Auntie, and apparently came to the conclusion that I was stealing his mother from him. She always loved me more, you know. It was just a fact of our lives. I can't see how it really changed anything for him. I was out of his way, first at school, then I left the country altogether. He was a dutiful son. Auntie was a perfectly good mother to him. And yet it seems he never felt he got his due. He could never please her to his own satisfaction.'

'But they seemed so close,' Thea interrupted. 'My fiancé said that was obvious from seeing them together, last month.'

Martin nodded sadly. 'He was always determined to be seen as the perfect son. It was almost an obsession. When he finally discovered who his father was, it was the same there, too. He had to win affection and approval from a deaf old man, who had never much cared about his offspring. He more or less abandoned me as a small child, and I've barely seen him twenty times in fifty years. But the fact remains that I'm his legitimate son, and nothing can change that.'

'Is there a lot to inherit now?'

Martin puffed out his cheeks in amusement. 'Barely a cent. He was the fourth son of a grand family. As a youngster, he had a reasonable income from all the various enterprises. His father was a remarkably clever businessman, unusually for the aristocracy. When he died, there was a pretty handsome share-out. But that was a long time ago. They've been a prolific family. There's a dozen cousins at least all claiming their share. Besides, don't you think there's something very unsavoury about a man of seventy waiting for an inheritance from his father? If you can't make your way in life by that time, then it's a bit late to get started at my age. I don't need any more money. I've done quite nicely for myself.'

'So what happened with Richard, then?' she blurted. 'At the barn.'

'You really think I know the answer to that?'

'I really do.' She fixed him with an uncompromising stare. 'Who else?' It sounded much bolder than she felt. There was still every chance that an angry farmer had killed Richard, she supposed. Perhaps all the things she had gleaned from members of the family had expanded into a conviction that was quite wrong. But no, she couldn't believe that. It had gone too far for that.

'I will tell you,' he said, glancing up and down the little road. 'Will you walk to the church with me? I think better when I'm walking, and your little dog seems eager for some exercise.' Hepzie was mooching aimlessly close by.

'Okay, then.' The church was two minutes' walk away, but the suggestion made a sort of sense. They were somewhat conspicuous, standing in an empty road. It was somehow the wrong setting for a confession to murder.

Because she felt certain that this was coming. Why in the world the man should freely make such an admission remained obscure. He had said on the phone that he owed her something, but she failed to understand what or why. Nevertheless, she was more than happy to let him speak.

'Let me summarise,' said Martin Teasdale. 'Richard was always jealous of me, from the very start. Auntie talked about me all the time, rushed to open my letters as soon as they arrived, paid handsomely for my wedding and gave me lavish presents. It was foolish of her.'

'Indeed,' said Thea.

'But not my fault. However, as I just said, in Richard's mind there were countless reasons for hating me. And he acted on his hatred. He thwarted me in every way he could. He tried to poison Auntie's mind against me. He labelled poor Brendan a criminal.'

'Which made you hate him in return.'

'Well, no, actually. I always felt sorry for him. I spent a large part of last Friday trying to put him straight. Trying to make him see that we were both too old for such foolishness. He came to my place in Gloucester, demanding that I stop emailing Auntie and showing her so much attention.'

'All day Friday? So that's where he was. He let people down. He didn't answer his phone. He abandoned his dogs.'

'He got very drunk on Thursday evening. He'd come to meet me to talk about the house here. We met in a pub near my home. He just lost it, I'm afraid.'

Thea thought back to the man she had seen on her arrival at Chedworth. How he had claimed to be consumed with guilt. It would make sense for him to try to drink the guilt away, she supposed.

'So he stayed the night,' Martin went on. 'And in the morning he felt too ill for work. I took his phone away from him, because he would only make things worse for himself by trying to explain what was going on. And then we got into the most dreadful all-day conversation, going right back to the start, with Richard airing every grievance he'd ever had against me. He recounted his whole life. Then he drank more, and fell asleep at about seven in the evening. I didn't know what to do with him, quite honestly. He woke up at six the next morning, insisting we settle it once and for all.'

'Settle what, exactly?'

'I wasn't sure myself by that time. I was utterly sandbagged by the whole thing. But I knew we owed it to Auntie to try to clear the air. All that talk on Friday hadn't resolved anything. It just made everything worse. Richard kept talking about a day we'd both gone to the barn.'

'The barn where he died?'

Martin nodded. 'It has a lot of history for us, that barn. When Richard was six and I was about seventeen, we went there together. We had a little terrier and wondered if we could get him to catch a rat. Rather nasty boy stuff, to be honest. We'd been before, and regarded it as our own personal playground. Anyway, it was August and the place was full of corn waiting for the thresher. Mountains of the stuff, fantastic for climbing on. We stayed all day, with the dog. Never caught a rat, and I remember getting bored with such a young kid in tow. I'd got my eye on a girl in Yanworth and wanted to get over there. But for Richard it was a magical day. He said it was the only day he could remember that we were real friends. We'd got some pop in a bottle and bits of food, so we had a little picnic, right up on top of all those sheaves. I told him some stories about school. All slow and sweet.' His eyes grew moist at the memory. 'So I stupidly reminded him of it, and said maybe we could try to recapture that friendship, by going back to the barn. It was mad, I know. But I couldn't think of anything else to do, and it would at least get him out of my place. I was sick of the whole thing by then. I wanted to get on with my own business. Richard was maudlin, but not really drunk by that time. We took his car and decided to walk through the woods, just as the sun was rising.'

It fitted the facts thus far, thought Thea. Everything sounded genuine. Almost for the first time since Thursday, she felt she was being given unvarnished truth. 'Then what?' she prompted.

'We climbed up to the platform, pretending we were boys again. But we'd got a lot bigger and heavier. Richard banged his head really hard on a beam. That made him bad-tempered, and he started all over again accusing me of wrecking his life. Then he tried to push me over the edge. I was terrified. It seems a hugely long way up, you know. And I've never liked heights. I clung to him, and scrabbled for a foothold. Then I realised we were close to an upright strut, and reached out for it with one arm. The sideways movement changed the centre of gravity and Richard just went over the edge, head first. I didn't see him fall, but I heard him land. Just like a sack of potatoes. It never occurred to me it could kill him. But it did.'

'But ... the police have come to the conclusion it was murder.'

'Must be because of the knock on his head. And that might have done more damage than it seemed at first. It was quite a clout.'

'You didn't finish him off? Did you rearrange the body or anything?'

'I checked for a pulse, when I finally got down again. That took me several minutes. The ladder was wobbly and I was in a real panic. He was dead. I just left him. Nothing I could do would increase the impression that it was suicide.'

'But there were no signs of a struggle on the platform.'

'No. We didn't struggle much.' His voice grew

softer. They were at the church door, the light rapidly fading. Ninety-six hours, almost exactly, since Thea had last seen Richard Wilshire. 'You knew I was there,' he went on with a little frown. 'How did you?'

'I don't quite know,' she faltered. 'It just came together, somehow. But I thought perhaps it was Brendan and not you. I just got there by accident,' she said with a quick laugh. 'That's often how it seems to happen.'

'Well, you needn't worry any more. I'm going to slip in here for a little while, and then I'll phone the police. Nothing more for you to do, Mrs Osborne. Not a single thing.'

She gave him a searching look. 'They won't believe it was an accident,' she said.

'They won't be able to prove otherwise. I'll get a good defence barrister. And character witnesses. It won't be so bad,' he said with his customary smile. Then his face hardened. 'You said Auntie Rita had lost everything. That isn't true – yet. Only if I get sent to prison for the rest of my life will she lose both her boys. And that would hasten her death. If they do take Brendan in for questioning, there's nothing he can tell them. Those ridiculous stamps might divert them.'

'That might be what they want to talk to him about,' said Thea.

'Let's hope so.'

'What about Millie? And Judith? How did you get home again on Saturday? Did anybody see you?'

'I walked back through the woods, thinking I'd drive Richard's car back to Gloucester. Then I

330

had second thoughts. It had to stay where it was. I put the key in its little magnetic box, because Millie knew that was his habit, and I figured she'd find it eventually. I kept on walking, all the way down to Fossebridge. Then I phoned Brendan and he drove me home. I told him some bullshit story about a business acquaintance who'd been called away, leaving me stranded.'

'Did you take Richard's car key out of his pocket?'

'Of course not. I drove from Gloucester, so I had it already.'

'You wanted everyone to think Richard killed himself,' said Thea slowly. 'Wasn't that cruel?'

He shook his head impatiently. 'Enough,' he begged. 'These questions could go on till Doomsday. You don't need to know every little detail.'

Oh, but I do, thought Thea. Irritating, but true. 'Sorry,' she said, and then felt foolish.

She and the spaniel went slowly back to the car, wondering what came next. Was the case so easily solved, then? Richard's death had been an accident, it seemed. All his own fault. What would his mother feel about that? Would she continue to blame herself? Was Martin an adequate replacement for her son? *She's lost everything,* she thought unhappily. *Unless I leave it all alone and just go away.*

She looked around as she walked the few yards to her vehicle, at the house, and the thin scattering of cars parked along the road. One was Martin's. And on the back seat, if she was not much mistaken, was the painting of the two young sisters. He had got it from Brendan, then. Was he planning to sell it, or what? Like everything else, it must belong to Rita Wilshire, who could leave it to anyone she liked. It wasn't Martin's to sell – or even to hang in his house in Gloucester. But it seemed a small detail now.

She let herself and Hepzie into the car, but sat motionless for another minute. She wanted very much to phone someone. Just to hear a voice and feel less alone with such a terrible burden of knowledge would be a great relief.

But then something better happened. A car appeared, and pulled up beside her. At the same moment, the door of the house opposite opened and Norah Cookham approached her. She wound her window down.

'I called them,' Norah said, nodding to where DI Higgins was getting out of the vehicle just arrived. 'I didn't want to, but I saw no alternative. I've had a long email from Rita, just now. And another from Brendan Teasdale. I saw you talking to his father. And then you came back, looking so downcast. I couldn't just leave it all alone.' She gave a rueful smile. 'I expect I did the wrong thing again.'

'What did Rita say?' Higgins was close by now, and Thea opened the car door.

'She understands that the trouble is all her doing. She's shouldering all the blame. She mentioned you. Said you'd been a very good listener and she was hoping you might be able to put a few things right.' Norah looked at Higgins with exaggerated deference. 'Inspector,' she said. 'I have a feeling this lady might want to talk to you. She's carrying quite a load, I believe.'

Then she retreated to her house again, and nobody tried to stop her.

'She called us, and I've dashed over here, and now she just leaves us to it,' said Higgins, rubbing his head. 'That's not the way it's meant to go.'

'Were you at the barn?'

'I was, as it happens. Wrapping it all up for the night. Nothing more to be gained there.'

'Have you got any new evidence?'

He sighed, and gave her a schoolmasterly look. 'You know I can't answer that.'

'I take that as a no,' she said. 'You haven't arrested Brendan Teasdale, have you?'

'We haven't arrested anyone. I doubt if we're going to. If we did, it might well be you, for wasting police time.'

She didn't argue. 'That'll please Millie, at least. The thing is, Drew and I were wrong. That means you were right. Nobody murdered the wretched man. He brought it all on himself.' She deliberately avoided looking at Martin's car, hoping he wouldn't come back from the church just yet.

'And yet his head contained fragments of wood. How did that happen?'

'Have a close look at a low beam up in the roof. I think perhaps he bumped his own head up there, and that made him wobbly. And then he fell off and died. Accidentally.'

Higgins scowled at her, more angry than she had ever seen him. 'Which would have been our conclusion, if we had never listened to you.'

'I know. I'm sorry,' she said humbly. 'I feel awful about it.'

'Well, that's the way it goes sometimes,' he said reluctantly. 'Nobody's really guilty, after all.'

Nobody, except Rita and Martin and me and Drew and Brendan and even Bloody Norah, thought Thea.

Epilogue

She didn't phone Drew, but drove down to Somerset, arriving just before nine o'clock. The children were in bed, and he was showing signs of following them before very long. He opened the door before she could knock, and swept her in without a word.

He made her some coffee and stood back while she emptied the last of some dry dog food into a dish for Hepzie. It was gone in seconds. Then all three of them sank into Drew's old sofa, and gradually relaxed.

'I have to hear the end of the story,' he said after a little while.

'The short version is that Richard picked a fight with Martin at the barn, and fell off the platform. The fall killed him. We were wrong from the start. He wasn't murdered.'

'But neither did he commit suicide.'

'True.' She went quiet, before going on, 'The real guilt lies with Rita, originally.' She explained. 'But Richard was a fool to hold onto childhood jealousy like that, just because Rita had a special affection for Martin. Richard

334

didn't lose by it. Finding out who his father really was didn't help at all. It just reawakened all the same old grievances. He put everything onto Martin, quite unfairly. He wrecked his marriage for nothing. He was an idiot.'

'You're too hard on him. Where does Brendan fit in? And Millie?'

'Nowhere, really, as I understand it. They've both been affected by the animosity between the half-brothers. Brendan was the key to Richard discovering the secret about his father. Millie has been too self-absorbed to notice her father's state of mind. She might have done something to help him if she'd been a better sort of person. She's just a giddy girl, enjoying the reflected glory of her famous friend.'

'So Norah turned out to be a goodie. What else?'

'Remember that picture from the attic? Martin's got it in the back of his car. Or something very like it.'

'I suppose it does rather symbolise the whole miserable story. The two sisters, with the world at their feet. Men were going to fall for them, they'd marry well and remain good friends. And then one of them dies leaving a sad little boy to be rescued by the other.'

'And a useless man who fathered two boys and didn't do a bit of good to either of them.'

'Poor Rita,' sighed Drew. 'She's the one I care most about.'

Thea turned her head and looked at him. She had heard depths and echoes in his voice. 'What are you thinking?'

'That I have a few things in common with her. I'm in danger of making the same mistake, aren't I? Favouring one child over the other. Building up all sorts of future trouble as a result. I've got to change before it's too late. There's no excuse for it. It began badly, and I never did enough to put it right.'

'I'll help you. There's plenty of time. Kids can be very forgiving.'

'Unless they turn out like Richard Wilshire. Poor Rita,' he said again.

'I know. She's in a bad way. I doubt it'll be long before you have to do her funeral.'

He sat up straighter, one hand clamped decisively onto the arm of the sofa. 'Then that settles it,' he said. 'We move heaven and earth to open the Broad Campden burial ground within the next six months. No more procrastination or excuses. Whatever it takes, that's what we'll do. I'll phone Andrew Emerson tomorrow and tell him he's got a job if he still wants it.'

'I've just realised you'll be Drew and Andrew. That's funny.'

'We can make a thing of it, somehow. I think he's going to be a keeper. We'll need to generate enough business to justify him, of course.'

'We?' she echoed. 'That's definite, is it?'

'If that's what you want.'

'Of course it is. My life is worthless, pointless, empty without you.' A tear slid down her cheek. 'I was afraid I'd blown it this time.'

'So was I. I don't know how I could have just gone off and left you the way I did this afternoon.'

'You had no choice. I should have come with you.'

'We do what we have to do. You know what I keep thinking about?'

'What?'

'The way you spoke up to that Mr Shipley. Remember? At the Broad Campden house. You gave him a clear manifesto for the rest of our lives. I keep hearing your words in my head.'

'Well, we'd better be sure to live up to it then,' said Thea.

No more house-sitting, she thought joyfully. Instead, a whole new chapter, working with Drew, the green undertaker. Any lurking apprehensions about dead bodies, demanding clients, night-time calls and financial straits were quickly dismissed. It would be *fun,* she decided. The Cotswolds had earned a large place in her heart over the past three years, despite encountering so many dark seething reasons for committing murder lying behind the handsome stone facades, the ubiquitous human mixture of malice and benevolence causing so much confusion. None of that would change, but with Drew by her side, she might achieve a better relationship with the place.

With Drew by her side, she repeated to herself, what could possibly go wrong?

The publishers hope that this book has given you enjoyable reading. Large Print Books are especially designed to be as easy to see and hold as possible. If you wish a complete list of our books please ask at your local library or write directly to:

Magna Large Print Books
Magna House, Long Preston,
Skipton, North Yorkshire.
BD23 4ND

This Large Print Book for the partially sighted, who cannot read normal print, is published under the auspices of

THE ULVERSCROFT FOUNDATION